More Praise for *The Paper Man*

"Michael, the Paper Man, is a highly unconventional and persuasive hero, and David Doppelmann among the strangest—archnemeses? father figures? manifestations of the self?—I've ever seen in a novel. Gallagher Lawson is a weird and wonderful writer."

—J. Robert Lennon, author of *Familiar* and *See You in Paradise*

"*The* Wizard of Oz *on laudanum, a Björk musical in letters,* this devastatingly powerful debut challenges us to imagine what it would be like to be made of nothing more than paper, to live in a world where mermaids are murdered and art is the only path to actualization, a world, in many ways, not unlike our fragile own."

—Samuel Sattin, author of *League of Somebodies* and *The Silent End*

"Only in the purity of paper, in its essence of nothingness, is it possible to create a truly literary character."

—Mario Bellatin, author of *Jacob the Mutant*

THE PAPER MAN

A NOVEL

GALLAGHER LAWSON

The Unnamed Press
Los Angeles, CA

The Unnamed Press
1551 Colorado Blvd., Suite #201
Los Angeles, CA 90041
www.unnamedpress.com

Published in North America by The Unnamed Press.

1 3 5 7 9 10 8 6 4 2

Copyright 2015 © Gallagher Lawson

ISBN: 978-1-939419-22-4

Library of Congress Control Number: 2014948160

This book is distributed by Publishers Group West

Printed in the United States of America by McNaughton & Gunn

Designed by Scott Arany
Cover art by Tracy Kerdman

THE PAPER MAN

CONTENTS

Part One: MAIKO 1

Part Two: MISCHA 63

Part Three: DOPPELMANN 137

Part Four: ADAM 189

Part Five: MICHAEL 245

Acknowledgements 269

Part One:

MAIKO

1

AT MIDNIGHT THE LAST MOTORBUS PULLED INTO THE STATION.
While the driver busied himself in the rearview mirror with an
inspection of his teeth, a single passenger boarded. He was a young
man wearing a gray suit with a butterscotch tie and felt hat; his
jacket sleeves hid his hands that carried a cardboard valise and an
accounting ledger. Had the driver paid more attention, he would
have noticed something peculiar about the passenger. But it was
dark, and the driver, who suffered from unevenly spaced teeth and
had just finished a packet of sunflower seeds, was preoccupied with
checking his smile. In the mirror's reflection he only saw the back
of the young man, who chose a window seat halfway down the aisle
and immediately pulled the curtains shut.

As the bus's engine roared and they departed along the single-
lane highway, the young man's apprehensions grew. The dry inland
wind blew through a cracked window near the front and flung his
hat to the floor. He closed his eyes. It should have been a relief to
be on his way, but his mouth was parched and the shredded-paper
soup he had eaten earlier churned inside him.

The young man, named Michael, had lived his entire life inland,
the dry center of a large peninsula. He had never been on the bus
and had never passed the mountain range that cut off the inland
from the rest of the peninsula. If it had been daytime, he would
have watched the change in geography, yet it was crucial he left at
night—he needed the darkness to keep himself from standing out.

For two hours, the motorbus continued along the highway. At
the next station, two women boarded, reeking of lemons and laurel.
They sat behind Michael, and as they settled, their citrus odor made
him feel worse. He pressed his jacket sleeve to his painted lips until
a wave of nausea passed. The other passengers whispered while the
wind whistled through the cracked window. From his valise, he

3

removed a knitted scarf and left his accounting ledger in its place. The scarf he bunched up and tried to use as a cushion, leaning his head against the window. It wasn't particularly comfortable, but he was extremely tired and the rhythm of the road eventually rocked him to sleep.

The bus stopped five times throughout the night, where other passengers boarded. In a half-dream state, Michael observed liquid shadows that quickly spread in empty seats like sprouting fungi. At one stop, the shadow of a man chose the seat next to him, but within a few minutes he was snoring and his shaggy head was propped on Michael's shoulder. Michael didn't want to bring any attention to himself, and so he stuffed the knitted scarf between his shoulder and the man's head and accepted his new role as a pillow.

———————

At dawn, the motorbus stopped at an inspection point sitting at the base of the mountain range. During the night, they had crossed over it, and now they were about to join a highway that cut through a region of rolling hills. From the small impromptu shack that was the inspection point emerged three men wearing uniforms. They had short, thick necks with shaved heads like stumps that they lowered as they boarded the bus. In the dim morning light, their oiled boots gleamed, and with each heavy step they took down the center aisle, the bus tilted to the left and then to the right. Flashlights held aloft, they illuminated the faces of the sleepy passengers, their own shadows sliding across the roof.

"What do they want?" Michael whispered to the stranger beside him. After the night's sleeping arrangements, it felt odd, almost improper, to finally speak.

"Never been searched like this before," the man said. He had large hands that gripped the armrests between the seats. "Maybe they're looking for someone."

"Who?" Michael asked. He tried to get a better view of what was happening at the front.

The man shrugged. He yawned and clouded their small space with his sour breath. The inspectors continued walking in synchronized steps down the main aisle, to the left and to the right, painting each row of passengers with beams of light. One of the inspectors halted at their row and inhaled deeply. If it had been possible, Michael would have started sweating.

"Open your suitcase," the man said.

There must be a mistake, Michael wanted to say. But there was no time to explain. The uniformed man had already reached between his legs and plucked his case from under the seat.

The two other inspectors looked on as the first man undid the latches and shuffled through the contents. Michael stood to block the morning sunlight seeping through the curtains. He didn't need them to notice his unusual appearance. The inspector's fingers ravished the clothes and papers inside while Michael's own fingers trembled—he desperately wanted to snatch his belongings and stow them away—but he was the stranger here. He had to comply.

"What's this?" The uniformed man held up several bloated socks.

This couldn't be happening. His brothers, Michael realized, had called the checkpoint. Somehow, Michael imagined wildly, they'd already discovered he was gone—somehow, they had awoken early and announced to their father his escape. He opened his mouth to speak, but there was no story, no excuse that would get him out of this.

The uniformed man shook out the contents of one of the socks. Into his palm, strapped by a blue rubber band, plopped a bundle of cash.

"Why hello." Michael's neighbor welcomed the money with sour morning breath. He leaned closer to get a better look. Michael pressed his jacket sleeve to his lips again.

This was all the inspectors needed. One of them sniffed the case and then reached in and withdrew Michael's ledger. He flipped through a few pages before glancing at Michael, who was now bracing himself for the worst. The inspector passed the sketches of a shimmering city skyline and splayed the ledger to pages with crude drawings of his brother choking on a scorpion tail.

Before he could help it, Michael's hands went into action and snapped the ledger book shut and pressed it tight against his stomach. The inspectors ignored him, but he still tried his best to stop shaking and stand his ground, to make himself an imposing silhouette against the window.

"Any coffee beans in this case?" the inspector asked.

Two stowaway silverfish crept out of his suitcase, dropped to the floor, and scurried away. No one seemed to notice this except for Michael, who accepted his belongings back. The inspectors began sniffing again, deeply inhaling, and continued along the main aisle of the bus.

"Wrong guy," the neighbor said to Michael. "This time." He laughed and slapped his legs with his large hands. "Apparently, that chump change of yours wasn't even worth taking."

One row back, a woman jumped when the inspectors lunged at her and searched her bags. Michael held the curtain in place to block the light leaking in, but it was pointless. The sun had risen and daylight spilled into the bus. He glanced back. The woman held her face in her hands while the men revealed several pillowcases inside her luggage. They were full of lemons and laurel leaves, all of which were immediately confiscated.

Once the bus departed again, Michael was kept awake by imagining the scene he feared most: the surrounding passengers turn, see him, their eyes widen, unable to stop staring, and they ask—Where did you come from? Why are you alone? How old are you? And then, the key question: What happened to you? The few strangers who had happened to catch a glimpse of Michael at home always believed at first that he was encased in a kind of decorated body cast. More than anything else, it was terrible to watch their expressions change as his father admitted the truth. Michael pressed himself against the curtain until it undulated around his head, allowing him to sink into its fading darkness.

The man next to him, now fully awake, began to ask the basic questions politeness required. Michael mumbled responses, hoping to end the conversation, but soon realized that the man really didn't want to converse; he wanted to tell a story, and so Michael had to take on another role he was comfortable with but nevertheless somehow resented—the role of listener.

"I'm on my way back from a funeral," the man said. "My father passed."

Michael said nothing.

"But that's not the worst of it. I went all the way south, and when I got to the funeral home, they told me there was a terrible mistake. They sat me down in front of this large wooden desk, with a vase of beautiful flowers and a stack of papers on top. They hemmed and they hawed about telling me. Apparently, they had their paperwork wrong, and so they followed the southern custom to bury him at sea. I had purchased a plot of land in the north, where my mother is buried. They tried to apologize, but sorry isn't exactly good enough, is it? Not for that kind of thing! So I demanded they bring his body back, and they said that wasn't possible. Before I knew it, I had that vase filled with flowers in my hands and then it was gone. Smashed it on their floor."

He turned and said, "When my mother died thirteen years ago, I bought the two gravesites up north. They were supposed to end up together. Now he's in the sea—fish food, can you believe it? Don't you think I had a right to smash things up? Tell me, kid, what would you have done in my position?"

"You're from the north?"

"Originally, but I live in the city now." The man glared at Michael and leaned in closer. "Come on now, don't change the subject! What would you have done?"

This was when it became apparent the man only had one eye. How had Michael not noticed this before? Covering the man's right eye was a white patch that curved like the shell of an egg, held in place by an elastic band disappearing into his shaggy mass of hair. Michael had the advantage of a face that showed little emotion, and hiding in the shadow of the curtain, his surprise was muted. The one-eyed man stared at Michael, his face full of sincere patience, waiting for validation.

"I wouldn't know what to do," Michael said. He clenched his feet around his valise.

"I'll tell you what to do. You destroy everything within your reach." The man grunted, as if approving his own statement.

Michael imagined those large hands before him—snapping the stems of calla lilies, stomping on the ceramic vase, tearing the pages from the guestbook.

"The final blow," the man said, smiling, "was tossing some plaque with an engraved prayer through the front window of the funeral parlor. The shattering glass was the most liberating sound I have ever heard."

While the man spoke, Michael continued fidgeting with the curtain. The bus was filling with light; soon the people would single him out. And yet here was someone who also looked different, who was completely comfortable talking with a stranger. He even seemed to disregard his difference, or possibly even flaunt it, by highlighting it with a bright, white patch. Michael took this as a sign of inspiration.

"I'll be glad to have that behind me," the man said. He lived in the city by the sea, which he said was tolerable since it was close enough to his hometown in the northern continent. Perched at the top of the large peninsula they were crossing, the city, though still technically southern, had a lot of northern influence, the man noted. The patched eye faced Michael again. "And where are you from?"

His last word was accompanied by a fleck of spittle that landed on Michael's face. Michael hastily wiped it off with his coat sleeve. Moisture that sat on his skin for too long, even the smallest of drops, was always a problem.

"I'm from the inland," Michael said. He cleared his throat. It felt as if he had not spoken in days. "But I'm on my way to the city, too."

Every time he said the words "the city" it felt like he was uttering a secret password to another world—to a place meant exclusively for him. Over time, the words themselves had taken on a magical significance, and even in this moment, while talking to this stranger, he was swept up in the idea of entry into the city. But the man sat up. He became very stiff, clenching his armrests and puffing his chest.

"The last thing the city needs is more visitors. It's best you turn around at the next stop."

Michael was stunned. "That doesn't seem very fair."

"Fair? You think that last checkpoint was bad? The north has started doing everything to bring order to the city. Not just anyone can stroll in and pretend he's always lived there."

"Since when?"

"You inlanders follow the news? Listen to the radio?" As the man spoke, he tapped out each word on his knee. "The city's a mess. Full of immigrants, anarchists, and libertines. No real government, everyone doing whatever one wants. They call it autonomy. I call it chaos. It's about time the northern continent won some representation down here."

"But isn't the peninsula autonomous?"

The man shrugged mysteriously, and Michael realized that he hadn't really paid much attention to the papers. He only glanced at what was happening in the city—art galleries, movie houses, all-night bookshops, concerts.

"Is it dangerous?"

The man laughed. It was so loud people nearby glanced at them. Michael tried to lower his head.

"The city's anarchists are the problem. Criminals have been in the pockets of the politicians for too long."

It was Michael's turn to shrug.

"That's right," the man said, grinning. "Just like all the others, ignore all the problems and pretend everything is okay. You got your entry form squared away, right?"

Michael didn't say anything. The man scoffed.

"Good luck in the city!"

The possibility had never occurred to him that he would not be permitted entry. What would he do then? He couldn't go back. He had often heard his brothers complaining about the city's problems and how it prevented them from expanding their coffee business, but he had always reasoned that they were intimidated or scared. Perhaps their truck's axles could not handle the drive over the mountains? What little he had read in the newspaper never mentioned the situation had turned. The city, as he understood it, was a place where he could finally fit in, and this news prompted him to sit up anxiously, as the curtain in the window shifted and splashed sunlight onto his expressionless face.

The man's single eye widened. His lip curled as he finally recognized something was different. "Do all inlanders look like you?"

If Michael had real skin, he would have blushed. He would have given away that he didn't like talking about his appearance or being singled out as representative of inlanders—a term he hated and hoped to leave behind. If he had real skin, he wouldn't need to say a single word to explain all of this—it would all have been said through his body. But he didn't.

"I don't look like them, and they don't look like me," Michael said.

The man continued to stare, but a cruel little smile rose on his lips. This confused Michael—after all, the man himself sported an eye patch, so why would he stare as though he didn't understand? Michael pulled the curtain to hide again in the shade.

"There was an accident," he finally said. "I didn't always look this way."

"So what happened?" The man raised his hand to touch

Michael's face, an echo of the uniformed man reaching toward him. Michael leaned against the wall, realizing how trapped he was in this small space. When the hand, large with filthy fingernails, attempted to reach forward again, Michael panicked and heard himself lash out.

"And your eye? You did all that damage at the funeral office, but what did they do to you?"

The man's skin rippled with rage, something Michael wished his own could do. Inside was a distant building of some feeling; since his mind was so separated from his body it took time to register what was happening within.

"Or maybe you're wearing a patch for the fun of it? That's certainly why I'm this way. Just to be different." His own voice was trembling. He hated himself when that happened. He identified the feeling inside—he was terrified and completely vulnerable. Overwhelmed, he surrendered his nostrils to the surrounding smells: coffee from his case. Lemon and laurel. Diesel and dirt. Camphor.

"Excuse me!" The woman across from them was now awake, grimacing. A few others in the surrounding rows turned, including the woman who had her lemons taken away. Michael shriveled from all the attention.

The woman, whose blanket smelled of camphor, continued: "Will someone shut this boy up!"

He grabbed his valise and dashed for the back of the bus.

The last row was a single broken chair missing the seat cushion. By propping his case over the armrests, he was able to make his own seat. There he pulled out his ledger and began to draw the face of the one-eyed man. Michael's hands were clumsy, and most of his drawings, made to calm himself or release any unwanted feelings—a habit that had turned instinctual—would have appeared to most people to be made by a child. He exaggerated whatever he saw. Sketching the man, Michael added—instead of an eye patch—a large egg lodged in the man's face. This was Michael's style. Style, he thought, was what made you unique. And to create things, whether on paper or with paint or metal, required style. He drew to develop his style but also to take out his frustrations and anger on his subjects. Acts he could not commit in real life, therefore, were staged and practiced on the page.

He tried to ignore what the man had said. There had to be a way for him to enter the city. Leading up to his departure, he had already begun to imagine himself living there. Perhaps as an artist, perhaps as someone with friends who looked different too. Any situation was better than rotting away inland.

For several hours, he watched the road and changing landscape. The inland was far gone. No inspectors were looking for him. Inside he continued to daydream, while outside the sparse shrubs and hills of sediment began dwindling. Finally, as the sun was setting, the bus descended the highway down the last hill, revealing the first glimpse of the city. Michael's fear faded, and he tucked his head under the curtain for a better view.

The city rose from the top of the large peninsula, which was shaped like a ragged ellipse, with a bay on the east and the vast ocean to the west. A thin isthmus attached this autonomous southern region to the northern continent, a vast sprawling land filled with a network of cooperatives and city-states. But they were all uniform and had no real presence, Michael had heard, nothing to compare with the dazzling city that overlooked the great eastern bay. Towering buildings with impenetrable glass shimmered with the setting sun, matching the ocean beyond them. What was inside them? The north coast was a sharply rising hill with a cliff that faced the bay, covered by a canopy of trees. In the middle of the trees stood a white lighthouse, overlooking the ships entering and leaving the harbor. Michael took a deep breath, imagining the scent of salt water and secrets buried deep in the ocean. He was no longer an inlander. He would be an urbanite.

Yet as the highway off-ramp curved and his anticipation grew, something appeared in the road ahead: a slumped body with a sickly iridescence.

"Look out!" he shouted. The heads in front of him looked in every direction.

He was thrown forward. The bus skidded and swerved to the right. The wheels moaned louder than any dying animal he had heard inland. They slammed against a cement wall. A moment later something broke, a heavy sound of metal separating from metal, and the bus fell forward. Suitcases pinwheeled down the aisle, and bags from the storage shelves above dropped like falling fruit. Passengers on the left were flung to the right, screaming, salmon-pink mouths gaping.

As Michael plunged through the air toward the front of the bus, along with the suitcases and bags and newspapers from other passengers, he was surprised to find he could see everything very distinctly at once: he saw a stray lemon tumbling down the aisle; he saw a series of hats and scarves climb over seats; he saw, through the windows, the iridescent body in the road that lay motionless, and at the same time he saw the other side of the canal they had fallen into and that the bus was teetering on the cement wall that divided the street from the sewer; and he saw himself, in mid-air, somersaulting, snagging his blazer on one of the armrests, sensing a sharp tear in his body; and then he saw himself falling slowly, past the two stowaway silverfish, and it seemed to him that he could die, if not by smashing into the glass at the front of the bus then at the moment when the bus would finally fall into the canal and be swept away by the waters. At that moment, a sadness, a heavy feeling of regret, sank with him to the ground, as he understood that just when he thought his new life was beginning it was already over.

A blast of humid air entered the bus.

An overzealous young man with a barking voice had opened a side window as an emergency exit and commanded that everyone waste no time and climb out. Michael, though, lay on the ground, watching this exodus, numb, trying to make sense, inhaling the new smell of the open sea that seeped in. Then he detected another scent. Someone, out of fright, must have urinated—soaking into his scalp was a trail of liquid that started several rows back and, because of the angle of the bus, crept into his hair. He quickly dried himself on one of the seat covers. Liquids were constant enemies he had to avoid.

Where was his valise? He raised his hands to explore his head and ensure there were no soft dents caused by the urine but instead he felt something else.

His left arm was missing. It should have registered as a bigger problem that he was missing part of his paper body, but physical pain was something he no longer experienced. His paper skin had always seemed distant, so distant that he never received messages in his mind of any sensations of pain. The only hint was in his vision, when things lost their shape and blended their colors and textures. Land and sky would mix into each other, blurring borders; edges bled into their surroundings, and he would swim in a concave pool of colors until the sensation passed. This usually only lasted a moment. It was how he recognized something was happening to his body.

However, with the commotion and the increasing urgency to escape, it gave him less time to pause. The seats and windows were blurred into one puddle of colors, of lights and darks, and then the moment passed and details returned. Nearby, the remaining passengers scrambled to the emergency exit and out into the salty air. The bus lurched forward again, and those inside cried for help.

With one arm, Michael searched under the seats. He found his valise toward the front. Because he was so light, his own body weight didn't tip the bus forward as he wandered up and down the aisle. Beneath the old woman's wool blanket, still smelling of camphor, he located his missing arm. Some stout person must have stepped on his fingers, for they were smashed flat.

He clumsily dragged the arm and case to the emergency exit,

only to discover he could not lift himself. He was the last one inside. Through the front glass of the bus, he could see the swift muddy waters in the canal.

A shadow from above fell over his face.

"It's true, then. Inlanders like to stay on the inside." There grinned the man with one eye.

Michael humbly smiled back. Why shouldn't they be friends, after such a horrific accident? The man put out his large hand, the same one that had tried to touch Michael's face.

"Give me your suitcase first."

Michael hesitated.

"Give me the suitcase first, and then we'll pull you out. Hurry."

Michael raised the valise with his good hand, and the one-eyed man grabbed the handle.

"Thank you," Michael said. He was learning a valuable lesson now that he was on his own. He told himself not to be quick to judge others and was thankful that the man was forgetting what had happened. "Can you take this as well?" He held up the broken-off limb, embarrassed to look the man in his one eye.

The metal of the bus creaked again as it started to lean further. "Hello?"

The man was gone.

2

ON THE DRY PAVEMENT LAY THE BODY: A NUDE GIRL WITH WHAT looked like seaweed for hair, with fishing line and beaded floats tangled in it. At first, Michael thought it was a body risen from the dead, southern custom dictating that all bodies be buried at sea in the great Bay of Bones. Perhaps there had been a mistake, and she had been buried alive and tried to swim back to land? But the triple set of gills—crusted with sea foam and bursting from each side of her neck, told him this creature had not originated on land. Her skull—crushed, the bones piercing the skin of her face. One of her webbed hands held a rusty knife; the large fin that extended in place of legs had been severed down the middle and was filled with a canyon of dried blood. Her bluish lips had a taut smile, exposing two sets of small, serrated teeth. The stench of her body overpowered the lingering gasoline from the bus. Around her an elastic cloud of flies stirred as people approached, and then returned to cluster onto the soft spots of her iridescent skin.

The bus finally gave in to gravity and disappeared over the low cement wall. The passengers paused as it slid below the canal's trembling surface. Several fragile passengers whimpered; a few ran away. Michael stood back. Two clean-cut young men had pulled him out after spotting his detached arm waving like a flag outside the window of the bus. They had nearly tossed him across the highway, misjudging his weight so badly. He thought they were heading toward him for a better look, but the corpse of the fish girl was far more intriguing.

The man with the missing eye was nowhere to be seen, Michael's valise gone with him. It was as if another part of his body had broken off. There was too much going on around him, though, to think about this. He neared the crowd, wobbling past a few sweating passengers who lay on the ground, pressing cloths to cuts on their foreheads and forearms. Michael saw flashes of bright red. Blood always thrilled him, not because he was sensitive to it but because he no longer bled like that.

Leaning for a look, Michael wondered aloud: "It's a dead mermaid?"

"Should've run her over," someone complained.

"And we were almost home." The woman who had smuggled lemons and laurel leaves was crying. "Typical city trash! Get me out of here."

"She was dead before we got here," said a woman with red hair, frizzy as if she had been electrocuted. She put her hand out to touch the body but pulled back when a pair of mating flies landed on her palm.

The bus driver became defensive: "I couldn't tell if she was alive or dead. I had to swerve out of the way."

"Of course she was dead. Who lays in the middle of an off-ramp?" the woman with red hair said.

"Has anyone seen a man with an eye patch?" Michael asked.

They ignored him. All of his concerns of being noticed in the city faded. He had always wanted to blend in, and the time he needed to stand out to get somebody's attention and assistance, he was no match for a dead mermaid. He looked around, and for a moment he wasn't sure if he wasn't simply dreaming. With his one functioning hand, he touched his face and stroked his ears, and for a while he waited in vain to wake up.

Soon, several ambulances arrived. The men inside were volunteer paramedics who set up zebra-striped barriers around the body and covered it with a black tarp. Littered around everyone were their blue entry forms, flopping on the pavement like gasping fish. Then a fire truck arrived and passengers began arguing over who would get a ride to the hospital.

The sky was turning past evening—a brilliant expanse of pinks and blues, like nothing he had ever seen inland. In a way, the accident had served a purpose: he was now free from his past by losing all of his belongings. As the paramedics struggled to write with dull pencils what passengers were saying, he longed for his own ledger book. They never glanced over at him, and so he decided they didn't need him—there was no one here to ask for his entry form—and he walked away.

The exit off-ramp led to a road that connected to a main street that stretched as far across the peninsula as he could see. Buses and taxis sped beside cars and bicyclists. The street was lined with tall buildings, many starting to turn on their lights as the sky darkened. Michael stuffed his detached arm in his jacket sleeve and used his good hand to hold it in place by clasping the elbow. At a stoplight, he stood beside a flyer that said:

SAVE THE CITY: SAY *NO* TO ANNEXATION!

He joined a loose crowd of restless pedestrians and strolled as if he had always lived here. He had told no one at home he was leaving. At this time, his brothers, Leo and Ralph, had probably returned to the house after all of their deliveries of their coffee beans in town, and their father was leaving the high school where he taught. They probably thought he was still in his room. His younger brothers had turned their backyard into a coffee farm and sold their coffee to local coffee shops and grocery stores. Michael was their bookkeeper, and the day before, after counting the bags they had taken away, he updated their accounting books, went into his bedroom, and then packed his cardboard valise with a few belongings, including two socks stuffed with money and some clothing. He wore his one suit and walked their long driveway, past the apiaries and syca-more trees, to the town's single bus stop.

The big secret was this: his brothers knew nothing about bookkeeping, and for the past several months, Michael had used an account he had created, called Offsets, where he had placed small amounts for himself. Life inland had become intolerable. Ever since the accident, his life had become stagnant, never leaving the house, watching the same trees lose their leaves and then burst into green again, never knowing any other smells than those carried by the wind; before he knew it, ten years had passed. His younger brothers grew bigger, hairier, and fatter, and although Michael technically was an adult, he was treated like a cloistered child because he was the same size he had been at fifteen. He listened like a child by placing a glass on the wall to hear the sounds from their rooms, and he hid whenever his brothers' girlfriends stayed overnight and ate breakfast in the living room. His family was constantly worrying he would be swept away by the strong inland winds. They never let him go outside unless he had a heavy metallic belt with him, like a paperweight, to hold him in place. The few outsiders who saw him were always so startled and overly sympathetic, as if he was in constant pain. They never understood. No one understood. But after ten years as a kind of pet, he was on his own, and there was no way to stop him. They would never know he had come to the city. *Did the wind take him away?* they'd ask, searching the fields and inspecting the scarecrows for evidence of Michael's body. But they would find nothing. He didn't even leave a note. He didn't want to waste the paper.

He could be anyone now. The one thing that acknowledged him was a crow that yelled at him from a tree. He wandered the streets of the city and thought about the new life he would start. He imagined living in an apartment that overlooked the ocean, painting the images on large canvases, much larger than any work by his father. And in the corner would be paintings of his memories back home, with a dark streak beside the collapsing barn to represent his father's shadow. From this apartment, he would study the ships entering the harbor and how the pedestrians moved like ants on the sidewalk.

Here he was, one of the ants, someone unknown in the buildings above studying him. He looked up, searching for that window with a light, the hope that he could one day be up there.

Instead, he was hit in the eye.

It began to rain.

3

THE OTHER PEDESTRIANS HAD BEEN PREPARED. THEY POPPED open their parasols, which had been conveniently stowed inside their bags, strapped to their belt buckles, or in their hands. Everyone had the same style: a short, wooden handle with black fabric for the canopy. A few men loosely tented newspapers over their heads and dashed for cover. A stocky woman lowered the hood of her stroller and tightened the blankets around a baby. The only parts of the baby that could be seen were its hands, in motion like little pincers. Small nomadic groups of hooded people were headed in all directions—he had no sense which way led to the best place for shelter. Some hid indoors; some huddled beside a bus stop with a small overhang only large enough to cover a bench that could seat three. He stepped into the crosswalk and tried to duck under other people's umbrellas. Underneath them, the stiff faces of the umbrella owners glared at him, recoiled, and hurried on.

It was summer time. Weren't the rains over after spring? But then he realized he was assuming the rest of the world was like the inland. The inland: known for hot, dry summers and wet winters and springs. The city had its own climate, and he couldn't believe that he had not thought of this before.

Every minute the rain seemed to transform. It started as fat sporadic drops of water, splashing dark dots on the sidewalk and pavement. Then a wind blew in from the sea and shifted the drops to assault people and buildings horizontally. And then the drops turned into drizzle, finally settling on a steady shower. The rain felt warmer than the surrounding air, the clash of temperatures making the streets muggy. Wind picked up and set flight to loose leaves of newspaper across the street. Wheels of cars mirrored the wind, spraying beads of liquid from their tires, like moving sprinkler heads. Taxis honked and bus brakes squeaked. In the distance he saw a small traffic jam at an intersection. A man, his mustache drip-ping with rain, was yelling at a driver. He stood waving his deflated umbrella and spoke in a language that Michael did not recognize.

The gray cloud cover muted the colors of everything—except the blue trash cans on street corners, which seemed like columns of topaz; gray glass and gray walls; gray pavement, tinged with the swirling rainbow and starbursts of oil slicks; and the rolling water that stretched down the gutters like gray tentacles.

Michael grabbed a newspaper from the bus stop and tented it over his head. A new learned behavior. He was briefly excited for this innovation he had acquired. His jacket and shirt were damp. His detached arm snug in its sleeve. Water was something he had learned to avoid over the years. Whenever it rained inland, there always was a clear sign. The clouds would collect and darken in one spot of the sky, or they could be seen migrating from a distance, rolling forward like sheep. Here, it was as if the sky had suddenly given in to the weight of the water. Like nature's accounting: the credit of water in the air had transferred to the debit column of raindrops.

Up ahead, he could just make out through low-lying clouds the verdant hill and its luminous lighthouse. Far behind him were the highway and the bus accident. He had no plans to return. He had no entry form, no luggage, no money. But those things didn't matter right now.

He followed a few soaking people to a teahouse. Yet he was too late—the teahouse was packed, and the wet pedestrians who were pressed against the window steamed up the glass from their never-ending supply of body heat. A crowd indoors seemed like a place where he could have blended in and waited out the storm. Michael reached for the door handle, but a crinkle-nosed waitress saw him. She shook her head and shut the lock on the door.

"Please," he said. He knocked on the glass. "Please let me in for a minute."

She had tired eyes that might have been kind had she not been squashed in a room full of anxious people. She mouthed something. He stared. She mouthed it again and walked away. *No more room.*

Another restaurant kicked him out when he admitted he had no money and asked only to use the bathroom. Sorry, the waitress had said, the bathroom is for customers only. He sputtered a laugh. How funny that she would think he wanted to expel things from his body when all he was trying to do was keep his body intact. At another street corner, he passed the display window of a department store. The lights clicked off as he walked by. He scurried ahead to the entrance, where a few customers ran out into the rain. A biscuit-faced little girl stepped in a puddle that splashed onto her socks. She screamed—a mix of shock and delight. A new sensation, around his neck, extended to his waist. When he peered inside his jacket, he found a river of ink and paint that started at his neck trickling down his torso. He was losing his color. A taxi pulled up, and the girl and her distracted mother climbed in. As she was shutting the door, the girl paused and stared at Michael. Her eyes were large like goggles. She pointed and Michael turned away, embarrassed. While adults were too absorbed in their own lives and situations, children were always the first to notice when something or someone wasn't right. The mother's tapering arm around the girl's shoulder drew her in, and then she slammed the taxi door. He realized he must look like a monster to them, falling apart in the rain.

The door to the department store: locked. The place had closed. This time when he let go of his detached arm, it fell out of his jacket sleeve. He stuffed it back inside. Did bad weather always affect the city like this? He didn't understand why everything was closed or full. It had been so long since he'd been in a city, he didn't know the protocol. If only he'd had more time to learn it. Why did it have to rain his first day here? He leaned against the building next to him, but there was no cover above, and each minute he felt his body grow heavier—liquid seeping inside his paper skin.

The rain was relentless now, punishing him—it seemed—for entering the city. Hardly anyone was on the street. A bus arrived at its stop across the way, and a small shivering crowd boarded. Michael ran over, and the water that his feet kicked up soaked into his legs.

"Please, I need to board, but I don't have any money," Michael said to the bus driver. "I'll pay you back."

"Get lost!" The driver scoffed and waved him off. Michael stood back as the bus drove away, generating a wave of water that shot out of the gutter and across Michael's legs. Inside, the windows immediately steamed with the breath of passengers. He suddenly missed the relative comfort of the motorbus he had been in earlier that day. His vision began to blur, and the falling rain blended with the cement to create a giant sheet of gray surrounding him. A moment later, he was able to see clearly again. Behind him, on the bench and under the awning, a fidgeting man with an open, saffron-colored mouth was trying to curl up.

"Find your own bench," the man scowled before Michael had time to speak, exposing his gapped teeth and releasing foul-smelling breath. His hands were claws nearly as terrifying as the rain.

The sunlight faded; darkness filled the city, and the rain bit like sharp teeth. He looked up. Another drop in his eye. Perhaps this was how the one-eyed man had been blinded—he had stared into the sky and something had fallen, something as simple as a raindrop but with just the right composition to destroy his sight.

His detached arm felt like putty in his other hand. Michael started to run, spotting an alley ahead that he hoped could provide cover. There he located a dumpster, and for a moment, he recognized the fact that he was willing to hide inside it. Had his life this quickly come to this? But the lid was locked. His feet had become heavy, like bricks that he had to drag. A man in an elegant trench coat passed the alley, and Michael put out his good hand, already bent in a pose familiar to any beggar. There had to be one person who would help.

"Please, do you have any cover?" he mumbled, but the man casually veered away from him without stopping.

He would not hold up much longer. In the strange painless way his body worked, it was telling him he was falling to pieces. The visions of blurred surroundings came in stronger waves. Soon, he thought, he might be blind.

A cluster of umbrellas marched past him and disappeared around the corner. There were no trees on this street. No awnings, no overhead covers. The only trees visible were north, on the hill, too far away. There would be nothing left of him by then. And so he reluctantly headed south, past the locked doors and occupied benches, where further along the street Michael finally found hope: a large bridge that scalloped along the city skyline. He used a building wall to support himself but then saw that he was smearing a streak of black ink across the stucco. His painted fingernails were gone; he now had white tips for fingers—it was as if he was seeing bone. His legs became as heavy as bags of coffee beans. Yet a voice inside remained optimistic: *a few more steps.*

It was an extreme effort to make it across the street. The water was ankle deep, and his feet became heavier with each step. The water seeped up his legs. He was absorbing it fast, and he only saw everything below him as one mass of dark colors. He rushed to the bridge. To avoid a large puddle, he had to go back a half block to find a spot where he could cross onto the sidewalk. Then he ran, past discarded wrappers of trash and bones of dead fish that had been glued to the uneven pavement and were now being loosened and were floating away.

Under the bridge he celebrated deep breaths of dry air. He loosened his tie and squeezed out some water, but his body was too heavy. He fell to his knees on the curb and had to steady himself. It might be too late. The water was inside him, and he had become a sponge. His detached arm fell out of his sleeve again. He gave in to the weight and lay on the sidewalk. Above him, several rats and a flock of pigeons huddled near the stone arches. He felt strangely at ease. Just to make it to the city seemed like enough of an accomplishment. Perhaps that was all he was meant for. Or perhaps all along he had made a terrible mistake. He thought about the rare times it rained inland. How was it possible, he wondered, to be awake and aware of his body disintegrating before his own eyes? Inland he had watched the rain coat the coffee bushes and form the small streams that flowed between them, never afraid of the rain because he was always inside, safe behind the glass of a window. Two contrasting worlds connected by clear material. Here there was no glass.

Just then, the glowing headlights of a bus materialized through the curtain of rain, roared along under the bridge, and splashed a large puddle that had formed in the gutter and spread into the street. It coated him with slime and debris and shoved him to the ground. He vomited water. As he leaned over, in the small puddle forming before him he saw the reflected outline of his face—it was not a shape he recognized. Perhaps his ability to see details had permanently vanished.

He thought he might be able to step out of his body and suddenly be so light that he could fly like a pigeon in the rain. The drops would roll off his wings and he would find that apartment in the high rise he was meant to live in, and below he would see the mash of pulp and pile of clothes he had once been. He would only need to splatter open the spot inside himself that would liberate those qualities capable of transforming him.

On the ground, he was dying—he was certain of it—pulpifying. The few details visible were rats and pigeons watching with their small, reflective eyes. One of the rats broke from the group and ran across him, sniffing like the uniformed inspectors on the bus. Then, emerging from the mist that shrouded the bridge, a vague pair of thin human legs approached. Someone had been out in the storm longer than him. No one here would help him, he had decided, so he thought it best to blend in with the surroundings and let the pedestrian on his way.

He didn't have the strength to move. The pedestrian would have to either step over him or—more likely—on him. His mouth opened. The person approaching was wearing high heels. Above, she had a strangely shaped head—but then he realized she was covering herself with some kind of square or panel. The panel was removed and lowered toward him. Then softness—fur—brushed him with gentle strokes.

She was doing him a favor. He was sure of it. She was going to suffocate him and put him out of his misery. He wanted to say thank you, but his mouth would not close for him to speak. The fur moved across his face; he coughed once, and realized he had stopped breathing. A moment later, he closed his eyes.

4

FIRST THERE WAS DARKNESS, THEN IT WAS FILLED WITH SOUND. Soothing orchestral music entered his head. A slow string section played a waltz, a clarinet moaning the melody. Then his vision returned. He found himself lying on a kitchen table, wrapped in a mantle of fur, staring at a ceiling covered with brown blossoms of water stains. The fur quickly slipped off when he sat up, as if, once released, it was trying to escape from him.

The music played from a radio on the kitchen counter. He focused on what he thought was his heart beating but then discovered it was a steady stream of drops into a body of water. Behind a thin curtain drawn across one side of the kitchen was another room, filled with rainwater. The curtain fanned in time with the rhythmic dripping and the waltz on the radio. He glanced to his right and there on the stove sat a baking pan holding his detached arm.

His body's newsprint had dried like a crisp shell, shriveled with a skein of tiny wrinkles spreading across it. He stood up and learned that his feet were soft; he could not stand without holding on to the dining chair. The room, he noted, exuded a whiff of fungus.

He staggered down a narrow hall that led to a bathroom, its wall displaying several framed photographs. One was a family photo, a father and mother with two girls, but the rest were of a pretty woman, probably the one who had rescued him. Some looked professionally taken, glamor pictures, and others were blurry self portraits almost purposefully out of focus. In the dim light, he thought of home. He had grown up in a decommissioned primary school that his father had purchased at auction. The long hallway that connected all the classrooms to the former office was decorated with drawings, paintings, and photographs. These were the pieces his father—an art teacher by profession—had been unable to sell. In some ways, it should not have surprised anyone that Michael's father used his own artistic skills after Michael's accident. He distrusted medicine and blamed pills for the cause of his wife's death. The subject of most of his father's unsold work was the change of his own sons, so when Michael had walked down that hall, he passed pictures of himself from the time he was a baby to the young man he was now. While the photographs illustrated the growth of his younger brothers from boys into men, Michael, from the age of fourteen on, appeared the same in each one.

Inside the bathroom, Michael stood before an egg-shaped mirror, bracing himself against a small sink and preparing to see what had happened to him. A moment passed as he listened to the pipes groaning within the walls. Then, with a single desperate motion, he flipped the light switch. It flickered several times, humming loudly, emitting a very dim glow. At first, it gave everything a milk chocolate overtone, and Michael could make out in the mirror, staring back at him, a familiar young man. Across his face, still frozen in the bland, impassive look his father had created for him, a jagged fault line now spread down his forehead and faded near his nose. His yarn hair still framed his face, but instead of being parted neatly to the side, it was a curly mass.

When the light finally reached an antiseptic brightness that could burn any mold or soft-shelled insect, the true damage became clear. The entire upper right side of his face had been caved in, dented, as if a crater had exploded around his eye socket. The flesh-colored paint that made his skin had faded to a dusty rose and in many spots was completely gone so that he could see the newsprint underneath, a pulpy sinew of smeared words from ten years ago. While most people could recover from an injury—a bruise or a cut always healed on its own—his body had not been designed to heal itself. That was a kind of art beyond the powers of his father. In a frenzy, he removed his clothes and examined the rest of himself.

His paper coin nipples: gone. His belly button: caved in, leaving a gaping tunnel to his innards. His paper coin roll penis: still fully intact and flaccid as usual. He moved his hands along his body and skin: dents, more dents, and occasional soggy spots. All of it was a close approximation of what he used to be. His elbow and knees: pins still between the segments of his arms and legs, except for the missing arm. He fingered his empty socket, hoping for any kind of physical pain, but of course, it didn't register. The sensation caused was purely visual. In the mirror, he saw his reflection fade into the colors of the wall and tile for a moment before his shape defined itself again and returned to normal.

This was how his body would be for the rest of his life. After the accident, when he had been rebuilt with paper, he'd at first imagined it would be temporary, even refusing to believe his father when he confessed that there was no going back. And now after ten years inside the paper cast, here he was, in a strange city, in a stranger's home, a strange creature himself, disintegrating into something hideous.

He no longer wanted to be alive like this. To be made of paper was bad enough; to be made of deformed, defiled paper would be unbearable. He considered sitting under the shower in the tub that was too small for him until he had melted away like a piece of soap. He was, in fact, reaching to turn on the water, when a phone began ringing, so loud it shook the toothbrush off the edge of the sink.

In the kitchen stood the woman, her back to him, the phone held to her ear. Her hair was tied up, revealing an elegant neck.

"Only one room is flooded," she said in a hushed voice. "The same one every time it rains. Can you come tonight?"

On the kitchen floor lay the fur cape. As a guest, he knew he should help keep things tidy, and so he crept into the room and with his one hand draped the fur onto the tabletop. But as he did this, one corner snagged under the foot of a chair, which squealed in surprise. The woman reeled around and dropped the phone to the floor. She squeaked like a mouse.

Michael darted into the darkness of the hallway. The woman

scrambled to untangle herself from the phone cord and then held the receiver back to her ear. "It was nothing," she said. There was a long pause while she smoothed the hair around her forehead. Finally she added, "I saw a spider, that's all."

She spoke for a few minutes, negotiating a time for someone to inspect the flooded room. Then she hung up, undid her bale of brown hair so that it cascaded over her shoulders, and stared at the fur on the table.

From the hallway, he waited a long time before he said: "I'm sorry if I scared you."

She approached, but he stepped further away, past the pictures and back toward the bathroom.

"It's all right. Come out," she said. He paused in the doorway, and she stopped before him, a silhouette against the light from the kitchen. She stepped closer. She was young, with tired eyes, and had a small mole on her jawline like a mushroom. Her frame was petite, and yet her posture made her stand as if she were much taller. A moment later, he noticed that he was touching his own face, tracing the dents around his eye socket and the torn edges of his cheek.

"How is it," she began, then hesitated. She rubbed her temples as if she was trying to break loose the thoughts that were jammed in her head. "I've never seen anyone like you."

"I wasn't always like this," he said quickly.

"Will you be all right?"

"I don't know," he said. He didn't want to talk about himself. "Who was on the phone?"

"The engineer. You're not from the city, are you?"

"I just got here, from the inland. Today, actually."

"What will you do now?"

"Start over," he said.

"It's not easy," she said. "Just when you think things are fine, your life can change—like that." She laughed so hard he thought she was laughing at him. She covered her mouth, stifling her trill of a giggle. When she recovered, she sighed and stared at the floor.

"Today I lost my job, and I don't know what I'll do. All I think I can do is laugh at myself. Sorry." She looked at him until he turned away. "How old are you?"

"How old do you think I am?"

"Why, with skin like that you must be a hundred years old!"

He bowed his head.

"Relax, it was a joke," she said.

"You're not afraid of how I look?" he asked.

"Why should I be?" She smiled and he found this very comforting.

"I've fallen apart."

Before he knew what was happening, she was touching his dented eye socket and brushing her fingers across his cheek. He tried to stay still, but it was the first time in years that someone had touched his face. He retreated into the doorway.

"I could fix you up," she said.

"You've already done so much for me," he said. He wanted to say more, that he thought he would have died today if she had not rescued him, but he couldn't shape the words in his mouth. Besides, he had seen the damage and knew he could not go back to how he looked before.

"Don't be silly. I'll fix you. Then you can go your way. But you don't seem prepared. Where are your things? Do you have any money?"

His head sank, remembering the one thing he missed: his notebook.

"Someone stole my money. A one-eyed man."

"I'm sorry," she said, reaching to stroke his frayed head of yarn. "You poor thing."

He wanted to run away. He was tired of real people reaching out at him. But where could he go? Outside it was likely still raining.

She asked, "Are you hungry?"

He explained what he liked to eat: newspaper soaked in milk. This seemed to give her a new purpose. She went through the curtains that separated the kitchen from the drawing room, which was flooded, and climbed a set of stairs. He realized they were in a basement apartment, and the only window was at the top of the staircase. She returned with the evening edition of the *City Mirror*.

"Look at that," she said, pointing to the front page. A photo of a crowd of people was below a headline that said DEAD MERMAID CAUSES ACCIDENT.

She used scissors that shined in the overhead light to chop up the newspaper. She shredded it into bits that she put into a bowl on the stove before adding a splash of goat's milk. For herself, she made noodles with mushroom broth. Was this the source of the persistent fungal smell in the apartment? Through the strands of her hair hanging over, her eyes blinked rapidly like a camera.

"What's it like," she asked him, "to eat paper, when you're made of it?"

He nearly choked on his first bite. He cleared his throat and said: "I imagine it's the same as people eating meat. Is eating meat strange to you?"

She grinned. She tipped her bowl for him to see the noodles.

"I don't eat meat."

Underneath the table their stomachs moaned like two whales singing in the sea.

5

HER NAME WAS MAIKO, AND SHE WORKED IN THE DISPLAY WINDOW of Willard's, the largest department store in the city. Three days and three nights a week she was a fur model, wearing anything made of fur: rabbit berets to foxgloves and mink stoles to weasel earmuffs and muskrat-trimmed boots. Sometimes, she shouldered a sable purse. She and two other girls modeled in a display not larger than a small waiting room, and smiled and waved at those who walked by.

"There was no notice," Maiko said. "This morning, when I climbed into the display window, ready to work like any other day, I found two new women waiting for me. They gave me the cold shoulder."

Michael blinked uncomprehendingly.

"They were actually mannequins, Michael, and I soon learned they were to replace all the live girls who worked as fur models. My supervisor who had hired me a year ago—she was a family friend—explained that it was a way to cut costs. It came from the top, and she had no say in the matter. Fur sales were slow in the summer. She offered a position at the perfume counter, but I turned it down."

"Why?" Michael asked. He pushed his empty bowl toward the center of the table, a habit from his life back home. Michael had been exempt from washing dishes because of his paper hands.

"At the perfume counter, you have to talk to people. And they want you to tell them what scent is best for them. It's a lot of work. I know because I've talked to the girls who work there. But as a fur model, you don't have to say anything. The customers just look at you and wish they could be you."

She sat back and her chair creaked. She looked extremely tired now that she had eaten, but she continued.

"I stayed late, this last day. After all the other models left, I stayed to walk between the arms and legs of the mannequins and act as if we were all at a rooftop party. Normally the other girls and I walked and posed to an unspoken rhythm we all followed, always giving each other distance to take a turn at the front of the glass. The mannequins wouldn't allow this. They stayed in one spot, commanding the center. I was like a hamster in a maze.

"Modeling had been my dream, and after failed auditions for fashion shows, I had settled for a job as a fur model. I say 'settled,' but I loved being the sophisticated girl in the window. Everyone recognized me, and everyone wanted to be me." She smiled to herself.

"That's got to stand for something," Michael said. "Couldn't it help you get a job at another store?"

"Willard's is *the* store here in the city. Anything less and I might as well be a waitress. Or a girl on the street."

That last day, she said, only a few shoppers who passed by paused to watch her. As she clumsily squeezed past the tall mannequin with outstretched arms, the frosted mink scarf draped over her shoulders caught on the thumb of another mannequin and was yanked off. The shock of cool air on her exposed neck made her freeze in place. The other girls had never done something like this to her. Just then an older woman walked by, glanced once at the scene, and saw Maiko, motionless as the mannequins. The woman, scowling with boredom, moved on.

"I panicked," Maiko said, massaging her damp hair. "But I realized something. I realized that the perfect model is one whose expression never changes."

Outside the window, she had seen the rain begin to pour. It streaked the glass, and the last of the people outdoors ran for cover. The sky darkened. The mannequins continued to stare out into nothingness. Maiko watched them watching nothing until a hot current boiled up inside her chest.

"I had to do something. So I smashed them. They all broke apart at the joints, losing their wigs and fake eyelashes. Then I sat down and...." She shook the thought out of her head.

"My supervisor paid me in cash for the remainder of the month. I gathered my things in my purse, took one of the store's umbrellas, and then decided that I deserved a real going-away gift. I put this maribou cape inside my coat before buttoning it up. Maybe this is a good thing for me, losing the job."

They listened to the music muffled by the rain. In the next room, the steady dripping continued.

"Do you like the music?" she asked.

"It's very nice. Is there a city orchestra here?"

"Not yet. This music is from the north. All radio stations are up there."

He imagined going to a concert hall for a live performance by an orchestra. The lights would illuminate the players and hide the audience in darkness.

She bit her fingernail and it produced a searing memory in Michael of doing the same to his own real nails when he was still a boy of flesh and blood. Maiko marched away.

"Would you like to see my mushroom collection?" she shouted from down the hall.

"Excuse me?" He went after her, where she stood with a closet door open. Inside, the bottom shelves had racks of planters filled with a variety of mushrooms: tall, spindly ones with miniature white caps, large ones the size of a tea saucer, and some with their dark, purplish gills curled around the edges. The smell of them was overwhelming. He stepped back, worried that he would take on the scent, absorbing it permanently into his skin, as paper was want to do.

They returned to the kitchen with a cardboard shoebox, where she unpacked several balls of yarn, a cushion, shaped like a mushroom that was stuffed with pins, and a handful of spools of thread. With her chin, she pointed for him to sit closer.

"It just so happens that I'm a very good seamstress," she said. "You don't know how many other fur models were rescued from shame and ruin because of me."

"Shame and ruin?"

"They could have lost their jobs. When their outfits didn't fit right, they would ask me to do quick alterations to them. Take out the hem here, tighten the darts there. You'd be surprised how small alterations can make something the perfect fit. Take off your shirt."

"My...?"

"I'm going to fix your arm," she said.

His segmented fingers loosened his tie and fiddled with the shirt buttons, but he couldn't do it with one hand. She waited for him as he struggled. Eventually, he turned away to have a modicum of privacy.

"Don't worry. I don't care what your body looks like."

"It's not that," he said, thinking of the dents and soggy spots he had discovered on his torso earlier.

"We should check for more damage. Here," she finally said, and quickly undid the buttons. She opened the two panels of his shirt like a book. Michael's reflex was to cover himself with his hands, but he only had one arm to do this. She calmly lowered his good arm and said, "You still need to dry. Look here, you're soaking wet." Her fingers grazed his ribs; he flinched. "Are you ticklish?"

"No," he said quickly, then: "I don't know."

"Relax." She tilted her head to study his shoulder socket. Michael, to avoid seeing his body in the light, glanced up at the water stains on the ceiling. "I want to keep the repair as close as possible to the original."

First, she popped the flattened fingers of his detached arm back into shape. Then she began to sew.

"Does this hurt?" she asked.

"Not at all," he said. He held his breath as the thread moved in and out of his paper skin, and saw how the arm became loosely connected to his shoulder. Despite her commitment to stick to the original construction, he worried that he'd never be the same. This new stitching would make him move differently, and like the alterations Maiko gave to the clothing for the other models, this one alteration would make the difference between survival for another day and being sent away.

A few times, she rested her free hand on his leg. She held extra pins between her lips and exhaled through her small nose. Michael could feel his body trembling—he figured it was because he was cold. He didn't want to dwell on how vulnerable he was, in this foreign kitchen, with a strange woman making changes to a body that didn't accept change so readily. When she was done, she had him move both arms, up and down and then left to right, to test the new stitches.

"How is it?" she asked. She hovered around his shoulder with the needle, a long trail of thread twisting around her small waist.

He walked the hall and could sense a slight shift of weight with each swing of his arm. His body seemed to lean on the left shoulder, whereas before his weight always sat in the center. When he explained this to Maiko, she had him sit again, but she could not find a solution other than tightening the thread.

"Any tighter and it might break."

He walked again, and it felt no different. It wasn't bad, for he could still walk, but it wasn't the same as before. She stood before him, and for the first time, he noticed that he was taller than her. She was glancing at each shoulder, he guessed, in order to ensure they were even, but her breathing had changed, and her gaze was no longer on his shoulders, instead trailing down his soggy torso. This time there was no hiding the fact that he was shaking.

From the staircase above came a harsh knock on the door.

They both leaped back, Michael knocking against one of the dining chairs and Maiko spitting the needles she had clamped in her mouth onto the floor. Without thinking, he ran down the hall and hid in the bathroom. He listened to a man's voice talking to Maiko. A few minutes later, she knocked on the door.

"It's only the engineer. He's here to clean up the flood water. It always happens whenever it rains."

Michael opened the door to find her smiling at him, his shirt draped over her shoulder.

"Did you see yourself run? You're as good as new."

He waited in the hall, disturbed by the sucking sound of the engineer's vacuum tube, which snaked from the front door along the length of the stairs. It writhed around every so often from the large globs of water it gobbled up.

"It sucks anything in its path," Michael said.

"Cover your ears, and pretend it's not there," Maiko hushed him.

He raised his hands, his left shoulder tightening as he did so, and placed his palms over his ears, but the sound of the vacuum still seeped inside.

6

THE NEXT MORNING HIS BODY, AS WELL AS HIS CLOTHES, HAD dried and he prepared himself to go. But Maiko explained that she was lonely, she missed her sister, and suggested he stay at her apartment until he found a place of his own. He felt, nearly, happy and almost forgot the mushroom smell. She offered to help him too: she could repaint his skin.

"Then get dressed. We're leaving," she said, and gave him a straw hat to cover his head.

"This is ridiculous. Now I'll really stand out."

"Let them think whatever they want." Maiko pushed them out and locked the door. "We're going. Here, take my arm."

They linked arms and Maiko laughed. She teased the hat a bit and then they set off, her maribou mantle clasped around her neck.

The sun was beaming, the sky clear, and the road dry. The only evidence of yesterday's rainstorm sat in the gutter—a pile of wet leaves. Once outside, he was relieved to be free of the musty apartment.

"Has it really only been a day?" he asked.

"It's always like that here. One day, it's one thing, and the next day, like nothing's ever happened."

His reattached arm still felt strange to him, but even stranger was that he had no control of his movements, linked as he was to Maiko. When she stopped, he had to stop. When she turned, he followed. His body didn't have the weight to alter their path.

Although he wanted to see everything—the shops for hatters, druggists, and the cyclists, the pedestrians, the people inside cars—Michael kept his gaze mostly focused on the ground. Occasionally he looked up to take in what everyone wore. Everyone was dressed slightly strange. Colors that seemed mismatched made up a single outfit. And his straw hat turned out to be the least unusual headpiece. Some pedestrians had hats with large feathers or oversized eyeglasses with thick, tinted lenses. And the hairstyles! Several women had elaborately shaped hair, held in place by wires, vines, even bird nests.

"This is Willard's," Maiko announced after they had crossed many busy streets. Suddenly, they were standing before the doors where only yesterday Michael had watched the young girl splash in a puddle before being swept away by her mother in a taxi.

"Wait here," Maiko said. "I'll be back in five minutes." She unclipped her maribou mantle and wrapped it around him. "Don't talk to anyone, and don't move."

He continued to stare at the ground, counting the number of spots where gum had been spat out and smashed into the concrete. Maiko returned ten minutes later with her purse bulging with small cans of touchup paint. She put her mantle back on, and then led him to the side of the building.

"Look at them," Maiko said, as they passed the mannequins in the display window, furs draped across their still necks. "No one will buy furs from these girls. They're lifeless."

Michael paused before the window. One of the mannequins had a broken thumb. In the glass, he saw the outline of his dented face.

"And look," she said, "No one's even stopping for them. No one will ask them for autographs later."

She was agitated, her maribou mantle sliding off and exposing her bare shoulders. She sucked in her cheeks and pouted like a fish. For a moment, he thought she was going to begin competing with the models, posing in the street, but they kept walking. In the sunlight, he noticed that Maiko's mantle, which had appeared luxurious and rich in the dark apartment, was actually quite tattered, and the fur was flat and had missing tufts. He was swept along with her long strides, and they were almost back home before he realized she had been crying.

Back in the apartment, he stripped to his underwear, standing on sheets of the day's newspaper, shy of the exposed parts of his body. Maiko painted on a glowing, fresh coat. It was slightly off from his previous skin tone color, making him appear somewhat gray under the kitchen light. Just as the repairs to his arm transformed him in a small way, the new paint altered him too. Each of these was a good thing, he told himself, believing that underneath these temporary changes he was still the same.

He had to stand for several hours to dry. While he stood, he listened to the programs on the radio: a concert, then a radio play, and finally the news, read by a fiery broadcaster who didn't hesitate to interject his own opinions about things. It was a voice Michael recognized immediately.

"This is how bad it's become in the city," the anchor ranted. "Now even mermaids are trying to live there. But they obviously can't survive there. They're just another kind of immigrant. Too many are flooding the city and causing more harm than good. One flopped onto the road the other day and caused my bus to crash. And does the city know how to respond to emergencies like this? If you were on the highway anywhere nearby, you'd have your answer! Put it this way: I didn't make it back to the studio until the next day."

So he's a radio host, Michael thought, his heart drumming.

"We don't need to listen to this dreck." Maiko came into the room and snapped the radio dial off. Michael sighed and continued to wait to dry in the silence. Of course the one-eyed man would be a radio host. He could hide behind the airwaves to share his opinions. *Why would someone like that steal from somebody like me?* A radio personality should have plenty of money.

At the kitchen table, Maiko flipped through the remaining sections of the newspaper. She was holding the classifieds section when she paused to study his features again. "What will you do here? Once you've recovered?"

"What do you mean?"

"Here in the city. For work."

He shrugged. He glanced at the brush she had used on him. "Paint."

She stared. "You're an artist?"

He shrugged again.

Her gaze grew hard, her mouth turned down. "That may have been fine when your were a man of means. But now you need to survive. What kind of work do you do? Actual work?"

He was silent. Even the thought of saying it pained him.

"You'll need one. You'll need money." She appeared very serious about this.

"I used to work in accounting," he blurted. "Bookkeeping."

It took a few years, but one day his father gave Michael an occupation to go with his new body. Since he couldn't risk going outside and damaging himself and he didn't want to see anybody (which was his father's coded way of saying nobody wanted to see him), Michael was given a pile of bills to go over. Why don't you go ahead and compare them to the checkbook ledger, his father had suggested. At the time, Michael had been drawing for hours a day and growing frustrated by the crude results. This, he realized, was his father's way of telling him to give it up.

Despite the sad facts of the story, Maiko's face brightened. "Perfect. A city always needs bookkeepers. But wait, you need a work permit."

There was a long pause. He wasn't ready to make a decision on working in the city. The possibilities of his new life were already narrowing; on the bus, it had seemed like an open field, and now a portion of the landscape was receding inside this mushroomy den. He wasn't one for analyzing his emotions in the moment, only after, and usually through drawings in his notebook that were violent or otherwise transgressive. He was beginning to feel afraid, and excited, and hopeless all at once—and he felt a faint crack within a previously inaccessible region. He had never asked himself "What do I want?", only "How can I escape?"

"I wouldn't know where to begin," he muttered, though his

thoughts kept returning to the one-eyed man and the signal broadcasting his voice into the apartment. There was a starting point.

"Don't worry. I'll show you how to survive in the city," Maiko said. "You'll learn from the mistakes I've made."

7

THAT AFTERNOON, ARMED WITH JARS OF WHEAT PASTE, MICHAEL
and Maiko plastered flyers advertising his services as an accountant
on telephone poles and trees, streetlights and street signs. Without
paying much attention, they covered posters advertising cigarettes
and records and hamburgers. They hid posters insisting the south
Stay Independent! They buried fliers declaring *Annexation is the Only
Way.* He felt self-conscious, at first, but no one seemed to mind. Fly-
ering was a way of life in the city—and for the first time, Michael
felt like he belonged.

Two teenagers in filthy clothes lingered on the steps of an
empty shopfront. One of them, a boy with red hair, carried a backpack. The other, a girl dressed in black and wearing a beret and
black gloves, motioned for Michael to come closer. He could no longer see Maiko across the street and hesitated. They had been flyer-
ing for hours and he was tired.

"Hey, you," the red-haired boy said.

He nearly dropped the glass jar of wheat paste. The wooden
applicator was becoming soggy. "Me?" he asked.

"Yes, you! Come here. We have a question for you," the girl said.

Michael took a few wary steps in their direction. "Yes?"

"What are you doing?"

Michael thought about the trouble with the inspectors on the
bus, and then the one-eyed man. He didn't know how to answer
these two now. Anything he said could make the situation worse.
So he stood. Why were no other pedestrians on the street?

"What is that?"

"It's paste," Michael said. "I'm trying to start my own business."

"Do you need help?" the girl with the beret said. Her hand
reached for the jar of paste. Michael stepped off the curb and stood
in the gutter.

"Careful, you might get hit," the red-headed boy said.

"You should listen to my brother," the girl said. Michael nodded. He wished just then he had had a sister instead of two brothers. He liked how the two were a team.

"Maybe you can help me," he said. "Do you happen to know a one-eyed man?"

They shook their heads.

"Or where the radio station is?"

"Near the lighthouse," the boy said. "You can't miss it. Look, do you mind if we borrow some of your paste?"

"We're not really borrowing it if we're going to use it," the girl said. "Borrowing means you're going to give it back!"

They all laughed.

"What do you want it for?"

"We're trying to start a business too."

"What kind?"

"Hey, what's wrong with your face?"

Michael turned away. He dropped a sheaf of flyers. The adolescents ran to him and picked up the sheets of paper. Michael was secretly thankful, and when they put their hands on his shoulders, comforting him, he had an intense desire to make them his new friends. And they had given him critical information to help locate his notebooks. He was already planning to draw them once he got his things back.

"I can't give you all of it," he said, motioning to the paste.

"That's okay. Half should be enough."

The boy with the backpack produced a small empty container for butter. They used the wooden applicator to plop in half of the paste.

"Thanks."

Michael eyed the boy's hand—he was holding an elegant pen.

"What about your pen?"

They looked at each other. Bargaining was essential here, in the city. He couldn't let people, even kids, simply walk all over him.

"Give it to him," the hatted girl said.

They handed Michael the pen. It was beautiful: black metal and with a fine nib. Michael was already imagining the things he could draw.

"See you around," the red headed boy blurted with a laugh.

The two ran off. Michael was pleased. He went along several more blocks, posting more flyers. When he was out of paste, he headed back. Eventually, he saw Maiko and crossed the street to meet up with her.

"You still have a lot of flyers left," she said.

"I ran out of paste."

"You must have used too much, then. Oh well, let's move on. But first, let's stop at a pudding shop. There's one a few blocks that way."

They walked on her side of the street, past jewelers, laundries, seed companies, and lithographers. Michael warmed inside. What would it be like to have his own friends to visit? His reverie broke when Maiko gasped.

Across the way, he recognized parts of his flyers by the corners of blue paper, but now they were covered by new flyers, scrawled in calligraphy: *THE NORTH IS RIGHT!*

There were hundreds of them; overwhelming the telephone poles and streetlights and clipped under the windshield wipers of parked cars.

"I can't believe this!" Maiko said. "They won't leave us alone."

Michael was stunned. Ashamed, he didn't say anything.

In the pudding shop, they sat at a table in the back, encased in shadows. Maiko scooped tiny bites from her bowl of rice pudding while Michael stirred in a page of shredded comics into his.

"Can you tell me something? What's all this business with the north? What are they trying to do to the city?"

"Don't you read the papers?"

"I try to avoid politics."

"The north," Maiko began, but then glanced in each direction. She lowered her voice. "They're very interested in annexing the city."

"But why?"

"Many reasons. This peninsula has a natural harbor, and if it was controlled by the north, they would be able to tax all the goods that enter. And then there's the fish market. There's a lot opportunity to make money from the city. And of course on the south end of the peninsula are the beaches. Right now, fishermen use it each fall. People from surrounding fishing villages show up for a week and try to marry off their daughters. But if the north had the beach, it could become a resort for northerners, and you know what kind of money that would generate. There are lots of rich northerners."

"Have you been to the north?"

"Don't tell anyone this," she said, "but I'm from there. My parents still live there with my sister. They keep asking me to move home, but there's nothing there. There are no pudding shops. Only ice cream shops, and they all serve the same boring flavors. That's the saddest thing—if the city is taken over by the north, sure there will be good things that come of it, but all the stuff that makes the city unique will disappear. Things are already disappearing. Like fur models."

"Do mushrooms grow in the north?"

"Don't make fun of me."

Maiko grew serious. "I'll tell you this: the north is infiltrating the city, buying our officials. They are also starting to hassle people who stand out. It's not safe to be different."

"I see," he said, and nearly choked on his last, large bite.

8

TWO WEEKS WENT BY, SLOWLY ERODING HIS HOPE. THERE WERE several phone calls searching for a bookkeeper, but they all inquired if he already had a work permit.

"Ask them to sponsor you," Maiko whispered into his uncovered ear.

Each caller refused. Despite the recent optimism that had risen inside him, it became apparent that living in the city wasn't easy. Still, he lived for going out, and quickly grew used to the straw hat. To be around people, tall buildings, and smell the salty air was thrilling. On several occasions, he spotted the radio tower near the lighthouse, and he continued to listen to the one-eyed man's rants whenever Maiko wasn't there to shut off the radio.

On the streets, he often imitated people walking in front of him. What he wanted was to blend in so well that he was almost invisible. He practiced different gaits, swings of his arms, hunching his shoulders or pulling them back. Listening to their voices, he even tried on their vocal patterns, including the ones with megaphones demanding that the city secede on its own. On an empty street, he shouted their demands with their same intensity, where only the mockingbirds listened and nodded with approval when he sounded just like the original.

He blended into the frequent demonstrations and protests that flared up everywhere. Before a tall corporate tower, a teenager began throwing anchovies at its windows. Then from the crowd came bodies of squid and octopus, fresh from the fish market that stuck to the glass and slid down, leaving streaks of slime. Michael dodged the falling sea creatures, afraid their wetness would ruin his newly painted skin. Police arrived; the crowded erupted, and Michael hurried away unscathed and proud of himself.

They'd lost track of the rejections when a call came from a fish cannery in the harbor. It happened one morning while Maiko sat at the kitchen table altering a shirt she had found in the street and then had washed to give to Michael.

"M&M Bookkeeping," Maiko said when she answered the phone. "One moment." She covered the mouthpiece. "Another customer!" she whispered to Michael, who was leafing through the classified ads of the *City Mirror*.

"A client," he corrected her.

He spoke in single word sentences. Maiko waited. "Ask if you need a work permit," she said. But he didn't. When he hung up the phone, he sat at the table and said nothing.

"Well?" she finally asked, holding his hand in hers.

"I might have a job," he said to Maiko. "No work permit required."

She leaped up and hugged him. He stumbled back from the impact, reeling from the closeness of her body to his. Despite her vanilla perfume, in the curve of her neck he smelled the scent of mushrooms.

"What did they say?"

"They want me to come by tomorrow morning. What will they say about my body?" He pawed at the dent on the side of his face. At a job interview he would be under scrutiny, and each imperfection would be a debit against him.

Maiko observed his face, turning her head to take him in from all angles. He lowered his hand and allowed her to stare at the dent. Her look was never malicious—it always had genuine concern, and he was becoming comfortable around it.

Her cheeks brightened as she smiled.

"I know! I'll make you a mask. To even out your face."

In the bathroom, he looked at his face one more time. It was the last part of him that still had damage from his first day in the city. He turned to his good side, then to the dent. It still shocked him when he saw it under a light. The day of the rainstorm, the one-eyed man, and the dead mermaid—everything seemed like a dream from long ago. He had been so afraid then. What would have happened if he had not made it to the bridge? Where would he be if he had not crossed paths with Maiko?

He decided that she would be able to approximate his true face again by mirroring the good side. He glanced again in the mirror, wondering what his father would say if he could see Michael now. Using the lid of the toilet as a table, Michael smoothed down a piece of paper from Maiko's desk and began writing:

Dearest Father, I thought you should know that I have started a new life.

With a sharpened pencil he had taken from the kitchen, he wrote slowly and carefully to make his writing as clear as possible.

I have found work, and I already have a new home. I live with a woman who cares deeply for me. She prepares my meals and washes my clothes. She has improved my body and made me more resistant to the elements.

In the bathroom, things were warm and stuffy. He wanted just then nothing more than lots of water poured on his body. It was a dangerous desire, but that was the energy of the city, the only thing that would have a calming effect, because the energy inside him was so hot that he might set his paper body on fire from the inside out. A douse of liquid, so seductive and so necessary. He ran out, scared by his own desires.

Maiko was in the kitchen waiting for him. He tucked the letter in his pocket.

She unbuttoned his shirt; then reclining him against the kitchen table, she rubbed a sticky, cold jelly on his face that made his entire body shiver. She began layering strips of newspaper across his nose. He lay listening to the sound of her tearing paper, in the dark, before he finally opened his eyes.

Eventually, he asked her, "Did you ever want to be an artist?" If he had better hands he would have liked trying sculpture. Seeing

Maiko's fingers stirred this vague desire to do more art.

"I don't know. I like to make things, but I just think of myself as more into crafts than art."

"What's the difference?" He had never distinguished the two; now it seemed there were two methods to achieve the same thing.

"I suppose it's how serious you are about what you're making. Don't move your mouth now."

He watched her, and it was strange and exciting that he could observe her so close and she didn't seem to mind. She hummed out haikus and brushed her bangs, and glue stuck to the strands of hair.

"This needs to set a bit before I can remove it," she said. He continued to lie on the table, waiting. Then, like most sensations in his paper body, it took a few moments to realize that her hands were resting on his stomach. He stayed still, for it was more important to him in this moment to show that he wasn't afraid, even though he felt himself trembling inside; it was more important to no longer be like an adolescent from the inland but like a city dweller who could handle any surprise thrown at him. Her hands moved in ever so slow strokes, and through the eye holes of the mask he saw her head turn to look at him.

"You're so lucky," she finally said. "You'll always be young. You don't have to worry about getting older."

"But I want to be older. I want to look my age. Someday I want gray hair and aches in my joints."

She laughed. "You say that now." Her hands brushed along his chest.

He didn't know what to say. With the mold on, it was as if a huge weight pressed upon his entire body. He thought he might be suffocating until finally she pulled off the mold and wiped away the jelly. Then, the mask in her hands, she added more paper pulp to the mold to shape it and compensate for the distorted, dented side of his face.

"This needs to dry," she said, "before I can paint it."

Despite having the mask removed, he still felt he had a huge weight pressing upon him. "I'm going for a walk," he said, sitting up.

"But it's night time," she said. "It's not safe."

"I'll be fine. I won't talk to anyone." She frowned. He tried to ignore her stare. After putting the straw hat on, he pocketed his pencil. As a substitute to a shower, he decided, he would walk at night where the coastal air felt like cold water. If he stayed inside any longer he would explode. "I need some air after having the mask on."

She studied him, looking for a reaction, he assumed. He didn't know what to give her as a response.

"Don't be too long," she said.

9

In the evenings, we drink wine from the north and watch the sun set over the city. This is something you will never see because you never made it as more than an inland artist. It's time you know that all of your failures hang from our walls. We had to see them every day. Even when you made me, your other sons laughed and made fun of it. The most terrible thing for me to realize is that I am your greatest creation. An object that is trapped in a stifling body and is forever ruined because of your "vision" is the best thing you ever gave to the world. And that is why you will never see it again.

As he wandered the neighborhoods and passed more pudding shops and coffee houses, he remembered at home the scent of the stacked bags of coffee stored in the gymnasium. He walked by restaurants that reeked of fish sauce and sandwich shops with the perfume of onions, and he took in all the sights of the people inside and out. How they moved behind the glass, how they interacted with their surroundings on the sidewalk—he imagined how he could act like them, how he could be any one of them.

He hiked the hill at the end of the city and sat under a crop of apple trees. Maiko had said that years ago a farmer had tried to start an apple orchard, but the city claimed the land as theirs, and the farmer had to give up his property and eventually became a poor shoe shiner. From this view under the branches, Michael was shocked to see how dark the city was. Most of the lights were turned off now. He wondered what time it was. Behind him, the lighthouse occasionally panned its single eye of light across the city before swinging it over the dark ocean, splashing its beam over the radio tower not that far north. Below the tower, a blue police light mimicked the motion of the lighthouse. Once he got a work permit from his new job, he would be equipped to cross into the north.

The darkness of the ocean was no different than the darkness that spilled onto the hills inland. So far apart and so similar, he thought. What had frustrated him most of all about his situation was to have time stopped in his own life but to have seen his brothers, all younger than him, grow into adults while he was stuck. They had transformed from skinny sticks to full grown men with facial hair and dry knuckles from working in the coffee field. They ate like lumberjacks, even though they were coffee farmers, and they were responsible and loyal to their work and each other. Michael's paper body stayed the same, and no hair grew on his painted jaw or above his rolled paper lips. His arms never changed, stunted in this shell of a body he had to wear, no matter how many bags of coffee he dragged across the gym floor to the scale.

But now here he stood, above the compact city, its lights and sounds and smells below him, all within his grasp. He had been afraid upon arrival, but of course there were bumps along any road. They made sense, he told himself, only when he had some distance to look back. The sensation of a line, from his feet to his head, pulsed inside him, the beginnings of a sense of control. He wouldn't be like the dead mermaid. She had tried to change too much, from a fin to a set of legs. He now understood that he would always have limits with his body, but at least he could mimic others and slowly blend himself into the city.

Below the lighthouse, he imagined himself and Maiko drinking wine, watching the whales from a rooftop apartment. That version of himself was not fully inside him yet. But somewhere in this city it existed, and he could absorb it as he had absorbed the rain and the energy around him.

To the east lay the darkness of the bay. In bookkeeping, the point was to find a balance in debits and credits. Here, the balance was not visible. The small lights all over the city did not equal the darkness, especially of the sea. He pictured what lived inside the water, what was just below the dark, flat surface. He pulled out the pencil and added to his letter. *I've seen whales at sunset; their fins silhouetted against the sun.*

When he returned to the apartment, he saw a large man in an unbuttoned coat leaning against the wall, holding himself up with one hand. Someone was crying—or the night wind was howling. A car drove by and its headlights illuminated the man's shirt, stained with bright red blood.

"Are you all right?" Michael asked. As he approached, the man let go of the wall and tried to walk forward, but he instantly collapsed. Michael's first instinct was to step away, afraid that his paper body would be crushed by the weight of the man, but something overtook him, a kind of courage he had not felt before, and he braced his legs to absorb the impact. The man's body balanced itself on Michael's shoulders, and Michael was able to use his arms to hold the man. During all this, the man moaned several times, and his bloody shirt swept across Michael like a giant paintbrush.

The apartment door opened and Maiko appeared. She stood for a moment, registering what had happened, and then she cursed. She ran to the man's other side and helped balance him. The man kept muttering words that made no sense.

"No-no-no," the man said.

"Who did this?" Michael asked. The man looked into Michael's eyes, and before Michael would have been terrified of the attention, but this time he told himself not to look away and held the man's gaze.

"Northerners," the man said.

"Stay away from northerners," Maiko said, but she was staring at Michael.

"Did they get you too?" the man said. His face was glossed with sweat and his eyes were focused on Michael's dent. Michael said nothing, but the comment lingered inside him. He wished the damage was because of a violent act upon him, instead of something as simple as rain. They helped the man to his apartment. After they returned him to his wife, who had thrown the key so they could bring him into the apartment above, Maiko rushed Michael downstairs.

"We have to get that blood off you before it soaks in," she said. She tore off his shirt—some of the blood had already stained his skin like a birthmark.

10

After dealing with the blood on him, Michael wanted to see the mask she had made. She blocked him from looking at the kitchen table.

"It's not ready yet. Don't look. You should go to bed. You've had a long night and have a long day tomorrow."

He tried to move around her, almost as if they were playing a game, and she broke into her trilling laugh.

"All right," he said. "But wake me up when it's ready."

In the bedroom, he crawled under the sheets and listened to the strokes of the paintbrush lapping at the paper mask. It had been a long time since he had slept in a bed. He wondered if she would object. The steady, rhythmic stroking reminded him of his first night in the apartment when the water from the rain dripped in the pool of water flooding the drawing room.

I'm sorry I left without saying anything. It was time I try out life. Ten years was enough time to stay in one spot. He inhaled the scent of mushrooms from the pillow. Against the night stand, he wrote the last line to his letter: *I hope you found a suitable replacement for me. Regards, Michael.* He dropped the pencil as the sounds of the paintbrush lulled him to sleep.

───────────────

Later in the night, he woke with his hands pressed to his chest. Through the floor vent, the shrill call of a train whistle rang and its pulsing, chugging sounds. He put his ear to the vent and listened. How could the sound of a train travel through these pipes? He wondered where it was in the city and where it was going.

Maiko was beside him. She shook him, as if he were sleepwalking, trying to bring him back to reality.

"I'm awake," he said. Her eyes were luminous.

"Were you thinking of your accident?"

He nodded, and then added, "I was thinking of Mischa."

Maiko had gathered the sheets around her, exposing his legs to the cool air. "Your girlfriend?"

In his mind, he played back the memories he had tried to forget many times. Maiko shook him out of his reverie. She looked ready to cry.

"Who is she?"

"It was a long time ago," Michael said. He swallowed the cool air but wanted nothing more than a shower. "She was the only girl I talked with in high school, and she had liked to call me at all hours and say cryptic things, clues that were instructions on where to meet. In front of others, she pretended that she didn't know me."

"That's terrible. No one should ever be so mean to a papier mache boy."

Michael wanted to smile. "This was before. When I had real skin." He continued to stare at the dark ceiling. "She was all that I thought about when I was in high school. We talked about poetry and art all the time. She was the nicest girl."

"But what happened?" Maiko said. Her hands sat on his shoulders, her hair draped over one eye, and he remembered the hands of the one-eyed man on the bus. For a moment, he wasn't sure if she would strangle him or hug him. He was fresh from sleep, though, so there was no filter in his mind. The thoughts passed from his head to his mouth. No layers of paper got in the way.

"We would go to her bedroom."

Maiko dropped her head on his chest and sobbed.

"Why are you telling me this?"

He gently pushed her away. She used the sheets to wipe her eyes. As the train whistle faded in the distance, he listened to her sobbing, the guttural sounds of living things in the vent and the creaking of his body from each deep breath. Maiko was the first woman he had spoken with in years. He didn't mention what happened in the bedroom with Mischa—which was nothing, really. They had read poems to each other, and all the while, even though she knew he was in love with her, Mischa treated him like a kid brother.

"Why are you crying?" he asked Maiko. "You barely know me," he paused, "I could be lying."

"Stop that."

He tried to think about his new life, the one he was shaping on his own terms and that the future was bright as a blank sheet of paper. He sat up and folded his letter on the nightstand. Maiko stopped crying and looked him in the eye: "So what happened?"

"The day she left, I took her to a train station. I never saw her again."

He turned to Maiko. He put her hands in his. His thumb stroked her palm, and she blew her breath toward her pillow.

"She's the reason you are like this. No wonder. Why didn't you tell me?"

"She didn't do this. I did it myself. I went back there to look for her each day until one day, I got tired. And I..."

He started again. "And that was when there was an accident."

They sat holding hands. The confession hung heavy in the room. Then she leaped up and ran down the hall.

"Maiko? Where are you going?"

It seemed as if he were still asleep, or underwater. She returned slowly from the kitchen, her peignoir flapping behind her like a tail.

"It's ready," she said and presented the mask. When they climbed into the bed, a spring squeaked like a voice.

The mask. It had the same vague, sickly gray paint as his skin, with a slight redness near the cheeks; eye sockets that were cavernous; a mouth with complete lips, and one corner of the reddish paint she had used extended, a small brushstroke, into the cheek area. The nose looked a bit larger, but he assumed that was so his real nose would fit. The best thing about the mask, as far as Michael was concerned, was that it was symmetrical. There was no dent. This mask, despite its small imperfections, was closer to the face he'd had before.

"It looks just like me." He could have said something more, something affectionate. For a moment, he was unsure of how he felt, and if he hesitated, this uncertainty would become apparent to her.

"Put it on," she said, but she put it on for him. She tightened the painted string around the back of his head. "Face me, now."

He panicked at first and thought he was suffocating. He reached to pull it away, but the string was too tight. He felt Maiko push his hands away and then stroke the cheek of the mask. It was so distant—in fact, he didn't really experience the touch at all, only heard the dry fingers caress the dry paper mask. Then he realized he couldn't see properly out of the eye holes. He turned to her.

"Let me adjust it a bit. Hold still."

"Okay," he said. His voice sounded muffled behind the mask. As if it filtered the tone of his voice to become the voice of someone else.

"Is that better?"

"That is better," he said. "My voice, though. Do you hear the difference?"

"I hear nothing."

"It's just the sound of my own voice, then," he said, more to himself.

The new job would work out. His new life would smooth out. He believed these thoughts as she had placed the mask up to his face, and from the eye slits, he watched her grin spread wider. She pulled him close and they were hugging. She held on tight, tense, taut—he was going to be crushed. Then he felt the softness of her lips pressing against his forehead.

"I barely know you, and you're already so close to me," she said. She squeezed him lightly again.

He was waking up—everything was real now. With the mask and the cool air and quiet night, something inside him loosened, and a wave of sensations and emotions crashed in the paper chambers of his body. With the mask, she looked at him like no one had looked at him in a long time. Could he be in love again? Inside the mask, he leaned into her, seeking her lips. She averted her face and, enveloping him, tucked him into the crook of her arm.

"Now, now," she said. "It's time for sleep." She stroked his hair and he pretended, behind the mask, to sleep.

Part Two:

MISCHA

11

His job was on an enormous ship, parked in the harbor beside the fish market. Each morning he pressed his way past the poles that had his flyer posted, through the bustling aisles of shoppers eager to buy the fresh sea creatures set on ice or swimming in small tanks. He was careful to dodge the puddles of melted ice or sludge that formed from loose fish skin and scales; he secretly enjoyed stepping on the discarded shells of crabs and lobsters. The shells were thin enough that his weight could crack them, and it sounded to him as if he were cracking bones.

His new client, a tuna cannery, was nothing like the work he had done inland. His brothers and their coffee farm had kept him busy not only with the bookkeeping but also with checking the inventory and weighing the bags of beans that were stored in the former gym. Like most clients, though, the cannery was oblivious to how much was required to get them on track. But whether it was coffee or tuna, the same accounting language would work.

His first day, he had crossed a small bridge over the harbor water to a black ship that glistened like a freshly emerged whale, with the words HOLLOWAY & HOLLIDAY TUNA painted across the side in red. The ship was parked next to a fleet of hearse boats that belonged to one of the city's many funeral parlors, which shuttled bodies and people out to the center of the bay.

Inside, a man whose clothes were stained with fish blood directed him to the controller's office. Michael walked a low-ceilinged hall, its steel walls bubbling with steam and drops of condensation like diseased skin. He stayed in the middle to avoid getting wet. The smell of the ship hit him that first day and each day thereafter whenever he passed by the boiler room—a mix of seawater, fish rot, and diesel. The controller's office door was open, with a single, exposed light bulb hanging over a desk. A large man with a cigar was scribbling out some receipts, and with the bulb before his face, it looked as if he had one eye. The paper of the cigar glowed around its edges.

"Who's there?" the man asked.

"My name is Michael," he said through the mask. "We talked over the phone about the bookkeeping position."

"Step inside," the controller said as he spit the cigar into a bucket of gray water. He proceeded to ask several basic interview questions, ending with, "So you think you know how to make sense of a mess?"

"It's my specialty," Michael said.

The controller leaned over the desk and squinted to get a better look. Michael touched the nose of his mask.

"Are you a foreigner?"

"No, sir. But I recently moved to the city. I'm from the inland."

"Has the city given you a work permit?"

Michael clasped his hands tightly behind his back to brace himself against this interrogation. No job seemed interested in helping him.

"I thought your ship said one wasn't required."

The man grunted.

"I can tell you're into accounting. And I'm guessing you're ugly, like me. Me, I've never thought to wear a mask to hide it, but maybe you're onto something. People are getting paranoid about who's watching them. All that northern scrutiny, makes you want to crawl under a rock!" The man laughed but coughed up some phlegm that he spit into a bucket.

Michael shifted his weight, his left arm—the one repaired by Maiko—heavier than usual. He didn't know what to say to the man, but before he knew it, his head was nodding like a puppet.

"You won't need a work permit here. But it's very important for you to know something. We have been accused by the NSA of transporting *more than tuna* to other destinations. They demand to see our books, which are nonexistent at this point. Your first task is to make sense of what papers we do have."

"What is the NSA?"

"The Northern Shipping Authority. The north has its hands in everything, and I'm not sure why we ever assumed we'd be excluded from that honor."

The man sneered. Without getting up he reached out, since his office was so small, and pulled open a metal cabinet. An avalanche of papers and folders crashed to the sticky floor.

"Once you sort all of this, we'll need books for each month for the past two years."

"Do you have a chart of accounts?"

This seemed like the right question to start with, Michael thought. There had to be at least one document from which to start that would be a key to this chaos.

The man laughed again and leaned out of the direct glare of the light bulb. Michael tugged the knot of his butterscotch tie. Maiko had washed most of the stains on the front of it, although the few left looked intentional, like a pattern on the fabric. If he had pores, he would have been sweating around his neck.

"If you have nothing for me to start with, this will take some time."

"That's fine. You might see things that don't belong. Gross invoices that need to be recorded in net amounts. I expect you to put them in the right columns to show we're doing nothing but tuna here. You'll be paid nicely for it. Understand, inlander?"

From then on, his daily task was to go to a storage room that was further down the hall, a room lined with shelves filled with rows and rows of black vests, black helmets, and shiny guns. He used a bucket to occasionally scoop up pages in the controller's office and then dump them in the storage room, where he sorted them into chronological piles. The bucket reminded him of the barrows of coffee that were recorded in the ledger book he once managed back home. Again he remembered the scent of the stacked bags of coffee, which always had a vague hint of vomit. Here, though, the smell of the buckets was of fish and rotten organic material, bits of fish bones fossilized along the rim. He worried if the stench would seep and settle into his paper skin.

———————————

He returned to the ship each weekday, during which he created a new chart of accounts for Holloway & Holliday. This would be the system that explained where all the money went and was received—in theory. His own accounting tricks back at home that resulted in him acquiring extra money for himself were helpful for this new task at the cannery. The controller seemed pleased and told him to proceed and left Michael on his own.

Each day his work usually began with one invoice that he pulled from the pile. It was normally for the purchase of thousands of tuna cans (any paperwork that wasn't related to tuna was to be thrown into the furnace at the end of the day in a single pile, although he never did it because of the heat). The invoice was simple, with only one line item, but the quantity column had the number 5,000. For some reason, this always made him think of himself. He was one person but had the capacity for 5,000 different people he could become. Already, though, he was beginning to notice his number had been reduced because his body was damaged, and he only had one skill that made him money. There were so many other people he could possibly become, perhaps only 3,000, but he tried not to let this reduction discourage him.

In between tasks, when he was bored, he would draw, just as he did in his old notebooks. He drew the controller and the rows of helmets around him. In the back pages of the journal ledger, he sketched other figures. He tried drawing the city's buildings and the people he encountered each day, cataloging the things he liked or didn't. Sometimes he exaggerated a feature, such as a nose or slouch. Their clothes, their eyes, women or men, he included them all.

While the work was slow and uneventful, there was one problem. When he emerged from the ship each evening, shocked from leaving one environment and entering another, he would wipe his mask with a handkerchief to remove the condensation and find streaks of paint. In addition, the heat on the ship caused the paint on the mask to bubble, and every night Maiko would have to repaint it. Eventually, after his first pay check, paid to him by the controller in cash, Maiko bought enough supplies to make a cabinet in the closet full of masks. She seemed pleased to have a role in helping him prepare each day. They developed a routine where she rotated the new ones out from the top shelves and left those awaiting repair on the bottom.

Each mask had slight variations. Sometimes he had a grin on his face; other times his eyebrows looked angry. One mask had cracked while it dried, and it was too late to notice that an eyehole was large and exposed his dented eye socket until he was at the bus stop and a young girl pointed at him.

"Sorry about that," Maiko had said when he told her that night. And because they had a reserve of masks, she threw this one away. To see his face on top of the trash in the bin next to the refrigerator made Michael sink deeper into his seat at the table.

In the kitchen, the radio was airing another of the one-eyed man's rants.

"Their buildings are unstable. Their streets have no logic. There's no monitoring of resources. The city is doomed to destroy itself if the north doesn't help. And that's what the north wants to do most of all: help. If you city folks are listening—and I know you are!—please remember this: there's a reason why the great northern continent is known for having citizens living the best life today. They have the greatest education system, which your children could have access to, the greatest doctors and hospitals with the latest treatments, the best musicians and poets, and the safest streets from a robust police force..."

He shot up from his chair.

"Michael, what is it?"

"I forgot to do something at work," he said. His voice sounded normal in the apartment, where he went without his mask. The next day, he decided, he would try to find his notebooks. He didn't care about the money, which was probably already gone. He only wanted his drawings. "I may have to work late tomorrow."

12

HE WANDERED THE STREETS, AVOIDING THE MUSHROOM AIR OF Maiko's apartment. In the windows—the hall of records, the ice and cold storage shops, and the bustling but barricaded canteens—he observed his reflection; he touched the mask to remind himself that it was not a permanent part of his body. It sometimes felt odd to have on another layer, and other times he completely forgot. On several occasions he went too far from the center of the city, and people immediately stopped him and asked for identification. The controller had given him a fake work permit, but once when some official-looking man on the street demanded to see it, the man laughed and tore it up. After a while, he learned which streets not to cross that led into the stricter neighborhoods. In the city's center, he found he blended in better and was mostly anonymous.

As he wandered—the overpowering scent of honeysuckle in a stray wind, perhaps from the north—he thought about the night he had put on the mask, the final seal of protection around his body. But recently he had begun to worry that his new life had too quickly turned into something routine, something static. And that was exactly why he'd moved away from his father and brothers. It had taken him ten years to build up the courage to be on his own, and now it had been a little over a month and already a similar, dull ache was forming inside his armature.

After his accident, he never went back to school, and no one ever tried to contact him. This was how he learned that he had no true friends. The only person he wanted to see was Mischa, but she had left on the train and had no idea what had happened to him. The only girls he saw after that were the ones his brothers brought to this house. Once, while walking down the hall past his father's artwork, a blonde girl emerged from Leo's room and froze when she spotted Michael. He stopped too, and they stood there, the split of paintings and photographs between them.

"You're the boy who jumped onto the track," she had said. He shook his paper head, still a bit floppy at the time.

"I didn't jump." He said this every time, but nobody, not even his brothers, believed him. She didn't believe him either.

"They thought you were dead."

––––––––––––

A truck passed by and blacked out his reflection in the window. He continued on his way up the shoestring street, the wooden heels of his shoes clicking against the pavement. He kept his face low as a crowd of young men rumbled past him. They were carrying long wooden poles and buckets of paint. Michael hurried on.

He eventually switched to a smaller road two blocks up. Too many people seemed on the main street, and he was afraid there might be an inspection point higher up. This road wound north then narrowed to a row of shacks. Several children with dirty faces came out to see who was there.

"I'm looking for the radio station and can't find the road to get to it. Do you know?"

The children ran away.

He kept going. It was nearly dark. The road now was lined with houses illuminated by their porch lights. His head low, he avoided the brightness and made it to another road that joined what he assumed was a main street.

And there, across the way, sat a square building of three floors, dark except for the windows on the middle floor, crowned by the glistening radio tower.

He was going to storm in and ask for the one-eyed man. He was imagining the confrontation when something else caught his eye. Stuck to a telephone pole was a flyer that rustled in the wind. He paused, stepped closer, and leaned in to read *ABC: Adam's Book-*

keeping Company. We'll Help You Mind Your Ps & Qs. It looked almost identical to his flyer, except that the typeface was printed, rather than hand-lettered like the ones he and Maiko had done. And it was stapled, not pasted. He tore it off the pole and the large steel staples clung tight, keeping the corners of the paper.

A new panic spread from his gut. Someone was trying to displace him from the city. He reviewed the situation, and of course it made sense that these moves were allowed living in the city. Anyone could displace you, and your place would be lost.

Maiko was in the apartment, sewing a torn sleeve on one of his shirts. She had found several in dumpsters that she laundered and then altered to fit Michael's small body, too large otherwise. He presented to her his rival's flyer. She took one look at it before resuming her sewing.

"It's nothing," she finally said.

"This was in front of Willard's," he said. "We only have one client."

"For now. Don't worry. This will work out. I'm being optimistic now, like you."

"What happens after this assignment ends?"

"Are you ready to eat?" She stood and her dress unpeeled from the couch cushion. Since the drawing room flooded, all the furniture had a sticky residue that clung to their clothing.

"I have to remove every one of these from the city," he said.

She ignored him and added mushroom broth to a pot.

"I could lose my place here."

"That's impossible."

"Look what the mannequins did to you."

She froze. She tightened her grip around the ladle.

"That's different. Michael, it's impossible to remove all the flyers. I refuse to encourage that. Besides, it's not safe at all to be out much. You're supposed to come home right after work. What were you doing by Willard's?"

"I didn't come to this city to hide out in a ship all day and basement apartment all night. I need to be around sunlight, plants, the sea, people."

She stroked his cheek and pouted again like a fish.

"Soon, my dear. Just wait until all this mess blows over in the city."

He tossed the flyer in the trash. In the closet cabinet, he exchanged his worn out mask from that day for a fresh one. He no longer spent more than a few minutes without a mask. Even when sleeping he wore one. In the bedroom, he scribbled another letter—*Dearest Father, today I stayed out all day in the sun*—placed it in an envelope with no return address, and threw it in the mailbox.

The next day he found another flyer for *Adam's Bookkeeping*. He tore it off. Down the street, he saw another and tore that one off; but two blocks later, he discovered another one. The little posters were both pasted and stapled. Soon he was racing through the streets and was amazed and horrified at the number of flyers. At first, he held them, crumpled into small rocks of paper, but soon his hands were full, so he littered and tossed them into the gutter, into the pots of plants, into the branches of magnolia trees, and at the windows of passing cars that flashed his reflection.

Around one corner, he found the same flyer posted three times to a newspaper vending machine. As his painted fingers picked at the edges of the flyers to peel them off, he finally noticed a crowd approaching from one end of the street and another group running toward them, shouting slurs and epithets. They crashed together and the scuffle turned violent. A man in a tank top with tattoos along his arm swung a pole and knocked an older man unconscious. People began throwing rocks. More people fell. Michael kept tearing at the flyers and was so close to removing the last one that he stayed, noting that Adam obviously had not used wheat paste but something stronger, something manufactured. The mixed crowd, shouting and screaming, tossing debris at each other, suddenly enveloped Michael and the vending machine. The man with the pole struck the machine, the tattoos on his arm twisting and writhing, riding his muscles and tendons as his arms flexed. Before he could escape, Michael was grabbed by several hands that lifted him up.

"What's this one hiding?"

Someone was reaching for his mask, but he held tightly to it, covering his face with both hands.

"Leave the kid alone!"

"He's so light!" someone shouted. More hands grabbed at him, and then they were pulling him in different directions.

"Let him go!"

"Show your face! What are you ashamed of?"

"Does he have papers?"

He tried to move but his limbs were clamped. Two buttons from his coat broke free. Someone tugged on his arm socket, the one Maiko had repaired. He did not fight back for fear of coming apart and instead offered no resistance to the flow of the crowd carrying him forward.

"I have a work permit," he finally lied, hoping it would buy him time to escape, but no one heard him. Hands burrowed into his pockets. In the blur of faces, he could clearly see Maiko's neighbor, the man who had bled on him not long ago. Did he not recognize Michael? The crowd became silent. Michael looked between the waves of fingers and balled fists surrounding him. His heart raced, his blood was glue.

"He doesn't belong here," the man shouted.

The fighting broke out and spilled everywhere. From the mass of hands came the covers of metal trash bins and a chain that smacked across his shins. He screamed. The hands dropped him, and he was kicked from all directions. Above him was the man he had helped, holding a chain, using his steel-toed boots to kick Michael down the street. The man's lips were coated in spittle that floated away like sea foam in the wind.

Michael absorbed the impact, and his sight blurred his sur-roundings into a mass of gray concrete and black smudges. His nose snapped. Luckily, he thought, it only belonged to the mask. Finally, he saw his chance and leaped up. But then he stumbled. His right foot was broken off. His sight turned fuzzy again—everything shaded a rich purple, then yellow, the forms of the crowd parting in two colorful waves.

"You broke him," the tattooed man said.

He found the broken nose on the ground, but as he hobbled over on his one good foot, the entire mask snapped off in a strong gust and fluttered down the street.

The woman screamed and the crowd reeled back. Everyone's expressions showed their disgust. His protective shell was gone. The cold coastal wind felt invigorating, but to have his actual paper face exposed and free of cover, was, at the same time, terrifying. A strange thrill shuddered through his body. They all saw the ugli-ness that was now stamped on him, forever. As the people stopped fighting to gape and stare, he used their moment of hesitation to grab his detached foot and hobble off.

He rushed across the street, limping as fast as possible. At the first open building, he went inside. In its dim hallway, he leaned against the wall, panting, covering his face, unmasked, with his hands. He was devastated. His body had been badly dented again. Now he had a torn foot. A broken nose. What would he say to Maiko? That she had been right?

Dearest Father, I need help to get home. I will pay back the money I took.

He wanted nothing more than to leave this place behind. He belonged someplace safe, even if it was terribly boring. Even if he was alone and suffocating. His brothers would understand it as a phase he had gone through. Even though he was an adult, he was still an adolescent trying to catch up. They might even laugh about it.

"You got in just in time. The fog's rolling in."

Above him stood a man with oversized black-framed glasses, gazing out the frame of the door. He wore a deckle-edged ultra-marine suit and on nearly all of his fingers were gold rings with different gems. The man smiled. Then he offered his hand to help Michael stand up.

13

"Do you need anything? You seem lost."

The man continued to hold out his hand, emerging from his deckle-edged sleeve. *If I was home now, I'd never leave again.* Michael presented his segmented fingers, and the man pulled him up. He peered consolingly at Michael's dented face but said nothing.

"Your foot," the man said, taking it from Michael's hands. He inspected the contents of the shoe. "You're in luck. This is an art gallery, and we have some supplies that can fix you."

"Really?"

"I'll be right back," the man said, and disappeared down another dark hall.

Michael walked into the first of the two main rooms and glanced at the paintings hung at eye level across the walls. The room felt warm, inviting—so unlike Maiko's apartment or the Holloway cannery ship. This room appeared to be ready for a show. The canvases each had their wires exposed, though, something he had never seen before. It was as if the gallery was acknowledging the illusion that artwork appears to hover on a wall. Here, the nuts and bolts of it all, or rather the nails and wires, were available for everyone to see.

As he walked around, peg-legged, his one shoe clicked on the concrete floor. With the fog outside and the danger passing, he felt warm and safe in this quiet place, filled with beauty. In a corner of the gallery, Michael discovered a fascinating piece that hardly looked like a painting. It was a circuit board with small silver blocks connected by yellow strips like roadways. The green of the board extended outside of the canvas onto its edges. The piece was labeled *The City*. Briefly, Michael considered if there was a connection to the layout of a city and its relationship with nature. Below this title was the artist's name: D. Doppelmann.

The next painting, though, was completely different in style. An elevator, piled with geometric shapes, triangles and cylinders and a circle standing beside the square buttons for selecting the floor. They were all going to floor 77, as that was the only button lit on the console.

Each painting was wildly different from the one before it. It was as if the artist experimented with every style available, from abstract splashes of paint to glowing blocks of color to more detailed and realistic paintings of the sea cliffs and the boats. There were several portraits, some with paint so thick it rose above the canvas. It was quite a shock for him—his father's work had always been realistic, perfectly capturing the shadows of the clouds on the hills inland and the patches of cottonwood trees shimmering. The variety of style and total disregard for matching reality surprised and thrilled him.

That was when he saw the final painting. A girl, gazing over her shoulder. Her short black hair was shiny, her face round and moonlike, glowing skin, but she had tiny blood vessels around her small nostrils, the faint hint of a mustache above her lips. Her flat, almond eyes looked at him so desperately. He wanted to reach in and pull her out. Her puckered rose lips held back something that was ready to come out, a scream or stream of words. Obscenities. He imagined her upset with the artist, who caught her in such a vulnerable state. Her neck was thin and a bruise stained her arm. It was her eyes, shimmering, that made him want to hold her.

What was most shocking was that she was a girl he had once known: Mischa. The painting had to be of her. Could she be in the city? What if she moved here after that day ten years ago at the train station? He wondered how the artist came to paint Mischa. Perhaps he saw her in a crowd, and her image burned into his mind. Or perhaps Doppelmann was related to her.

As he went over the painting again, noting the details of her hair, the shape of her earlobes, the corners of her puckered lips, she became more real. It had to be her: the piece was even titled *Mischa, darling.*

He imagined himself in his new life in the city, with this kind of girl. She had always been his ideal—sweet, artistic, slightly adventurous. She would feel sorry for him when she saw he was now made of paper, sorry that she had never called him after leaving on the train. And he would care for her, make that look on her face disappear and a smile emerge, and she would hold onto his elbow when they walked along the coast. She wouldn't be afraid of the city. The past, something Michael had tried hard to erase by moving here, would finally fix itself in the present, and he could have the relationship with Mischa that had been intended years ago. And they would help each other. The city had been harsh to her as well—she was someone he could trust to get him out. They'd eventually return inland and start over.

This possibility thrilled him. The painting showed that he was not the only one stuck in time. She had the same expression from when they were in high school and harassed by other students. The anxiety of the painting disturbed him. He could help; he would make her better than this.

A door shut. The man from the gallery appeared. He held a shoebox overflowing with rolls of tape and paintbrushes. He passed Michael and walked to the front counter, where a bowl of cloudy water housed two red goldfish. The spell broken, Michael took in the painting one more time and followed the silent man. His peg leg made a hollow tapping on the floor with each step.

"Excuse me, but how would I go about contacting the artist?"

———————

In the apartment, Maiko repeated herself. Why had he not listened to her? Why had he tried to remove the flyers? What would have happened if his mask did not fall off? What if this? Or what if that? What if the art gallery had been closed?

He wasn't listening to her, though. He was imagining the possibilities of life with Mischa. Where could she? What would she say about the turmoil in the streets? Having someone from his past in the city comforted him—perhaps she actually might help him leave the city. He remembered how alive she was, how she looked ready to burst out of her clothes. If she had been in that crowd, she would have held his hand and asked him to join them. With Mischa, they would throw crumpled paper rocks at the others and be a team.

After the attack, Maiko met him every evening outside the ship. She usually did some shopping in the fish market beforehand, and then they took the bus home together. The gallery owner had reattached Michael's foot, but he now had a slight limp while walking. And Maiko, who had inspected his dented sides from being kicked, could only paint over the cracked skin. Now he wore another layer of clothing to fill him out, so that he didn't appear too uneven. The mask with the broken nose was thrown away; for the new ones, she added strips of cloth to reinforce their structure.

Something had changed. He now felt different around her. Every time she cooked the same meal, he wanted nothing more than to eat what he couldn't. Each night she removed her slippers and then folded the corner of the bed sheets, he desired to ruffle them so that they were a mass like seaweed. The repetition began to grind on him. Only the brief fresh air they breathed while walking to and from the bus stop was his relief. He had an intense desire to jump in the ocean, and she seemed to sense this one evening: as he stood looking over the canal wall at the sluice gate with the waves banging to enter, she dragged him away and never let them walk by it again. He often thought of the dead mermaid as Maiko shuttled them to and from the apartment and how he understood what that creature of the sea had gone through to get here on land.

Then, one Saturday, he executed a plan to get out on his own. He held his briefcase in one hand and an umbrella in the other. In the briefcase was a letter, encased in a small envelope made from a page of newspaper comics, and on the umbrella was a pattern of colored triangles. The letter belonged to him; the umbrella to her. As he ascended the steps of the basement apartment to the entryway, he heard her bedroom door close below.

"Where are you going?" she asked. Her silhouette stood below him, a mound glued to the bottom step, which gave the appearance of a fin instead of feet.

"I'm going to work," he said. She climbed the stairs to stand one step below him.

"What if you get wet?"

They both listened to the rain falling on the street above; even though it was summer, it felt like a winter storm. The air in the stairwell seemed full of moisture, of steady thrumming from the rain, and was mixing with the heat rising from the kitchen below.

He raised the umbrella.

"And it's Saturday," she added.

"I have to finish the financial reports before Monday."

"You might get wet again."

"I'll be careful." He was wearing his mask, and an urge to pull it off pulsed from his center. He brushed the back of his hand, the one that held the briefcase, across the mask's cheek.

"Don't go." She hooked her hand onto his shoulder. "You can finish it on Monday. Or let me get dressed and walk with you."

"I'll be fine," he said and opened the door.

The gray outdoor light split across her face. She had a lovely face, despite the beige lump on her jawline, the mole like a mushroom sprouting.

"You look like a school boy," she said, and straightened his new thin black tie and smoothed his jacket's lapels. "Fine. Stay away from any puddles. And watch for any wind that blows the rain sideways." There hadn't been any news lately of violence in the streets. She wrapped her robe tighter around her body and braced herself against the cool air sinking in. He could smell her vanilla perfume. "If you're not back before dark, I'll be looking for you."

"I'll be careful," he said again, and popped open the umbrella. He walked the wet street, every time glancing back to see that she still watched him until he was around the corner.

It was true that the financial reports were due Monday. But he was not on his way to work. He was on his way to meet the sender of the letter, encased in newspaper comics:

Michael,

I appreciate your enthusiasm for my work and your incisive comments about style. I agree that everything begins or ends there. Certain methods better express ideas and feelings than others. Similar to how some statements in one language sound perfect but can't readily be translated into others. I would be delighted to discuss that one odd minimalist piece, The City. I think you would enjoy the story behind it if you are so curious. Let us meet this Saturday at the City Collectorate building. Say noon? I will be waiting at the top of the steps. You mentioned you have your own distinctive style—I look forward to seeing it.

Curiously,

Dpplmnn

14

THAT SATURDAY, MICHAEL WALKED WITH HIS BRIEFCASE IN ONE hand and the umbrella held over his head and passed the many shops and neighborhoods that were part of his new home. He had learned to avoid crowds and spot potential clashes of people if they were walking too fast or carried objects ready for a fight. This only made him feel more alienated from the city. His move here had been to fit in, and now all he could do was sneak into city life.

He tried to plan how to act around the artist, Doppelmann. He wanted to appear intelligent, casual, but he also hoped to exude enthusiasm for his work. There were so many possibilities. In the end, he knew one of them would take hold depending on the first words from David Doppelmann's mouth.

He headed for the City Collectorate building, a large asymmetrical structure that appeared like a mirrored diamond on a square plot of park. The headquarters for the city's government, the building had become a site for daily protests. Rumors had spread that the government had been infiltrated by the north's representatives, and that was why they were losing more rights to the city's land and soon the rest of the peninsula. To reach it and see it in all its shining glory, Michael had to climb a flight of long concrete steps. As he approached, he spotted Doppelmann, ten years or so older than Michael, standing like a monument himself, open-collared shirt, longish hair waving in the wind, a cigarette inches from his lips. Something below had caught Doppelmann's eye, and he stared so intensely that Michael paused and turned around to see what it was. Behind him, the weekend traffic had clogged the narrow street below, and the street food vendors were setting up their stations on the sidewalks. What was so fascinating down there? Perhaps Michael was missing it; perhaps it was right before his eyes and he didn't even know it.

"Michael!" Doppelmann shouted when Michael was only a few steps away. He switched hands for his cigarette and put out his right one to shake Michael's. "I've got it right, haven't I?"

"You must be Doppelmann," Michael said. They shook hands and then Doppelmann raised his index finger to his lips.

"Shhh, you mustn't say that out loud," he said, grinning. "They might hear you and come after me."

Michael glanced around at the few people descending the stairs and those further away on the benches that faced the square of park grass.

"What do you mean?" Michael asked.

"It's nothing. I'm becoming of interest for my neighborhood, and they want me more involved with their efforts to secede should the north continue down the path of annexation. But the truth is that no one cares about art. Every so often, they think art can teach them to survive, and so they come to me. But they never learn anything. Let's walk, shall we? And why is your umbrella open? It's stopped raining. Or wait, of course! It is part of your style! Excellent. You are masking yourself from the sun as well!"

They descended the steps to the sidewalk. He scanned the line of approaching people on the sidewalk and was relieved no one appeared to be a potential threat for attacking him. When he walked the streets with a companion, he found that people left him alone. He hoped Doppelmann didn't notice his slight limp. Nearby, fried food from the street vendors sizzled in steam and smoke that floated by in clouds shaped like ghosts of animals. His stomach growled, but it was covered by the squealing wheels of a passing bus.

"What a delight to receive your letter. It's not too often I get asked questions by an admirer. Usually they are from journalists who want to interrogate me and box me in to some art movement. They expect that I'm working within some framework of ideology, so I don't talk to them. You aren't a journalist, are you?" Here, Doppelmann flapped up Michael's tie, as if his tongue was hanging out.

"I'm a bookkeeper," Michael said. Did Doppelmann not notice

that Michael looked different, that his face was frozen into one plain expression, a mask, that his eyes were begging forgiveness for embarrassing Doppelmann in public as his companion?

"How can you do that? Looking at all those numbers."

"Sometimes I help them save money."

Doppelmann did not seem to notice Michael's paper condition, perhaps because of the overcast sky or perhaps because of the shade of his umbrella or, more thrillingly, he simply did not care.

"You probably see sensitive information."

"I do indeed," Michael said. He tried to loosen his stiff stance. Doppelmann seemed distracted.

"It's a front of some kind, I'm sure, but what isn't a front these days?"

Trying to capture the artist's attention, Michael heard himself babbling on about the cannery and its accounting practices. He stopped only when the artist fixed him with a hard, penetrating gaze.

"So what was it again, then, that prompted you to write me? You liked the piece The City."

They were now at the corner of an intersection. In the distance in the bay water, a boat slowly moved away from the city, a cloud of steam above it.

Michael tried to formulate what to say about that first painting of Doppelmann's he had seen. He wanted to sound informed and original in his statement.

"I think its sleekness, how it wasn't like a painting at all, is what caught my eye."

He was surprised at this coming out of his mouth. It sounded professional.

"Correct," Doppelmann said. He put his hand on Michael's shoulder as they waited for the streetlight to change. "I used a microcosm to illustrate the workings of a city."

"Fascinating," Michael said, and for a moment they looked each other in the eyes. He wasn't certain if Doppelmann was staring at him, or through him, for his eyes were so intense and busy he might have been thinking other things.

They crossed the street. Michael had no idea where they were headed, but he went along for the walk. For a moment, he was afraid since Doppelmann had stepped into the crosswalk before the light had changed, but he, with several other pedestrians, had followed him. Doppelmann moved like a natural leader. They passed another food vendor selling bright fruits, skinned and raw, the burst of citrus scent surrounding them. He had the urge to abandon the umbrella, but it belonged to Maiko, and she would ask for it later.

"The funny thing on that piece," Doppelmann continued, "is that I started with something completely different. A field, green, with piles of stones. The piles grew and shrank. The tips of the grasses, yellow. The sky was overtaken, the stone piles multiplied, the tips became lines. Can you imagine, starting with a field and ending with a circuit board? By distorting the image, I came back to a recording of the image."

"It's amazing," Michael said, but he was only amazed that he was doing this, talking with an artist as if he, Michael, knew much about art. Doppelmann would surely laugh if he saw any of the drawings Michael sketched in the back of the extra general journals. How would he bring up the other painting? He only wanted to confirm if it was based on a real person.

Doppelmann continued discussing the circuit board painting as they turned another corner. He said painters too often left too much in and that they always struggled to take things out. They were now walking on the other side of the City Collectorate building. More people were on the sidewalks, carrying plastic bags of food. The misty breeze from passing cars made the bags hiss like snakes. Michael clutched the umbrella as the wind tried to tug it free. They climbed the steps again and stood under an olive tree in the park square.

"Nothing is more beautiful to me than scaffolding surrounding a building under construction." Doppelmann pointed in the distance to an old brick building surrounded by scaffolding with workers, small as ants, scurrying about. "The coming into being of things, it's so lovely." He glanced at Michael. "You're losing interest," he said. "I've gone on too long. I apologize."

"Not at all," Michael said. "Perhaps you could tell me about another painting. The Mischa painting."

"Ah, yes," Doppelmann said, combing his hair back. Michael realized how handsome Doppelmann actually was. "That painting is one of my favorites. To capture the look of loss and desperation, a begging for hope. It was quite intense for me to paint that. To have worked in the abstract for so long, to suddenly switch to the real was like seeing the world in a whole new way. I thought that way was dead, long dead since the arrival of photography. But no, the rawness of it all can still be captured, even in the slowness of painting."

"Was it based on anyone in particular?"

"Why, every young woman today has that look, whether expressed outside her body, or kept inside. The look of pleading for help, for reassurance that life is worth living, can be found in every naive girl who has tried to love."

"But was the portrait based on a real girl?"

"Portrait?"

"It is a portrait, right?" Michael thought he had said something wrong. Doppelmann seemed perplexed.

"I do not understand where this question is going."

"Mischa," Michael said. "Is she a real person? Or did you make her up?"

"She's real," he said. "Very real."

"It must have been hard for her to appear so revealing to someone, an artist especially."

"She didn't even know she had done that. She didn't know that her face was captured in my mind. I didn't steal it from her. I simply transposed it."

"Has she seen it? I mean, does she live in the city?"

"Why are you so interested in the source of this painting?" Doppelmann asked. He tilted his head, studying Michael, who scratched behind his ear.

He was afraid of what to say.

"She looked familiar," Michael said. "I thought I knew her, but I wasn't sure it was the same girl."

"She lives here," Doppelmann said, and waved out at the city, the expanse of the city surrounding them. "She works as an art model."

Michael tightened his grip on the briefcase handle. The pressure was too much, for the briefcase was old, and it burst open, the letter from Doppelmann flapping out, only to be swept by the wind. Doppelmann watched it fly away as Michael scrambled to latch the case closed.

"Never mind that."

But inside he was burning to run after it—he wanted to keep it as a souvenir.

"Regarding Mischa, I would love to meet her, and find out if she is the same girl from high school," Michael said. "Old friends, you see. Do you know where she went to school?"

"I wouldn't know," Doppelmann said.

"Is there a way I might contact her?" Michael wasn't sure if this was working. If he linked his past to his present in the city, he truly thought she would be able to help him leave. Looking around them, he felt the city was pressing itself upon him, trying to force him to break.

Doppelmann stared at him again, or through him, and Michael was frightened that he was discovering things inside his brain that manifested themselves, somehow, through his face and onto his mask.

"There's a new exhibit opening next week in the museum, he blurted. I was wondering if you had any interest in going to it. You could shed much more light on the pieces, more than I ever could glean on my own."

Doppelmann pondered this for a moment, smiled, and said:

"Delightful. I don't get out often to see other art. I'm usually in my dark studio, which this place," and here he waved at the diamond building, "wants me to pay some rent. It will be nice to leave, like today. Even if it rains a bit."

"That would be wonderful," Michael said.

"And perhaps you could do me a favor."

"Anything," Michael said.

"All that bookkeeping you mentioned. Genuine accounting pages could be useful for a project I'm working on." The artist cocked his head inquiringly.

"I don't think I'd be able to take any with me."

"Just an example. They wouldn't be missed. There has to be some papers they wouldn't mind leaving for a bit. Like a library—I just want to borrow them, carbon copy them, and then you could put them back. My motives are purely artistic, to be sure."

Michael considered. He wasn't sure what Doppelmann was up to, and he wanted to trust him, yet it was a strange request.

"I'm sorry," he said and shook his head. "I don't think so."

Doppelmann waved him off. "Forget I mentioned it. As for our date to the museum, I will see if Mischa will join us."

Michael stopped in his tracks and his chest became heavy. "You know her still?"

"Yes, very well. She likes new things. She probably would go along with us, and you would be able to visit your old friend."

"Thank you!" Michael said, and then covered his mouth for fear he had spoken too loudly and showed too much enthusiasm. Doppelmann shook his hand, and they agreed to meet at the diner outside the museum the following Saturday. Michael agreed he would try to find some papers for Doppelmann.

And then, as he turned to leave, Doppelmann bit one of his nails and spit it on the ground. Michael stepped back, aghast.

"Always leave a piece of yourself wherever you go," Doppelmann said, and winked. He descended the stairs, a slim, fit strip of human in dark clothes scissoring down the steps.

15

HE ARRIVED EARLY AT THE DINER. A CROWD OF PEOPLE BLOCKED the entrance, so after putting his name in at the front, he did a quick review of the faces to see if any of them belonged to Doppelmann or Mischa. The city had so many types of people. Here were families with grandparents and young grandchildren, teenagers smoking cigarettes, a few businessman in suits and ties, and people his age who were dressed in tighter clothes and brighter colors than he had ever seen before. Across the street was the museum, a large church-like structure with an obelisk-shaped atrium, where more varieties were streaming in. There were thin people, short people, round people, overdressed people, but no one made of paper.

A few glanced at him, perhaps wondering if he was the someone they were waiting to join their group. He touched the forehead of his mask, and he directed his gaze to the sidewalk, which was scuffed with stains of smashed berries from the thin trees that lined the walkway. Any time he was alone he felt vulnerable. Someone laughed and his eyes snapped up. Was he the source of humor? It was only a girl listening to a guy imitating, in an exaggerated way, the voice of someone else.

Michael imagined the possibilities with Mischa. He saw them eating lunch slowly, his speech confident and relaxed about the things they still had in common, his imitation of the voice of their high school literature teacher, her laugh like the girl outside the diner, her apology for not keeping in touch, his deeply moving confession that he had long hoped for this day, his suggestion that they meet again soon, and finally, his request for help to get him out of the city. All week he had feared the worst, that Mischa wouldn't show or she would be disgusted by his paper body or she would be the wrong Mischa. Now that all those thoughts had cycled through him, he was empty and ready to be filled with imagined confidence.

More people arrived and formed a loose line behind Michael. He was becoming part of the crowd. Each time someone walked by, he looked up from the smashed berries to see if it was her. As the minutes passed, he scratched at his yarn hair and checked his pockets for scraps of paper and money to ensure they were still there. His shoulders slumped, and in the berries, he started to decode constellations that spelled out how much of a failure he was. A flyer, perhaps belonging to Adam's Bookkeeping Company, blew by in the gutter; he wanted it to take him away.

But then the crowd parted and Doppelmann appeared, his hand linked to a woman's elbow behind him. Michael's heart nearly stopped.

"Michael," Doppelmann said. "Say hello to Mischa."

She was not the same woman in the painting. Not at first glance. While the painting had short brown hair, this woman had long, wavy black hair. Her eyes were darker and shined. She had the faintest creases from her nose to the corners of her lips. Everyone around them looked at her, not because she was exceptionally beautiful, but because she held a presence that alerted people that someone different had arrived. Her arms, exposed in an olive tank top, were tan and sinewy. He mentally projected the image of the portrait onto her face and searched for the overlaps. Yes, there were similarities, but the desperation was gone, the near defeat of optimism missing. This woman appeared to have survived whatever it was at the time of the portrait.

"It's good to see you again," Michael said. "Do you remember me?"

She tilted her head, not sure how to take in Michael's staring and said nothing. He tried again, more casually: "Can you believe how we are meeting? Through Doppelmann's painting."

"Oh that thing. I can't believe that was me. I don't really like that piece."

Doppelmann, who was taller than her, put his hands on her shoulders.

"She doesn't like to be reminded of herself back then. I think it's lovely, though. It says so much, not just about her, but about a generation."

She leaned forward and pointed directly at Michael's face. "I do like your mask. I've been seeing more people in the streets with them on, trying to stay anonymous. You are part of an early trend."

Doppelmann's fingers, thick and stiff, pressed into Mischa's shoulders. The door to the diner opened and the hostess announced Michael's name.

"That's us. Let's eat, shall we?"

Michael let them go before him. He watched her walk—nothing spectacular—simple steps toward the door, which Doppelmann held open for her. He even noticed that a few scabs dotted the back of her neck, pimples from sweaty hair that was now swept up and captured by a clip. Yet everyone watched her as she entered, as if she were a celebrity. Michael hurried after them, glad they did not see his uneven stride. On his way, he broke the strands of a spider web.

Inside, they sat in a booth, Mischa and Doppelmann on one side and Michael on the other. Michael had to avoid a sticky spot on his seat, so he crammed himself closer to the wall. He asked for a towel from the waitress, who forgot and never brought it. He instantly closed up, his elbows pinned to his sides and his shoulders slumped forward. Behind them, another booth was full of large men who worked in construction. They reminded him of his past and his brothers. Each time they shifted around, it jolted all the booths, forcing Michael forward to knock knees with his guests.

"Michael says you went to school together," Doppelmann said. Mischa squinted and stared at Michael, analyzing him, probably superimposing images of other young men she once knew. Satisfied, she turned to Doppelmann.

"Yes, he was a good friend," she said. This made Michael want to smile. "But what happened to you?"

His gloved hands were patting his mask again before he knew it. This had become a reflex since he had started wearing it. How quickly new habits can be formed, he thought. Luckily the lighting in the diner was dim, and she had not looked repulsed when staring at him.

I was in an accident, he said. So much more was on the tip of his tongue. He pictured his tongue like an abstract painting, with tints of different colors in different regions, some deep red and dark blue, a tint of pink, a zigzag of black. He thought it might all pour out, but then the waitress arrived with a pencil and paper pad ready for writing.

"It was after you left," he simply said.

"Would you like anything to drink?" the waitress asked Mischa.

"Two glasses of water, please," Mischa said.

Behind his mask, Michael's jaw slightly dropped. "You must be thirsty."

"It's not that. I like to have a backup plan."

Doppelmann ordered milk, and Michael ordered orange juice and reminded the waitress he needed a towel.

"Where we lived, we called you Michael," Mischa said, "But your name was really Michelangelo."

"Ha!" Doppelmann slapped the table and the knives clinked with the forks and spoons. "Is that your full name?"

"I always thought that was such a strange name," Mischa said.

"Yes, but I never go by that," Michael said, and grabbed his spoon, which had nearly rattled off the table. He hadn't heard that name in a long time. It didn't even feel like it belonged to him. It had never been him, and he had no idea what it signified. His father said the strange name had come to him in a beautiful dream, and that was all.

Was that what she remembered the most about him? Not the time she tore up his essay for school? The hours they spent in her bedroom, talking about the books they had read? Or the games she played to make him find one of her poems hidden in the school library? She had seemed so sweet and energetic then. Was this really the same person?

"I won't call you that again," she said. If she sensed his discomfort, he was grateful. "We're different people now. So when did you move here?"

"A little over a month ago," he said. He didn't want to talk about himself. He wanted to hear her apologize for running away ten years ago so that he could move on to lighter topics and imitate their literature teacher's voice so he could make her laugh. That had been the plan. Instead, he found himself imitating her questions: "When did you move here?"

Doppelmann laughed at this, and Mischa glanced at him with a knowing look. The way they stared at each other and the touches from Doppelmann's hands, made Michael turn away. It seemed impolite to watch this secret language they had. He tried to imagine himself as Doppelmann. What if he was the one touching Mischa's shoulders, squeezing her closer, and brushing her hair? He could be the one who was an artist, a slim but solid streak of human skin next to her.

"I've been in the city too long," she said. "But I wouldn't want to be anywhere else. Not inland, not north. This is where I should be."

"I feel the same way," Michael said, and relaxed his shoulders. The idea of leaving now vanished. They had a connection now, and that was enough to start.

———————

They ordered their food, and Mischa asked for two coffees. Michael ordered a bowl of shredded napkins soaked in milk. Doppelmann told many stories. He rambled on about his paintings he was working on, and Michael tried to listen but lost his concentration. He was captivated by Mischa's hands, her fingers lifting a spoon to stir sugar in her coffee and wrapping around the handle of the ceramic cup and the flex of her arm as she pulled it closer to her lips. They were the same lips from the painting. Of course it made sense now to him. That painting had been one possibility of her. She didn't need help anymore. She was fine on her own, or with Doppelmann. And here she was watching him, causing him to shift in his seat and touch the sticky spot next to his leg. He removed an ice cube from his juice with a fork and rubbed it on the vinyl to erase the spot. Underneath his clothes, his dented body jerked suddenly from leaning over too much.

"I only look this way because there was a storm, and I can't really be out in the rain," he said to her. "I used to not need a mask."

Mischa peered carefully. "Is there really that much difference?"

"Be careful in the city," Doppelmann said. "Some people are looking for excuses to single people out. People with style are becoming less and less appreciated."

"Don't trust anyone," Mischa said. "It used to be that you could be whoever you wanted here. The city will end up destroying itself if they don't work together."

"I seem to be okay as long as I have company," Michael said, looking to both of them for a sign of reassurance they would protect him. They simply stared back at him.

"Let me feel," Mischa finally said, and her hand, the fingers that lifted the spoon to stir sugar, stroked his cheek and brushed across the bridge of his nose. Doppelmann stopped talking, and they all sat there while Mischa's hand moved to Michael's mouth. Her thumb plucked his mask's lower lip.

"You must be happy to be so unique." She sighed. "It's so dull to be like everyone else."

"If I didn't have to wear the mask, I wouldn't. It's humiliating."

She didn't seem to see it as the shameful object it was to Michael. She cited it as the potential to make someone great and better than what was normal.

"And besides your mask, may I ask, are you complete? Do you have hair everywhere you should?"

"More hair? Where?" Michael asked, touching his head. She

broke into laughter.

"Darling," Doppelmann said. "Leave the boy alone!" He gave an apologetic look to Michael. "As I was saying," he continued, and discussed the benefits of horsehair brushes.

She began to take more of an interest in him, it seemed, so he sat up straighter. The dents on his right side were the worst, but by casually leaning against the wall, there was less pressure on his distorted body. The men in the booth behind them were loud and complained about their orders to each other. One of them grunted, and then Michael was thrust forward again as the guy behind him got out. He bumped knees with Doppelmann, whose eyebrows jumped in surprise.

"What are you doing down there?" he asked, followed by an authentic laugh.

"Sorry about that." Michael imitated his laugh.

Doppelmann spoke of a trip that he and Mischa took to a tropical island. Michael watched Mischa as the story was told. Often, she looked at the empty plates of food, only to shoot a glance at Michael. She played with a wrapper for the straw to Michael's orange juice. She rolled it up, unrolled it, then folded the paper and finally crushed it into a ball and tossed it on the floor.

"It's just paper," she said. She looked at him again to see if he noticed and then smirked.

"Let me pay the chit, and then we'll be off to the museum." Doppelmann stood up.

"That's so kind," Michael said. "May I give you some money?"

"Nonsense. You get it next time," he said, and rushed off to the register. Michael was pleased. They seemed to like him and had implied they would hang out with him again. Mischa looked over her shoulder as Doppelmann walked away.

"A lot of us were mean to you back then," she said. "But that was many years ago. That was another life for me, inland."

"You were never mean to me. As for the others, no one knew better. Is life that much different for you now?" Michael asked.

"You know how it is," she said. "You live in a situation you have no control over. Then, one day you decide to leave. And you never look back. Then you can be whoever you want to be. Start over as many times as you need."

"I know exactly what you mean," he said.

She was a delight and he wanted to savor all of this: the words, the connection to their forgotten pasts, she alone on her side, he on his.

"Maybe you and I can meet soon. Catch up on old times," he said. "In fact, I was hoping to get your help with something."

He couldn't believe he said this. It just came out. She glanced at the register. They both watched Doppelmann remove his wallet from his back pocket, pick through the folded money, and select a bill. Michael waited for her response. Doppelmann swiped his index finger in his nose and then slid his finger across the counter. Leaving a piece of himself, Michael thought.

"I can't this week," she said.

"Of course, no rush," he said.

She pulled a napkin from the dispenser and brought out a pen from her small purse. "Do you still like poetry?"

"I do," he said.

"Do you remember my box of poems?"

"I remember," he said. He thought of the time they were on her bed and she poured the box of poems on him, and he read each one and stacked them neatly at the foot of the bed.

"You used napkins and receipts, often stained with coffee."

"And you didn't drink coffee. Only juice." She nodded to his glass of juice and then scribbled down words on the napkin as Doppelmann returned.

"Everyone ready for some art?" he said. He stood before their table like the monument he was, or wanted to be. Michael stood up and noticed they were the same height. Doppelmann had seemed taller the first time they had met. "Mischa? Ready?"

She finished scribbling on the napkin then handed it to Michael.

"I wrote a poem for Michael."

"Excellent, dear," Doppelmann said, and draped his arm over her shoulders. "You write excellent poetry."

Michael glanced back at the men in the booth behind them. They were beefy and packed like canned anchovies. One of them snorted. Michael brushed at his yarn hair, scurried to join Doppelmann and Mischa, and then, as they approached the door, the glass door with the sign that said THANK YOU PLEASE COME AGAIN, he unfolded the napkin in his hands.

The paper was dry and coarse. Written in ink, slanting to the right, was the first poem of Mischa's he had read in ten years. He read the inscrutable lines several times over as they walked across the street:

Why
oh why
did he serve us
cubism on rye?
Now we must lie.

He crumbled the poem and he ate it. He put it in his mouth and swallowed it, a small, white, paper capsule. Any other time he would have saved it, for such a thing deserved to be remembered. But if Doppelmann asked to read it, there would be too many questions, and he wanted this to be a secret. So he ate it, made it a part of his paper body, and breathed quickly to calm his fast-beating heart.

16

INSIDE THE MUSEUM, THEY PASSED ROOMS OF THE PERMANENT collection and headed to the back, where the new art was on display. It was an annual show of emerging artists that had a vandalized sign above the entrance: ENTER FOR FINE ARTS. The first word's missing front letter C lay on the floor that everyone stepped over. The museum itself seemed to be a facade—from one direction the walls appeared thick and stable, but passing through door frames, it was clear that they were thin boards that could collapse easily. As they walked down the hall, Doppelmann pointed at things they saw and quickly commented on them.

"Museums are normally graveyards for art, but now look at all of this. It's alive with art by living artists. This is why I love the city. I like that there," he said, and then, glancing at the other side, pointed again and said, "but this, here, is just wonderful."

Mischa would not look at Michael. He wondered if her poem meant something more or if it was a joke. The guessing woke up his brain and glue blood. Other men in the museum watched her as she walked by. She was beautiful, he decided, even though her walk was not graceful, her shoulders a bit too stiff, and her legs shuffling to keep up. How, he thought, would she move in a dress if they were to attend the opera?

They stopped at the first piece in the new art exhibit, a blob of yellow plastic embedded with dog teeth.

"Why look at that," Doppelmann said. "Now this is the kind of stuff I'd like to do. More variety in materials, and the smell." He inhaled deeply. "It's so manufactured."

"Those teeth," Mischa said. "They seem real."

"I think they are," Doppelmann said. "Michael, what do you see?"

They both stared at him. He glanced at Mischa, who was rubbing her eye. Was that a signal? Was it giving him the answer to the question? He inhaled near the yellow blob, noting its smooth curves, like a tongue. His own tongue felt around for any bits of the poem stuck in his teeth. The art piece below seemed too bright, bringing too much attention to itself.

"I feel like I'm seeing something that I'm not supposed to."

"Oh? How do you mean?"

"It looks very raw," Michael said. This was the first word that rose in his mind. He thought of the plate of food at the diner, where one of the men behind him had broken open a soft-boiled egg. He said so: "It reminds me of a raw egg, without a shell, the yolk filled with teeth of unborn ideas."

Mischa smiled. Doppelmann gasped.

"Correct," Doppelmann said. He leaned on Michael's shoulder. "That's exactly what my works lacks. It's not raw right now. It's all about ideas, ideas afraid to hatch. I like how he thinks," he said to Mischa. She rubbed her eye again.

"I don't know if I like it, though," Michael said.

"I agree. I probably feel as you did when you went to my exhibit," Doppelmann said, winking.

"I like your art, Doppelmann. But I do have a favorite kind of art. It's art that is flat," Michael said, and stared at their reflections in the yolk below. "It's simple and easy to understand. No distractions."

"No perspective," Doppelmann said, also gazing at their reflections.

"Like cubism on rye," Mischa said.

Michael choked. Doppelmann laughed. "Mischa will add an 'ism' to anything."

"Comes in my dreams. I'll be right back." Mischa stood abruptly. She headed toward the front, brushing past Michael.

"Very well," Doppelmann said. "We'll be here."

When they moved to the next piece, Michael was struck with the sudden urge to urinate. Where had Mischa gone? Perhaps it was a signal. He and Doppelmann talked about what stood before them, a collage of paint and newspaper and plaster.

"This is wonderful. It's so ugly," Doppelmann said. "Reproducing the effects of nature on the object." He began commenting on the size of the strokes in the paint before tilting his head to inspect Michael's mask.

"Is that made of newspaper too?"

"Yes," Michael said, and forced himself to keep his hands at his sides.

"Paper is very versatile." Doppelmann's nose was nearby, probably searching for a whiff of how he had been manufactured. But he would likely only notice that Michael had absorbed scents from the diner—coffee, bacon, burnt toast.

"Yes, it's versatile, but fragile. It can't get wet."

"Or burned," Doppelmann said.

They moved on to a bronze sculpture. Michael tapped his foot to fight the urge to piss. Then he remembered they had passed the restrooms at the front of the museum. Perhaps Mischa would be on her way back by now. He wasn't sure how to ask for her help but the sooner the better, he thought.

"I'll be right back," Michael announced. "I need to use the facilities."

"Fine," Doppelmann said. "I'll study the art by myself then. But I won't go back and add commentary for the stuff you missed."

"I'll only be a minute," Michael said. He didn't worry that the artist's comment meant Doppelmann was suspicious. Doppelmann simply liked to have an audience.

He walked to the front lobby and found the restroom. Mischa was nowhere to be seen. In the atrium light, his painted-on fingernails were glistening from the fresh coat of sealant Maiko had applied. No one seemed to acknowledge him, and he was relieved to be like anyone else in the museum. He entered the men's restroom and saw his reflection, a ghostly distortion of himself, in the metal walls of the toilet stalls. Inside was empty. He stood before the mirror and stared back at his masked face.

She was probably telling Doppelmann about her poem now, how Michael was thinking more would happen, and they were having a good laugh over it. She was so different from before. She had stayed the same in his mind but had grown up in real life. It was he who had stayed the same all this time.

"You won't see my feet because I'm standing," a voice said. Mischa, her head floating above a stall, laughed. He turned away from the mirror and stormed up to the door.

"What are you doing in here?"

"To tell you that we shouldn't do this," she said. She lowered herself as she opened the door and sat on the toilet seat fully clothed, smoking.

"We shouldn't do what?" He stepped into the stall. "What if someone entered?" He shut the door.

"We shouldn't know each other as adults. We'll just get ourselves into trouble."

"You were acting as if you hardly remembered me at the diner. Do I look that different?"

She lowered her cigarette and he moved away. He was in a tiny space with both water and fire inches from his body.

"I remember you."

"Then why didn't you say more? Is it because Doppelmann is with us?"

She blew a stream of smoke out of her nostrils. She studied his face again, and he turned away, ashamed, so that he was only in profile.

"I look terrible. I know it."

"Not at all. In fact, I like it." She stood and brushed the back of her hand against his jawline. She seemed to delight in the unusual, in whatever made someone stand out rather than fit in. A mask didn't only conceal, it also implied other possibilities.

"Careful, please, with the cigarette."

"Sorry," she said, and switched hands. "Will you take off your mask?"

"I can't," he said. He turned to her and sighed. "There's so much I've wanted to tell you since you left. I thought you would have come back. After the accident, all I wanted was for you to show up inland. But the years went by, and I finally gave up hope."

Was he giving himself away? Good, he thought, let it out, flood her with the truth and let her see what it feels like for once.

"How did this happen to you?"

He didn't say anything. How could he explain that he went to the station every day after she had left, hoping she would return? He remembered how her backpack was strapped to her back like the shell of a bug, how her hair was shorter than his, and how she ran from his car so fast he didn't have time to get out and chase her. Every day he stood there, studying the tracks for any sign, any smell, she might have left behind. He was so busy looking for signs of her he didn't notice other things, and that was how it happened. At least that's what he told himself.

She stepped off the seat and walked closer to him. He could smell her hair. He sniffed her scalp, and she reminded him of a ripe apple from the orchard at the top of the hill.

"Did you tell him you were meeting me?" he asked.

"Yes."

"Why?"

"Oh stop," she said, waving the cigarette smoke away from him. "I didn't tell him anything. Besides, he thinks you're light in the loafers."

"Did you tell him anything about the past?"

"You want me to? When he asked me about you after meeting you for the first time, I told him how people teased you, and how you pretended you were little boy blue and were different than all of us, and that you were always depressed and hiding."

"You were the one depressed and hiding."

"We were the same at that time. I hope you're no longer hiding."

"I'm here, aren't I?"

"If you say so." She paused. "And now? What are you doing in the city?"

He wouldn't tell her anything else. Not here. He tried to turn around and open the door, but there wasn't enough space with both of them standing, and she was in the way.

"Actually," he said. "I'm trying to get out of here. But I don't have any identification papers."

"Why would you want to leave?"

"I'm not wanted here."

"You're not wanted anywhere. Would you go back inland?"

He tried to decipher the expression in her eyes. She seemed to be challenging him, not the tone he had hoped for.

"There's not much to see here, anyway." She raised her eyebrows, something he wished he could do.

"Then why are you here?"

"To be seen."

"Is that why you work as an art model?"

"You and David have been talking a little too much about me." She sat down on the seat. "Modeling pays nothing. I sell this apple elixir that heals your body. Want to buy some? From the apple trees near the lighthouse. It might help you. Paper comes from trees, you know."

"You drink it? I can smell it coming out of your pores."

She sniffed her arm. He leaned over and sniffed her hair again. The odor of the toilets broke this spell, and he pulled away.

"You really want to go back inland?"

"I was attacked," he said. "I'm full of dents now. I can't walk without a limp."

"I didn't even notice," she said.

"It's there," he said. "My face is dented too—that's why I have this mask."

"You don't need to leave because of that. Just ask David to help you."

"Really?" This was not a possibility he had considered.

"Of course he can help. He's an artist."

"Would he really do that for me?" Michael wanted to believe her. He still felt he was talking to someone else, not the same Mischa from inland.

"He would do it. But what would you do for him?"

It made sense. Nothing was free in the city.

Michael shrugged. "What can I give him?"

"There has to be something," Mischa cooed.

"He asked for some papers for a project. Accounting ledgers, that kind of thing."

"That sounds perfect," she said, and smiled. The soft changes in her face were like stabs to his dented torso. She really was beautiful, and more than that, she seemed so sincere.

"Can you help me ask him?"

"Anything you want. I'm sorry this happened to you."

She pulled him close to her until he realized they were hugging. He put his gangly arms around her back. His fingers climbed up to her neck and felt the scabs he had seen earlier. It probably seemed strange to her that he wanted to touch them, but it was another reminder of what his body couldn't do.

Someone entered the restroom.

They both stood quiet and waited. They listened to a man urinate. Michael had the urge to piss again. The man outside walked to the sink. He washed his hands for a long time. Then he spoke.

"Michael? Are you still in here?"

It was Doppelmann. Mischa covered her mouth and crouched on the toilet again. Michael shuffled his feet, ripped some paper from the roll and tossed it between Mischa's legs into the toilet. He threw her cigarette into the bowl, flushed it, and motioned for her to wait.

"I'll be out in a minute," he said.

"I'll wait for you," Doppelmann said.

Mischa shook her head.

"One minute."

He brushed his fingers through his hair and right then decided to make himself appear ill. He tugged at the mask so that it was slightly off center; he undid another button at the top of his shirt. As he pulled the door in, Mischa crushed herself against the back wall.

"Oh," Doppelmann said.

Michael closed the stall door behind him. He leaned on the countertops before noticing they were ringed with water.

"I feel terrible. I bet it's something I ate."

Doppelmann put his arm around Michael's shoulder.

"I didn't like that food at the diner. Let's not go back there. Do you need anything?"

"Just some air. Can you get the door?"

Doppelmann rushed over and opened the door for them. Outside, Michael gulped the fresh museum air. He was breathing easier now that they were away from the stall.

"I'm sorry," Michael said. "It suddenly came upon me, and there I was, on my knees."

"Poor thing," Doppelmann said, and Michael was surprised how caring he was, touching his temples and stroking his back.

"I should probably go home, Michael said. Can we meet again soon?"

"Let's wait for Mischa, and we can walk out together."

"No, I must get back. My mask is suffocating me."

"Take it off, then."

"Not in public. Sorry." He scribbled his number on the museum's pamphlet and added, "Call me, but say you are asking for a bookkeeper."

"We will call you," Doppelmann said. "Take care of yourself."

17

AS HE WALKED AWAY FROM THE MUSEUM, HE DECIDED TO TAKE side streets through the center part of the city, far from the shoestring street and the coast, to get home. It was safer this way, and he also wanted the time alone. Cars flashed by and his clothes pulled against his body. He was in no rush. He replayed in his mind the scene with Mischa, how she smelled. It was artificial, but he would get used to it.

He thought about Mischa as the kind of girl he had wanted and Doppelmann as the caring friend he had hoped for. He wished he could stay with them all the time. They would be good friends and travel together. He imagined himself as the one with Mischa and Doppelmann tagging along, with his art supplies, while Michael and Mischa ran along the beach of a tropical island. Doppelmann would make repairs to Michael's body as needed, and Michael would help him with his projects. And as Doppelmann worked, Michael would watch Mischa swim in the ocean while he sat on the dry sand and sketched her as a creature emerging from the sea. He was never interested in tropical settings, but Mischa would convince him of its natural beauty. Michael would expand his interest from manmade things to things made long ago and still around.

As for Doppelmann, Michael was increasingly surprised. Sometimes he was so full of stuffy art details that Michael wanted to laugh and to reveal his pedestrian understanding and appreciation for serious works of art. At times, though, he impressed Michael, not only as a talented artist but as a caring human being. And sometimes Doppelmann scared Michael. He induced the kind of fear that Michael had of water and fire, that at any moment he could do something harmful and destructive if he liked, just in the name of art. If Doppelmann learned of his meeting with Mischa, would that unleash a side of Doppelmann he had not seen, but was certain existed?

On his way home, he passed through an industrial area that looked abandoned. He turned onto a road littered with paper in the gutters and stuck in the branches of the trees. Paper was everywhere—he was everywhere in the city. A door had the words DO NOT ENTER handwritten on it in red. The letters were uneven and descended down, as if the person who wrote it had shrunk while writing it. He came around to the front of the building to discover that it was an old theater with two large sculptures above the dusty marquee. One had the word DAY engraved in it, an angelic woman with a shield and birds on her shoulders, and the other had the word NIGHT engraved and was a sculpture of a male holding a spear. They stood, stained purple from bird shit, frozen from another time.

The theater had obviously been closed for years, and part of that reason may have been its location. Several large warehouses, abandoned, surrounded the theater and the main street a good distance away. He was uneasy looking at the theater, and he pictured the doors, with a chain strung through the handles, bursting open and sucking him in.

There was something ominous about this place. He imagined the face of Mischa on the DAY sculpture, surrounded by birds, and imagined that could be him on the other side, NIGHT, with a spear and a shield to protect her. But the statue now looked more like Doppelmann, and he was preparing to attack Michael, spear him in the heart and claim partnership with Mischa. Michael had a right to stand with Mischa because she wanted the life that Michael wanted, and regardless of her past, they could live an idealized life once they were together.

"I like how he thinks," Michael said to the statue, trying to speak in Doppelmann's voice. He tried a lower register in his voice: "I like. I like how he thinks. He thinks."

The statue didn't seem like a threat anymore.

"That's exactly what my work lacks. Lacks. Locks. Lacks, tacks, sacks." Michael tried different intonations. "It's not raw right now. Raw right now. Now."

To the statue, he said: "I like how he thinks." It sounded very close. Satisfied, he moved on.

―――――――――

Michael slinked down the apartment stairs. In the drawing room, he could not tell if the dark spots on the floor were shadows or pools of black water. He stepped lightly into the kitchen then drew the curtains shut. He didn't want to see the spots any longer than he had to. The clinking sound of the curtain rings across the wire prompted Maiko's bedroom door to open, and it released a wedge of light into the hallway.

"Michael, are you home?"

"Of course. Who else?"

"Where have you been?" Maiko stormed into the kitchen in her peignoir, even though it was afternoon.

"Did you know there's an empty theater in the center of the city?"

"What were you doing over there? That place is haunted—there's a ghost choir inside, and you can hear it all the way down the street. But why were you over there? What about your new client?"

"Why is the house so dark? Can't we open the window at the top of the stairs?" He looked away. Her hair was disheveled, and her cheeks were smeared with makeup. She must have been crying again.

"That's what you get for living in a basement apartment. Well, did your client meeting go well? Do you think you have a new job?"

"They said they will call us. I think it went very well. Things are going to be much better."

"Let me go with you next time," she said. "It's safer."

He didn't say anything. He sat at the table and removed his shoes.

"The neighbors said there was a scuffle under the bridge. It's spreading, and if you're alone, they'll go after you first. People are not sticking together—they're just turning on each other. Exactly what the north wants."

She rested her hand on his shoulder, like an icy clamp.

Later, he lay on the drawing room floor, away from the dark spots, replaying his encounter with Mischa. He tried to draw her in his notebook—a stolen ledger book from work. This time he did something he had never done before: he added a shadow to her jawline. Instantly, her picture went from a flat, cartoonish representation of her to something more lifelike. He added more, but then it was as if she had a beard. He crumbled the page and ate it. In the kitchen, the phone rang. Before he could get up, Maiko had run from her room and picked up the call.

"M&M Bookkeeping," she said. He went beside her and waited. Maiko turned to him, covered the mouthpiece of the phone, and whispered, "It's them."

"Give it to me," he said, and snatched the phone from her hand. He tried to stretch the phone cord to the drawing room, but it wasn't long enough. "Go to your room," he said.

"It's a woman," Maiko said, and sat at the kitchen table.

"How can I help you?" Michael said into the phone.

"How are you feeling?" the voice asked.

"Who is this?" he asked, even though he recognized it.

"Mischa, darling," the voice said.

"How did you get this number?"

"You gave it to David," she said, and laughed. "I wanted to know how you are feeling."

"Where is Doppelmann?" Michael's paper skin tingled.

"He's right here," she said.

"Tell him I'm much better. How may I help you?"

She exploded into laughter.

"He's not here, silly," she said.

"You laugh different," Michael whispered. He heard Maiko's chair creak—probably from straining to listen to what he said.

"Yeah, well you probably fuck different too."

"Why are you doing this?" Her coarseness made him suddenly nervous.

"Why don't we meet later? Just for a drink."

He was silent. He told himself to hang up.

"I can't," he struggled to say. How could he explain the dangers of liquids without sounding like his old self?

"You can too."

"I can't do it tonight. I'm finishing work for another client."

Maiko stood between the curtains separating the rooms. She appeared as a silhouette with two long, thin curtain wings.

"All right, then. Tomorrow evening. At seven. We can talk about getting what you want. Let's meet at the top of the city, the last street before the lighthouse."

18

THE EVENING WAS MORE LIKE AFTERNOON, HOT AIR STUCK IN THE avenues and streets of the city. Plants stood alive and vibrant, not held down or flattened, leaves soft from the heat. The cars and exhaust, the buses and trucks, the chatter of people on the sidewalk. As he walked to the corner, he imagined Mischa and him eating dinner, smiling as the waiter told them the special for the day. People nearby would think they were a couple.

He waited across the street. The lighthouse rose in the park above, and then further north stood the always-illuminated radio tower. If Doppelmann could help repair him, would he need to leave the city? He wasn't sure. But the idea of not having to wear the mask anymore, having the ability to feel the sea air and not be so covered from the world, this invigorated him and made him excited about living in the city again.

A taxi pulled up and a woman similar in shape to Mischa exited the vehicle then went inside the hotel, but she moved slower, more sleepy than slinky. He could already tell her apart from others, even though he had only known her for a day as the adult Mischa. He noticed that all the streetlight poles and building walls were blank here—as if the problems with the north had not infiltrated this part. Not even flyers for Adam's Bookkeeping Company.

A few minutes later, Mischa arrived. He waited for the stoplight to change, but as he did so, another taxi pulled up, and this time, Doppelmann got out. Michael froze in the middle of the crosswalk. She turned and hugged Doppelmann, who kissed her, and held her hand.

Cars honked. The light had changed, and Michael was still in the middle. Doppelmann glanced over. Michael ducked and covered his face with his scarf and retreated to the other side of the street. The cars that had waited for him to move sped off.

What was going on? Had Doppelmann become suspicious and shown up unexpectedly? He waited until the light turned green again and then crossed. They were already further up the street. He followed slowly. Doppelmann was constantly touching Mischa, and once they pressed against the shadow of a building and kissed, and Michael heard the pop of lips. They stopped at a restaurant, waited a few minutes outside, Michael hiding behind a tree, and then they entered.

He crossed the street and saw that they were seated by the window. Mischa glanced at him and smiled. So she had planned this. He didn't understand what was happening. Was this a game? Or was she rejecting him by forcing him to watch all of this? She ate her salad, and every time the fork went to her mouth she chewed each bite voraciously, like a very hungry creature. Doppelmann's back faced him. They were sipping wine, and Mischa smiled often, and her eyes would click shut and then open and shift their gaze over at Michael.

What had happened? This was supposed to be just the two of them. He didn't know what to do, so he stayed and watched. They finished their meal and left, and continued heading up the street to the park with the trees. They hiked the trail, and Michael followed at a safe enough distance.

When they got to the top, they ran among the trees. Michael listened to twigs snapping and leaves crunching. He hurried and hid behind a tree. He was crushed she had betrayed him. But then a hand reached around and touched his shoulder. At first he thought the tree had come to life and was grabbing him until he saw it was a thin, sinewy arm with light hairs, attached to the body of Mischa.

"Keep watching," she whispered, and ran off. She hopped over the thick roots like a rabbit. Michael crouched and hid behind the coyote bush to see what would happen next.

The air on the hill was as hot and moist as animal breath. The cliff dogs yapped nearby. Ocean waves crashed and crunched against the rocks below. The sounds of the city were blocked, and it was like they were in a different zone from below. He listened to Doppelmann and Mischa moving among the trees and bushes, so he stepped carefully over some roots and crawled on his knees to find them. He passed several fern stalks that unfurled from the lightest stimulation of his legs brushing them.

As he moved along, he detected a throbbing that became more distinct when he arrived near the northern point. There was steady breathing and the sticking and pulling apart of skin. They were on the ground, Mischa and Doppelmann. She was on her knees, Doppelmann behind her. She gasped when she saw Michael. He fell into a pocket of roots big enough to hold him. Doppelmann's sweater was raised up to his neck, so it was like he had four arms but only two of them had latched onto Mischa's hips. Doppelmann's back was surprisingly muscular. He was sweating all over; he sparkled, and Mischa sparkled too. They were reflections of the dusky sky. Their movements—so detached, so full of intent and focused, except Mischa, who occasionally would look toward him.

He collapsed into the roots and removed his scarf. Instantly, cool air wrapped itself around his neck. He opened his coat to release the buildup of body heat within him. He tugged at his mask and wanted nothing more than to take it off—his body was ready to internally combust.

She wanted him to see this. It was all planned. He nestled his head into the trunk of the tree and listened to their sounds, rising. And then he only heard the wind crashing through the tree branches. Michael popped up and watched Doppelmann stand and pull up his black underwear. Mischa went behind a bush. Doppelmann lowered his sweater onto his body, and it was now covered in sticks and leaves.

I want that sweater, Michael said to himself.

They paired up and walked, bouncily, down the hill. He followed slowly, trailing the odor of their bodies. They walked to the street, then continued to the hotel where they were supposed to meet. Doppelmann kissed her sloppily, his tongue flickering out of her mouth as he pulled away, and then hailed a taxi and left. Mischa waved goodbye.

_____

Michael approached the light of the hotel at the corner. He was ready to yell at her—the volume piled up inside his throat.

"You can smell him on my breath," she said into his ear. And he could. Her mouth smelled musky. He grabbed her shoulder as she turned.

"I thought we were going to be alone."

"That wouldn't have been so fun. Didn't you like watching us?"

"I didn't walk away," he said.

"I noticed. I kept my eyes on you."

"You're crazy."

She laughed. "Let's go."

They walked in silence to the abandoned theater he had passed in the center of the city. She said that she lived in the theater, and Doppelmann had just moved into one of the rooms. This alarmed him, but with the mask he was able to appear unfazed. What if Doppelmann saw them? She undid the lock and chain around the theater entrance and led them inside. He wanted to ask her questions but knew it would annoy her, and he didn't want to break the moment. In the hallway she rocked side to side, humming an unrecognizable tune.

"It's from an opera," she said, as if she had sensed his thoughts.

Nearby were faint cries of a choir. The ghost choir, he remembered, that Maiko had mentioned. He turned to her and pushed her against one of the doors. It was an easy gesture, and he assumed they were no longer strangers. Certainly not after how generous she had been in leading him to the forest to partake in an intimate act. She was neither nervous nor interested, pressed against the door, but curious to see what he would do next.

"You don't look the same," he said to her. He studied her jaw line and caught sight of the faint shadow, similar to the one in his drawing.

"I changed. You didn't." She stepped forward and was inside the opening of his coat. He leaned in and kissed her and was intoxicated with the taste of Doppelmann on her tongue.

"I can taste him. I can smell him."

She opened her collar, and he could smell the skin Doppelmann had licked. Michael kissed her neck, ran the tip of his papery tongue, protruding from the mouth slit in his mask, across her collarbone. It was something he had wanted to do when they were young, but then she was too pristine and perfect to ever let something like this happen. But now they were both ready. Around her neck was a chain and on it was a medallion of a mermaid. It frightened him, then made him slightly angry.

He pulled at her shirt harder, and a button snapped off. She smiled.

"You're funny," she said. "You didn't say anything to us."

"Did you want him to know? That I was following?"

"Why not? It would have made things more interesting."

"Do you think he can really fix me?"

"If you don't tell him about tonight."

He pushed her back against the wall. He smothered her mouth with his. It was as if he was a teenager and she was patiently waiting for him to catch up to her level. They stumbled down the hall, and somehow he found the key in her pocket and opened another door, only to slam it shut.

On the bed, she undressed him methodically. The radio played orchestral music from the north. She removed his shoes and socks and placed them near the foot of the bed. With rapid fingers she unbuttoned his shirt. When she exposed his paper torso, the air in the room pressed heavily upon him, and he collapsed onto the mattress. She unhooked his belt and stripped off his pants. In the darkness, only lit by the glow coming from under the door to the hallway, he observed her. She was so different from high school. While the intensity was there like before, it was now ten times stronger, and she was so focused. Her hands stroked his paper body, and he felt like he was an instrument that she was deciphering how to play.

"Your body, it's unlike anything I've seen before," she said. "It's so alien."

He pulled the sheets closer. Everything was awkward, and he wanted to cover himself. She grabbed his hips and then straddled his legs.

"Please," he gasped. "You might crush me."

She leaned close to his face. The weight of her body sank into him. He thought his cardboard ribs might crack. Her hands raced to his neck, fingered his jaw. A moment later, they were crawling under the edge of the mask.

"Take it off," she said. "Take off your mask."

"I can't," he said.

She used her knees to pin his shoulders. He couldn't move at all now. She reached behind his head and undid the string. Her body was sweaty, like fresh clay.

"Mischa, please," he said. "Don't do it. Not until Doppelmann fixes me."

He tried to move his hands, but he was paralyzed by her weight. In an instant, she had peeled away the mask. It was dark in the room, but Michael still blinked as if a light had been shined into his eyes. He imagined himself as a creature from underground brought to the surface. The mask had been more than a source of shame; it had given him a sense of security. He had never been so vulnerable before another person. Mischa placed the mask carefully on the night stand; she fingered the large dents on his face.

"I'm ugly," he said. "Don't look at me."

"You are," she said. "This is your real face?"

"I told you," he said. "The rainstorm did this."

"You did this," she said. "You didn't take care of yourself."

"Let me go."

She stood. He was surprised that she listened. But then she yanked down his underwear, looked upon his crotch, and cackled.

"You're so small!" she said. "How did you expect to do anything with that?"

She fell back on the floor and continued laughing. Michael was already standing, his underwear shackling his ankles. He pulled them up and dressed quickly.

"You're like a little boy!" She rolled on the floor where scraps of newspaper clung to her hair.

He put the mask on, turned to her, tried to think of something to say.

"It's not my fault," he said.

She didn't even stop laughing when he ran out the door.

19

THE WALK TO WORK WAS WORDLESS. INSTEAD, THEY WERE SUR-rounded by the sounds of buses and cars driving up and down the shoestring street. Radios played from apartment windows, the voice of the one-eyed man ranting about the dismal state of buildings in the city and their unstable construction. Occasionally, there were small groups at the corners, holding signs and shouting at cars. A bicyclist sped by and blew the tufts of fur in Maiko's mantle.

"Why won't you say anything? Did I do something?"

"I can walk to work on my own. I don't need a docent."

"Is that what I am to you?"

Michael didn't respond. He was thinking about the night before. The sound of Mischa's laughter replayed in his head, drowning out the surrounding city sounds.

"Everything I've done was to protect you. I'm not trying to suffocate you, I promise," Maiko said.

She placed her hand on his arm. He flung it off.

"Michael!" Her voice cracked, and she dabbed her cheeks with the corner of her fur. They stopped at the small bridge that led the way to the tuna cannery ship.

"Just tell me things will be okay, and I'll leave you alone for now. Michael, look at me."

He couldn't. He stared at the fish bones on the pavement and the seagulls waiting for them to move away so they could feast on them.

"Seagulls," she said. "Our nightingales."

"I'll see you tonight," he said, and boarded the ship.

He couldn't concentrate. Questions reeled through his mind over and over. Why? Why had she done this to him? Why did he think someone from the past would be the same person today? There really was no one to turn to.

Dearest Father, he thought. He was already composing a letter in his head. He stopped. Leaving the city was impossible. Staying in the city was impossible. Unless....

Before him was the pile of invoices and other documents he was told to destroy. They had stacked up in the cardboard box he was meant to take to the furnace each day but had never done. He looked them over. They contained the line items that he had recorded under intercompany transfers—details of helmets, vests, weapons, ammunition. Some even had the names and addresses of people in the city who were to receive the goods. He took an enormous stack, curled them, and stuffed them in his sleeves. Then he grabbed even more and tucked them inside his socks.

His only hope at this point, he decided, was Doppelmann.

———————

At the end of the day, he left the ship, his mask moist and slightly bubbling around the edges. He had tried to leave a few minutes early, but the controller had stopped by to ask a question about one of the financial statements. When Michael emerged from the ship, Maiko was already at the bridge, reading a newspaper.

Michael joined a group of workers leaving the ship, all of whom wore overalls blackened with soot and fish blood. A few glanced at him suspiciously. As they neared land, the group cracked jokes and slapped each other on their backs. He tried to join in, but one of the workers backed up and froze. He was ready to say something, and Michael feared his cover had been blown.

But then there was an accident. A forklift in the fish market crashed into a tank holding blue lobsters, making a sharp shattering sound. The water flooded out and the lobsters glided down the pavement. Maiko perked up and ran after a few. She moved them away from oncoming pedestrians. This was the perfect opportunity, and Michael slipped past her.

He looked back once. She was wiping her hands on her fur mantle. She stood up, and for a moment, he thought she recognized him in the crowd. But then she turned back to the ship.

He began to run. It was awkward at first, with his uneven foot. Then he had to clamp his arms to his chest or the invoices would flutter out. The sensation overtook him, and he wanted to jump and fly. No one looked twice at him. Sadly he recognized that the only way he had learned of avoiding or ending a relationship was from Mischa ten years ago—and that was by running away. He was doing the same to Maiko. He tried to think of himself as a happy businessman free from the shackles of work and on his way to visit his friend. He hoped Doppelmann was at the theater. And most of all, he hoped that Mischa was out.

He stood in the shade below the theater marquee next to the ticket booth. He could not remember the last time it had been such a clear day. Several birds pecked at the base of the trees that lined the street. The trees, he discovered, were what made the sound of a choir. When the wind blew through the branches, it sang. Further down the road, the main street had cars that drove by. Doppelmann leaned beside the theater entrance, squinting in the sunlight.

"Michael, is that you?"

"I have what you asked for," Michael said. He dug in his sleeves and slid out the pages of invoices. They unfurled before Doppelmann's widening eyes.

"How did you do it? This is fantastic."

"I realized these documents wouldn't be missed. They were meant to be thrown out anyway."

Doppelmann scanned several of the pages, nodding, then

gradually standing taller, brimming with excitement. He looked at Michael and grinned.

"These are perfect. How can I repay you?"

"That's what I was hoping I could talk to you about" Michael began. "I thought that perhaps, as an artist, you might have the skills to repair the damage that was done to my body. The dents and uneven limbs."

Doppelmann stared at him a long time, long enough that Michael twitched and looked around at the deserted street and still trees. He wasn't sure if Doppelmann was again looking through him or envisioning a new project.

"I don't normally work with paper," Doppelmann said. "It's painting that I do best. But I want to help you. Can you take off your mask?"

"Not here, please," Michael said. "May we go inside?"

"Yes, of course," Doppelmann said.

"Wait. Is Mischa here?"

"Why do you ask?"

"If she's here, I don't know if now is a good time for you."

"Who is that?" Doppelmann asked. They both turned to face the main street and watched a figure approaching quickly, nearly running. As it approached, Michael felt his heart jolt. He swallowed hard.

"Maiko?"

"I knew it. How could you?" she asked. "What is going on here? You lied to me."

"What is it?"

"You aren't a client. Who are you?" Maiko said between sniffs. Her eyes were red, and she wiped at her small nose with a paper tissue crumpled like a mushroom cap.

"My dear Maiko," Doppelmann said. He held out his arms to hug her. She ran behind Michael's back.

"This can't be," she said. "I thought you left."

"You know him?" Michael asked, amazed.

"An artist has to know every model in the city," Doppelmann said.

"Maiko, it's a big misunderstanding. Now is not the time to explain this."

It appeared she would cry, but nothing came out. Instead, her face crumpled tightly around her nose, as if she were about to sneeze or wail. Doppelmann leaped back and gasped.

"That look," he said to her. "It's gorgeous. I must paint this face. I must paint you. Right now. Michael, I will have to fix your face later."

"What?" Michael asked. Maiko's fingers pushed against his elbows.

"You're going to fix his face?"

"Yes, dear. He thinks because I am an artist I can do anything."

"Not exactly," Michael said.

Maiko stepped between them. She glared at Michael, and he felt awful in that moment. He really had not meant to hurt her. She seemed to take his refusal to fall into her fear of danger as a sign of betrayal, and he didn't know how to explain all this to her.

"After all I did for you," Maiko said. She turned to Doppelmann. "He can wait."

"What are you saying, dear?" Doppelmann asked. He cupped the side of her head in his hand and wiped a tear with his thumb.

"Paint me," she said.

"Bring her inside," Doppelmann said. He locked eyes with Michael and gripped his hand. "Do it."

She slapped his advancing hands. He worked to scoop her body into his, even as she kicked him and slapped his face.

"Stop it, no!"

"She's in pain," Doppelmann said. "Shhh, dear. Calm down."

"Please, please," Michael said, and wrapped around her tighter so that he was hugging her. It was as if he had real muscles with strength. All the tension in her body broke and she shuddered. Doppelmann waved them inside. Michael carried Maiko, surprised how light she was—lighter than his own paper body.

Doppelmann said nothing but seemed barely able to contain himself. He leaped a couple of times and skipped, rubbing his large hands together, mapping out how to paint a new canvas, one with the sad scowl that was Maiko's face.

Michael wondered what that face could mean to viewers. So many things, and really it was heartbreaking for him to see her this way. In many ways, she was like him, lacking the vision that he once lacked. When she saw her own face on the canvas, she would want to change who she was and would look upon the portrait the way Michael looked upon his masked face.

For a moment, he was overtaken by impatience. All he wanted was to be rid of the mask. Mischa didn't help him, and now Maiko was delaying him. Everything for him would change once the dents were gone from his body and he no longer needed to wear a mask. Perhaps Doppelmann could help Michael forge identification papers.

In one of the empty rooms off the long hallway, Maiko sniffled regularly—it was part of her breath—while Doppelmann shifted things around, clearing off his easel and mixing some paints. Maiko sat on a metal chair, and Doppelmann gently tied her to it with a blue ribbon. She didn't resist and it looked as though Doppelmann was only doing this to keep her safe. Maiko's eyes avoided Michael.

"Now, we will begin," Doppelmann said and, with a trapezoid of charcoal, sketched some lines across the prepared canvas. "She's just gorgeous." He breathed heavily and rushed to her, which frightened her, and lifted her chin. "There, there, that's perfect."

"This city has walked all over me," Maiko said. "I don't care anymore."

"Shh, now," Doppelmann said, holding the paintbrush to his lips like a silencing finger.

Michael watched the artist in action. His movements were necessary and practiced so much that they were part of his being. Doppelmann had his shirt off, and Michael tried to count the number of green dots of paint on his back.

Maiko's expression did not change. Sad, drooping eyes, brimming with tears, her small nose with hints of rosiness in the corners, her lips full and out, pouty, and the streaks of tears across the freckles on her cheeks, canceling them out.

"Water, please," Doppelmann said. Michael scrambled around the room, found an empty glass jar, and filled it. Doppelmann dunked his paintbrush in and swished it like a magic cauldron.

At some point, Michael fell asleep, leaning against the wall, sitting in his metal chair. It was in his dreams, or when he was almost awake, that things moved in his mind, images of not too long ago and the dark room he was in now. Things had changed, but were they for the better? It was hard for him to answer. All he could tell himself was that things were different. Simply different. Sometimes people fight and resist change as much as possible, and other times they accept change and adopt it as easily as if it had always been that way.

20

HE AWOKE TO SEE THE BRIGHT LIGHT FOCUSED ON THE CANVAS, and Doppelmann glancing at Maiko then back to the canvas. Without another thought, he left the theater. He walked in silence, and the silence spread inside his head for half an hour. Perhaps because of his confident attitude, when he entered the lobby of the radio station, he went by reception without being stopped or questioned. He exited the elevator at the second floor and immediately heard the voice. The hall had several doors, but one had an illuminated sign above it that said ON AIR. He didn't waste any time. If he hesitated, he knew he'd lose this momentary boldness. The door wasn't locked, and he almost laughed when he saw the face of the one-eyed man, obscured behind a large microphone, switch from a look of bemusement to one of terror.

"Where are my notebooks?" Michael said.

The one-eyed man was stunned. He turned a knob and a soap commercial began airing through the speakers. He glanced around, searching for anything he could grab.

"My notebooks. That's all I want," Michael said as calmly as he could.

"I don't have them," the man said. Then his cruel smile, the one Michael remembered from the bus, reappeared, and the man began laughing. He flipped a switch and leaned into the microphone. "Folks, you are not going to believe this, but an anarchist has just walked in demanding I give the airwaves to him."

"What are you doing?" Michael asked.

The man covered the microphone and hissed at him: "I threw that suitcase out weeks ago, into the canal. Why don't you go look for it there?" Then, into the microphone, "I'm asking this anarchist to join me but he looks a little timid. Stage fright perhaps? Or maybe he just can't get his two feet to agree on a plan for walking over here."

The man laughed and covered the microphone again, all mirth gone from his voice: "A lot of people, in the south, are tired of folks like you. Tired of paying for your messes. Your accidents. You should go. Security's on its way."

Michael stepped closer. The feeling he'd had on the bus, a sense of being trapped, afraid, and angry, rattled him. The inspectors rifling through his valise, the one-eyed man trying to touch his face. The scent of laurel leaves and lemon clinging to his skin returned as well—filling him with anger.

Michael's hand sprung out and snatched off the man's eggshell eye patch.

The man's howl chased Michael as he ran down the hall. "You won't survive this," the man threatened, still on air.

Michael hurried through side streets, eventually returning to the fish market. He couldn't shake the image of the man's desiccated eye socket, a well of skin in his skull, rimmed by a deformed eyebrow. Here in the market, despite it being later and all the vendors gone, many people still strolled through the area, couples holding hands and hiding in thin shadows of street lamp poles.

Of course the one-eyed man threw away his notebooks. He had been naïve to think they'd still be around. To have a single piece of his past had felt necessary to survival, and now he recognized that he was truly disconnected. He could start new notebooks, yes, but it wasn't the same. There was history in those pages. Proof of something. And all this time, they were in the canal—likely pushed out to sea. He dropped the eye patch and smashed it with his heel.

He returned to the theater to tell them what had happened, but one look from Doppelmann made him turn away. He shut the door and wandered the long hallway, noticing that from certain doors the sounds of the choir trees were more distant. Sometimes they sounded like an organ playing, with deep bass notes that vibrated the light fixtures in the hall, and other times as if they were a choir of wailing ghosts. Nearly all the doors were unmarked, except for their numbers, but eventually he came upon one marked PROJEC-TION ROOM.

He opened the door, which cried out as if its hinges had shocked it with pain, and stepped inside. The sound of the choir trees flooded the room, mostly because the wall on the opposite side of the door had been blown away. The projection room gave a wide view of the stage and the rows and rows of empty seats.

Standing before this open edge was a woman. Even before she turned, Michael knew it was her. When she was staring back at him, something in her eyes told him she was not done with him.

"You're still wearing your mask," she said.

"Doppelmann said he'd fix me. I asked him myself, but he hasn't."

"I'll tell you this now because I want to help you. He won't do it. He'll keep coming up with excuses. Do you know why?"

Michael shrugged. Behind her a slight draught blew into the room. One side of the room had shelves filled with supplies: buckets of paint, chicken wire, bins of screws and bolts, and stacks of reels of film. There was no film projector, though.

"Why won't he help me?"

"He doesn't do things for others. He only does things because he wants something out of it. You need to make him think that repairs to a paper man's body will benefit his work as an artist."

"What am I going to do in the mean time? It's not safe for me here." He was becoming desperate. "Can you help me, please? I want to get out of the city. We could go back to the inland."

"Both of us?" She laughed and sat down on the edge of the floor, her feet hanging above the theater seats. He wanted to pull her back. He realized, though, that he would sound like Maiko, and that was something he needed to rid himself of.

"Doppelmann will repair your face eventually and your dents, and your other, let's say 'undeveloped' parts, but then what? You'll find something else. It will always be something else you blame. I knew this about you when we were inland before all this happened to you."

"What are you saying?"

"It's what's underneath that needs repairs."

He sat on the ground next to some rubble from the broken wall. He wondered if someone had set off a bomb in this room. Perhaps this was why the theater had closed.

She was behind him. Her hands were shuffling something. He didn't look back. Instead he sat, staring out at the empty theater before them. The stage had looked very deep, but then he noticed on the side that there was a wrinkle, like the kind in a curtain.

"It's fake," she said. "It's a painted backdrop to make the stage look much bigger. The fact is this theater is very old and very small. It's like it believed in its own little world in here for as long as possible. Now it's over."

She pulled his hands behind his back. Although it was rough, he found her touch soothing and calmed his growing desperation.

And then she bound his wrists.

"What are you doing?" He sat still, waiting, not moving, not resisting.

It was black electrical tape, and she used it again to bind his ankles together. She removed his mask, followed by a blindfold that was lowered over his eyes.

"Trust me," she said. "You don't want to see this."

The door opened and then snapped shut.

"Who's there?"

"No one," Mischa said. "It's just you and me."

He sat on his knees, waiting. It was incredibly quiet. The choir trees had stopped at some point—the wind outside must have settled. He listened for any movement from Mischa, but she seemed to be standing very still.

"Are you watching me?"

After a long pause, she finally said, "Yes."

She approached him and he heard a metallic *shiiing!*—the sound of a blade opening. Then it was cutting his clothes off. Scissors. She cut from the collar down the sleeves and then down the back. She split it off him, and he felt exposed. The lights from the low ceiling were hot, and he thought he would melt, similar to the heat from the tuna ship.

She cut off the rest of his clothes and he was naked, bowed before her. He lowered his head. He couldn't bear the fact that she was observing him. It had been so embarrassing the other day, and here he was again. But she didn't laugh. Instead, she kicked his legs, and he fell over onto his side.

"Why don't you pretend to like yourself? You think that you are someone else, that your true self is waiting somewhere and that you don't know how to bring that person out. So, if you are already pretending to be someone else, why not pretend to be someone you like?"

"I'm trying to find a person I can be. Someone I can like. But it never goes according to plan. So I start over," he said.

"You could pretend to be the person you want to be, or you could pretend to be the true you. Isn't that being yourself anyway?"

"Not necessarily."

"You could be the Michael no one knows. You can be the one who gets invited out for drinks. The one who attends gallery openings with artists. Doppelmann will invite you out, but only if you plan to talk. He doesn't like to be surrounded by mutes. In fact, he only wants people who can contribute to the conversation. I'm going to give you a part of myself. A poem to make a part of you. I will always be inside you."

"You already are," he said.

She collapsed next to him. He was breathing heavily, suffocating from his own weight as he lay on his dented side.

"Please," he said.

"Shut up," she said, and kicked him so that he rolled across the room. His nose snapped. It swung loosely, brushing against his lips.

She opened the scissors again. An awful tearing sound. A bucket was kicked over. The scissors had just plunged into the top of his back, and then, using her fingers, she tore off two large panels of his skin. Rapid clicking or whirring from something mechanical rang in his ears. She poured liquid over his back, pasted something in its place. Even in the darkness of the blindfold, he saw firecrackers. Bright white outlined in the faintest blue appeared in quick bursts.

"There," she said.

"Please," he said. A piece of rope was placed between his lips and tied tightly behind his neck. It cut into the corners of his mouth and he leaked glue. He tried to spit, but the rope had widened his lips so much that the glue gummed up and slowly stretched to the floor.

She pulled more of his paper skin off, shredding the sides of his arms and fronts of his legs. A pile of paper shavings surrounded him, like leaves from the apple orchard trees he would jump into as a kid. More rapid clicking sounds.

"It's like a critical thinking class. You had one of those with me, back when. You talked a lot in there. I might as well tell you now. You were the only one listening. Everyone thought you were so boring because whatever it was you were saying, no one could decipher it. But that's part of the reason I became curious about you. I wanted to find out about you, see if that was truly who you were. But it was all just an act."

The rope was pulled tighter and his tongue fell out. More white and blue bursts appeared. The colors were brighter and pushing out the darkness of the blindfold.

"That's enough," she said, and kicked away his tongue. She slammed his head back and pulled an ear off. She stomped around, and with one ear, it became very difficult to understand what was happening next.

"And that's what we hate about you most. You try to be someone else, someone better than everyone. You're just the depressed boy in blue, who thinks no one understands him. You say you want to belong, but you shun groups. Doppelmann probably learned long ago he needed to be part of a community of artists in order to survive. You will shrivel away, and no one will know you exist. Only a few people know you are in the city. You think anonymity is good? Wait until now. I bet you don't even talk to anyone. That's so typical of you. And then you tell us you think you can start over."

After that, things became a blur of tearing sounds, mechanical clicking. It was like the opposite of the work his father had done years ago. Instead of soothing hands that held his injured body and applied layers upon layers, meticulous detail to threading and concern with comfort, this was Mischa undoing all that. She tore, she pulled, she cut and shredded. She stepped on pieces, including his fingers, flattening his hands. If his eyes were open, he would have seen nothing but blurred color everywhere. Even with his eyes shut, he felt his head spinning, dizzy from the constant explosion of colors—the white becoming more and more blue, a deep, mineral blue like clear water.

Then she began drawing all over what was left of his body. He felt a pen, stroking in circles, with pauses when it lifted before it started writing on another spot. What was she writing? Owned by Mischa? Designed by Mischa? Destroyed by Mischa? Whatever she wrote, he knew her name was being written.

Had he really upset her that much? Really, to be torn into pieces, was that a lesson he needed to learn?

"There are different types of people. You happen to be the type I don't like. Sometimes I only want to get to the bottom of people like you, yank out the things you don't want to talk about. But because I have made the effort to talk with you and listen to you, even though each minute I'm hating every word you say, you assume you have a friend. So when I say to do something, you'll do it, simply because you're a little puppy. You just want to be loved. We all want to be. Let me tell you something. You need to give up part of yourself if you want to get what you think you need. Leave a piece of yourself in the world."

Here, at this moment, he was afraid to think Mischa might be right. He had fallen into the same patterns with his new paper body. The job at the cannery had been briefly exciting, but it was him pretending to be someone else. Or was it? Maybe he was meant to be like that all this time. He had been hiding, vulnerable as a blank slate, and Maiko had given him a decent identity to wear. He had to ruin that for what? For this?

The scissors sawed at his neck and his head loosened, rolling and rocking on the floor.

Why was he so drawn to this woman? Was it because he had wanted someone to do this all along?

He finally admitted to himself, he had secretly desired for someone to take him and wake him up, make him face his hall of mirrors he had built, and then smash them so that he would have to find his own way. He would no longer project himself onto every-thing; instead he would pull it into him.

If he ever got out of this.

"So even though I tell you I don't like you and I don't like the way you are, you sit there and you listen and you want to smile. You hate not being able to express yourself properly. You know it's true, and it makes you sad, but when you're sad, you smile. Sometimes you laugh, even. I want to strip you down to the bare person who you are, and I want you to see it and fight with it until it wins. You will die in the process, but at least you will finally be happy. I'm say-ing all this for your benefit. You need to get out of your shell. And if you won't do it yourself, I'll crack it open. I'll get you out. I'll put you in front of the spotlights, and you won't be able to see who is in the audience. You'll cry, you'll collapse, you'll hate me, but in the end, you will be so glad. Because this fake you wants to die. He wants to go away. Why do you keep him around? He wants to leave you. Even he doesn't like who you are."

One of his legs, the same one with the broken foot from not

long ago, came off, and it was dragged away. Through the blindfold, there was a shadow slicing through the light, up and down. What could that be?

"Why can't you let go? Let go of everything and forget for a moment. Forget who you are, or who you think you are, and just do things by instinct."

Maiko had placed an image on him too. While it wasn't bad, it wasn't him. This was why he needed Mischa. She had an eye for liars, conscious or unconscious; she knew what Michael was up to, and he should be grateful to her for doing this. Was she killing him? That was probably best. He needed to go away. He was never wanted here anyway. The city invites but doesn't look after you. It accepts you if you're willing to pay the price. Most people here were probably just like those more inland. They accept whatever is projected on them, make some money to stay inside, and hold onto that for the rest of their lives.

"And now," she said, so close to him, as she flipped him on his back, "for the genitals."

He felt her hands, both of them grab onto him, claws hooked around him, and the tension of her pulling. She released slightly, and he thought she was reconsidering, but then in a dramatic pull, she tore them off, and he rolled over, as if a huge weight were removed from him and now he was nothing but a husk, blowing about from the slightest breeze. She threw the pieces at him. He couldn't move, couldn't pick them up and return them to his body.

She sat on what was left of him, holding his head up and shaking him with each word she said. He tasted the glue rolling back into his mouth. He gasped for air.

"If you can put yourself together again, you'll thank me for this. You wanted this all along, didn't you?"

She shook him so that he nodded yes.

"Good boy. Now I'm leaving. I hope to see you again, in one piece, as the person you wanted to be. If I don't see you, maybe I'll find pieces of you throughout the city. I'll think, how sad. That could have been Michael. Scraps of paper in the wind. I think this will change you, though. It will make you want to piece yourself into the you that you always wanted. Don't be afraid. You have to start all over. From the bottom up. That's what I did. Look what it has done for me."

She dropped his head, and through the blindfold and the bright light above, he saw a dark, blurred shape cutting between the light. It was her. She stepped away.

He rolled his head to the side so that his one ear was exposed. The door opened and then clicked shut. The silence that set in was so thick and heavy it pressed down on him. He felt as if he were at the bottom of the bay, weighted down by the heavy, heavy waters. No one else was down here. It was the place where things went to rot.

Part Three:

DOPPELMANN

21

THEY STARTED WITH HIS LEGS. A PAIR OF HANDS, MUSCULAR WITH coarse, rigid fingers, jerked his knees from under him and extended his legs. The fingertips pressed into him at regular intervals. He tried to scream for help, but his tongue was stuck to his teeth. The hands brushed back and forth the tops of his legs, and he thought the friction would set him on fire. He took a deep breath, or tried, and gasped. The hands returned to his legs, but this time they had brought something.

Ice cold slaps of cloth or other tissue, he couldn't tell, were whipped onto his thighs, one after the other, like a pile of wet tongues. The hands shifted these pieces around until they settled at their appropriate place and then proceeded with another layer. The cold strips were so soothing that he immediately became drowsy.

He opened his mouth to speak, or perhaps moan, but nothing came out. No words, no sounds, no air. He was suffocating. One of the hands caught him at the neck and thumbed his jaw to hold him still. Despite the firmness of the hands, they exhibited occasional lapses of gentleness. The other one inserted a finger into his mouth. Cool apple juice dribbled to the back of his throat. His moistened tongue clicked free, and he licked the finger as it exited his mouth.

"I can't see," he rasped, relieved to hear his own voice, though it sounded unlike him. A moment later, the finger was in his mouth again, and more apple juice dripped in. The hands returned to his legs, and soon Michael couldn't move his toes anymore.

After his legs, the hands moved on. They unfolded his arms, also pinned underneath him, and worked until all of his limbs were covered in strips of wetness. With his eyes shut, colors swirled in spirals of dark rainbows, twisting inside of him, trying to burst from him and take over his body—consume him. The hands glided to his torso. Then to his head. The cold strips around his nose and eyes seemed thin and delicate. He could smell the stench of thick, heavy glue. He realized his head was now fully encased in the wetness when he heard distantly a pair of heels echoing on a hard floor.

The room sounded large, airy, and near a street. He could hear traffic, pigeons, construction work. He was not in the theater anymore—certainly not the projection room. Something flapped when cars drove by, perhaps a tent or some canvas or plastic tarp. There were moments of intense silence when he sensed his body throbbing, probably in shock from the cold and the unfelt pain still crawling throughout him in blurs of color. The room didn't feel warm, but that may have been because of all the wet strips all over his body. *Dearest Father, the weather here has suddenly changed. I am chilled to the cardboard of my bones, and the city remains clouded in darkness. It strikes me now that I never asked you: How long exactly, does a paper man live? What is, I wonder, the half life of paper?* The cold made him drowsy, and with his eyes sealed shut, he fell asleep.

He awoke hours later, or perhaps a day or more had passed, his legs being plied by the hands. No, not plied—caressed. He welcomed this tenderness and listened, waiting for the helper to speak. Nothing was said; there was only an occasional sigh, from exhaustion, Michael guessed, but not boredom. He felt layers of new tissue being applied to his calves and thighs.

"I can't see you," Michael finally said. "What are you doing? What has happened?"

"There was an accident." This came from a whispering voice, and it spoke quickly, as if it had been waiting to say these words. It couldn't belong to Doppelmann—the voice sounded too gentle, too vulnerable. Doppelmann was always brash. Michael tried to sniff the air around the speaker for more clues, but he was overwhelmed by the scent of glue.

"Did I die?"

"Don't speak," the voice whispered, and one of the hands stroked his neck. It was intoxicating, the gentle brush of fingers.

At first, it felt odd to pronounce words, but he realized that was because his jaw wasn't closing right. The hands acknowledged this and had to remove a tooth to get everything to line up and close correctly. Then they continued to mold his new legs. Even with these new layers piling onto him, he had a vague sensation of the original space he occupied. He wanted this feeling to expand and fill the new layers.

The hands finished another layer of material, and then he heard the body they belonged to walk down a hall. The floor seemed hard, concrete, and the shoes clicked as they walked away. A door opened and then closed. He was about to fall asleep again when he detected whispering close by. A woman's voice. A man responded.

"Who's there?" Michael asked.

The sound of shuffling footsteps faded. In his solitude, he became very embarrassed. He didn't know if he was in light or dark, clothed or naked. When the voice returned, he would demand answers. He tried to sit and listen, but the concentration fatigued him and he fell asleep. He dreamed that his helper added antlers, then a fin, then fur to his body. With a sudden wave of panic, he strained to turn his neck or move his hands. Stuck.

Another unknown block of time passed. It could have been days, or for all he knew, a week. With no sunlight to pierce his paper lids, he was unable to tell. He thought about that theater and how his mind was like the inside of it. Perhaps he really was still in there. A space in the city stopped in time. It intrigued him. Maybe he'd been placed on the stage, hence the airiness around him, on display for the rows of empty theater seats. He tried to listen for creaking. Any sign of life.

A memory from the past climbed into his consciousness: when

he was a child, long before he had a paper body, he woke up one night with a terrible fever, his left side numb, as if it suddenly belonged to a different person's body. When he sat up and walked out of his bed to the hallway, bathed in cold sweat, it was as if someone else was compelling him forward. That foreign half of him was what forced the motion to walk. His original self seemed unable to move, even though he felt himself inside of it. It took the combined strength of all of his brothers, who heard him stumbling along, to carry him back to his bed. He's so heavy, they had exclaimed to each other, as if his weight had doubled that one night. And his father, who refused to resort to medicine, had used the coldest cloths to press against his forehead to make the heat go away.

After a long time passed, the voice returned.

"I have completed several layers. Now you are ready for the more critical elements"

"Excuse me?" Michael asked. He felt the hands between his legs and then a distant puncture. Something, a needle, was moving in and out. He held his breath while there was a slight tug from weight attached to him, and then the hands pulled away.

Someone nearby burst out laughing.

"Who's there?" he cried.

The laughing immediately stopped. Someone was breathing behind a hand clutched around their mouth. Large wheezing breaths were sucked in and pushed out of nostrils, probably through a deviated septum. Michael's brother had one and had a similar laugh.

The hands paused at his head now, and he felt another slight prick. It weaved in and out along his scalp. It took a very long time, and then a new row was begun. One of the hands rested on his shoulder. It was so gentle, so comforting. The laughter started up again.

"He has an erection!" It was the woman again. "You couldn't make this stuff up if you tried!" She shuffled off, a man mumbling to her.

Michael's body turned cold, and he tried to close his legs.

"Relax. It's perfectly natural," the voice whispered.

"Who's watching us?"

"Shhh," the voice said, and continued sewing around Michael's scalp. "Folks from the north want to see what the city is all about? Then let's show them."

It was too much to think about; Michael eventually fell asleep, and the voice left, returning later. Michael noticed his arms and legs finally felt less numb and that he was able to move his fingers.

"Almost done," the voice said. Yet the hands continued working on his body for a very long time. Michael asked questions, but the voice ignored him. Anger welled up inside his new tissue. He imagined the worst. They were turning him into a sea creature and would throw him into the water to see if he would sink or float away. Or, they were turning him into a paper boat. If he were inland, they would have made him into a scarecrow. He had been so stupidly vulnerable when Mischa had torn him apart, and now he was being covered up again. He would never leave this city, he thought. He was going to be crushed by it.

Much later, the hands were under his back and raised him. He sat up and moved his neck. His eyes, though, were still sealed shut.

"Very good," the voice said. "Now, I'm going to stand you up, and you need to try walking. It will be difficult at first. You'll think that you're falling. Just keep moving. If there's any tightness, let me know, and I'll make adjustments."

Michael was pushed to the floor. His feet landed, but his weight felt so different he toppled over. The pain flourished briefly again inside his body. Michael thought he heard murmuring, feet shuffling, but he couldn't be sure.

"Let's try that again," the voice said, and lifted him. He felt incredibly heavy. He was now standing when the hands slapped his back and he stumbled forward. "Keep moving," the voice said, so

Michael moved, certain he would run into something. The hands pinched his shoulders and changed his direction. He was running in circles—he was sure of it. More murmuring, shuffling from somewhere. His right knee kept locking, so he pointed to it. The hands stopped him, helped steady him, and then worked at his knee. The tension left, and then he tried walking again.

"I'm fine now. See?" Michael said. He laughed without meaning to. The room no longer felt airy, suffocating.

"Let's get you dressed," the voice said.

He was handed a set of items as the voice listed them off. "Socks, underwear, a pair of pants, a shirt, and some shoes. We'll put your coat on after."

"No tie?" Michael asked.

"No tie," the voice said. Michael struggled to dress blindly, so the hands helped him. Then he spread out his arms, and the hands put the jacket over Michael's hands and slid it up to his shoulders. His body had thickened. There seemed to be a greater distance between his core and the top layer of his skin.

"I still can't see."

"In a minute."

A door opened, and there was whispering. Many voices.

"Am I in the theater?" he asked anxiously. "I need to see. Why can't I see?"

"No," the voice said. "Your eyes have been sewn shut, but I will fix that now."

"Who are you?"

"Stop with the questions."

The gentle, tentative voice was gone, and in its place was the familiar bark of Doppelmann.

"You *are* Doppelmann, aren't you?" Michael asked. It made sense now. Only he had known about the repairs Michael had wanted, and only he would be interested in discarded paper. The hands grabbed his body, pulled him close to another body, much warmer, and the voice was at his ear.

"Yes, it's me," the voice said. "I've helped you get better, Michael. Now help me and stand still."

There was a sharp pull at his eyelids, something tearing through them. More real pain. He stumbled back, dazed, and nearly losing his balance. The shoes he wore were heavy and felt like anchors. He walked in small circles, holding his eyes until finally he let go and looked. It was not very bright out, for which he was glad. In fact, it was smoky. Before him, a large moving mass of colors first appeared like streaks of paint but within seconds became much more distinct.

He saw people, a variety of ages, men and women, some children, and a dog. The anticipation on their faces melted into joy, and they began clapping and cheering. Champagne flutes were raised. Bright cheeks exploded in smiles. Men shook their heads in astonishment. A woman pressed a paisley handkerchief to the corners of her eyes. The dog barked. The children leapt about hysterically. Doppelmann was nowhere to be seen.

Michael looked about quickly. The crowd, he saw, was held back by a black velvet rope. They reached for him, and they squealed when they made contact with his blazer or ran their fingers through his hair. He backed against the wall.

Over the shouts and murmurs, a woman's voice that wavered said: "So beautiful."

"I touched him!" a young boy said. A child began crying, saying he was scared of the monster. The dog wouldn't stop barking, and a woman tossed a napkin with lipstick at him. He continued backing up until he touched a sharp corner of something on the wall.

Staring back at him was the portrait of Mischa.

22

THE ART GALLERY. LAST TIME, IT HAD BEEN A PLACE OF REFUGE from the crowd and the one-eyed man. It was where he had first seen Mischa's portrait and had been inspired to find her. She had somehow brought him back to this spot, and now he saw emerging through the layers of paint Mischa's hidden smirk and ruthless eyes. At this point, it would not have surprised him if the painting were to come to life and try to tear him to pieces again.

He reached desperately for the portrait and pulled it off the wall, stabbing a corner of its canvas into the concrete floor, over and over again until the interior wood frame split and the canvas came undone. He watched Mischa's face bend and distort as it tore. The crowd was there for all of this. There were gasps and chortles. Michael tried to tear the canvas. He felt a new kind of strength in his new tissues. From the corner of his eye, he could see a figure quickly approaching, so he tugged harder at the canvas, ready to use his mouth to rip it into two.

"Stop this at once!" The man who worked at the gallery, the one with the deckle-edge suit and round glasses who had helped him, tried to intervene. His voice had none of the kindness from before.

"What have you done to me?" Michael yelled. "Doppelmann?"

He recalled the night the man didn't flinch at Michael's distorted face and broken foot. The man ignored him as if they had never met and took the wire that had held the canvas on the wall and wrapped it tightly around one of Michael's legs. He called for someone to help him, and a few men, faces flushed and celebratory, eagerly climbed over the rope and pinned the living sculpture to the floor. Michael kicked his free legs into the air, hoping to strike one of them, but they easily clamped his ankles together, pinning him to the floor.

The man in the suit returned, wheeling in a large display case made of clear plastic. One side of it was hinged as a door, which the man held open. He cleared his throat.

"Please place the artwork in here," he said to the men holding Michael down. They raised him like a delicate statue and installed him inside the case. The door was instantly shut, and the crowd began to break apart. Michael had no room to move around, and so he simply stood and watched as the others went on their way.

"This is the best art I've seen in a long time," a woman said. "I hope we can visit the city more often."

"Why anyone would ever be interested in this city confounds me," a man with a gray beard said. "What nonsense." He walked away, sighing.

"Is it true they bury their dead in the harbor?" the woman with napkins asked the man, her interest in the art waning as well.

"There's no cemetery here. So what do you think?" He scratched his beard and continued on his way. She squealed and followed him.

———————

The man eventually turned off the lights and left through the back door. Michael listened, his ears ringing in the silence. Later a large truck rumbled by. The sound vibrated in the still air, and he watched in surprise as the door to his display case popped open. Had it never been locked? And did he not think to check it?

He carefully stepped out and tiptoed to the front of the gallery. That was when he saw the damage done. Where there was once a door, large window, and wall, the gallery and the outside world were now only separated by a plastic tarp, taut and locked in place by a series of cords. The damage to the building, he assumed, was from another group of agitators.

He surveyed the room for other changes. All of Doppelmann's paintings were still here, apart from Mischa's, of course. At some point, the man in the deckle-edged suit had replaced it that evening with another painting: the new portrait of Maiko.

Despite the severe geometric shapes and violent strokes across the canvas, it looked vibrantly realistic: the usual resigned look in her eyes, her thick lower lip, the reddened nostrils, the freckles, the bangs that stuck together on one side, the mushroom mole. It was Maiko, and Doppelmann had finally got his way, to paint her and make her a representation of those who were afraid to live in the city. That was the overwhelming feeling of the painting—fear.

And yet, out of fear that he could get hurt, Maiko had altered his body to protect him, but in the end, it was pointless. Mischa had easily shredded him despite all of Maiko's best efforts. And now he really was an object, a thing, stuck in time, with no change and no say in how he would be perceived. He glanced at his new hands, his new arms inside new sleeves. Unlike his previous body, thin and undeveloped as an adolescent, his arms seemed larger and his fingers thicker. He touched his face and found the contours were different. Among all the paintings in this gallery, the one item that would help him fit in was distinctly absent: a mirror.

Automobiles roared past the tarp near the front. With one arm, he stretched the plastic, which bent and warped. He put all his weight against it until the plastic slowly opened, as if it were yawning. Using his hands, he pulled the gash wider until he could step through this large stretchy mass like bubblegum.

Outside, the air felt different on his new paper skin. He observed the empty street. The glowing streetlights were evenly spaced to the north and south. Everything sat completely still until another car drove by and kicked up the loose leaves and paper bags in the gutters. He set out, walking down several deserted streets until arriving at the shoestring street. South of him, in the distance, he saw the City Collectorate building, with most of its lights on. His first day there had been to meet Doppelmann, the one connection from the present to Michael's past. So many mistakes of his were right here, reflected in the buildings, staring back at him.

Another herd of automobiles screamed down the street. He wanted to avoid the main roads, and wandering down several side streets, he paused before rows of thin fences. They had not been there before. Upon closer inspection, he found they were made of corrugated cardboard and were tall enough to prevent anyone from climbing over. Had the city split? He followed the fence line and arrived at the trail that led to the hill overlooking the city. He hiked it, although it was difficult to see ahead in the dark. At the top, he knocked down a few apples, but he couldn't smell them, and they were too big to fit in his mouth. Apples, he decided, were his favorite fruit. It had been so long since he had eaten one.

He watched as darkness took over the city. It was a depressing sight, the balance of light and dark failing, and the darkness thickening its hold over the neighborhoods. He wondered where the theater and Mischa could be in that darkness. He just hoped to forget her and what he had seen her do in this forest. He wanted to lie down and go to sleep and have all of this be over. Mischa had influence that would now distort everything he saw, as if she had placed a convex lens over his eyes that inverted reality.

All along, she wanted him to be someone else. Here was his chance. She knew this was the only way for him to start over. Moving to the city was one thing, but there was a lot that he had carried over with him. So here he was, brand new, newly built by Doppelmann.

He patted his body, noting the thickness in his limbs and torso. With his bound hands, it was difficult to make much of an assessment of the changes. He needed a mirror now more than ever.

Higher in the hills, the shrubs began rustling. Then a group of young men burst out, yelling at the night.

"In you come! Join us! Join us!" one said.

"Down with northern darkness!" they shouted.

The cliff dogs howled louder, competing with the boys. As the group approached, Michael hoisted his new body up and hurried down the dirt trail.

23

AT THE BASE OF THE TRAIL, WHERE THE STREET BEGAN, HE DASHED into an alleyway and hid behind a dumpster. The group of young men continued down the street, shouting at the night, now flaring flashlights at darkened windows and curbed vehicles. Michael noted that the night's fog had descended and there was condensation on his blazer's sleeves. He wiped it off until it all fell in big droplets that stained the street. He examined his hand and found the painted skin was unharmed.

If he stayed out too late, he would be pulp by morning. He didn't need another night like his first one in the city, and curiously, this night felt somehow very similar. He rushed across the street, hobbling on his new legs, past the shops that he still recognized, avoiding the streets that led to the north and were now blocked by cardboard fences, and avoiding any pedestrians in groups of three or more. He had no idea what time it was, but he knew it was very late. The only solution was to keep going, never tiring, until he arrived at a familiar door.

He didn't even knock. It was unlocked, a rare occurrence. Empty boxes, stacked like blocks, lids torn off, lined one side of the staircase down to the drawing room. Black and white photographs floated in their colored frames randomly across the wall. The light at the end now had a new lampshade, and beside the sofa was a new sewing machine.

Someone was in the bedroom, tearing things apart. Cutting off the old to make room for the new. He listened and recognized the humming of haikus. The drawing room floor was still sticky. He wondered if it had flooded recently or if it was that way since his first night here.

He went to the bedroom door and knocked, timidly. No answer. When he stepped inside, the light made him blink. The room was warm and smelled like cardboard and body odor. In the middle of the room, Maiko was gutting one box lid with a knife. She wore a long t-shirt so that her legs poked out like a sandpiper, and her hair was combed back into a ponytail. Her face gleamed with sweat. He watched her, happy and humming. He almost didn't want to interrupt her.

"I'm home," Michael finally said.

Maiko's eyes narrowed, and she raised the knife. She looked different. Doppelmann's portrait had taken something from her. It may have been the fear she always had, now replaced by bitterness.

"Michael, is that you?"

"Yes, yes," he said, and then added, "I believe so."

"What happened to you?"

"I don't really know," he said. "I was hoping you could help me understand that."

In the kitchen, they sat at the dining table. Near his arm was a ring of water from a glass and a pile of coupons with a pair of scissors. She placed the knife on the table.

"Bring me a mirror," he said.

"You haven't seen this?"

He shook his head. He wasn't sure if he was ready to see himself yet. When she stood to go to the bathroom, he grabbed her arm, and she recoiled and backed against the counter.

"I changed my mind," he said. "How long has it been? Since you last saw me?"

"Two months? Three?" she said, as if asking herself. She looked at the nested bowls on the countertop. "It feels like forever. I was just getting used to the idea of you being gone." Her eyes clicked and locked onto him. "A lot has changed. The city is breaking apart. People are putting up walls to keep some semblance of privacy. Too many prying eyes are out there now."

Had that much time gone by? He thought about the waiting, in the dark, while Doppelmann repaired his body. Those hands. They stroked his legs and arms and adjusted the tightness of thread in his joints with the most care. Maiko's hands fiddled with a piece of tape from one of the boxes.

"I tried to change the apartment. I want things to be different around here. Brighter, less lonely." The outline of her body was so tense he was afraid she would spring out at him and stab him if he touched her.

Instead she approached him.

"Is it really you?" She stroked his face. "You're an adult now. You look different. Like a man."

He walked up to the metal toaster and turned it so he could see his face. Being here, in the kitchen, the oven door cracked for heat, he suddenly wanted to live the life he had before. The apartment exuded safety and comfort. He glanced at the stack of nested bowls.

"What happened that night? When he painted your portrait?" he asked.

"I don't want to talk about it. Go see for yourself in the bathroom," she said.

"Yes, of course," he said, as if he needed permission. He considered the fact that the reason for his disappearance had not mattered to her. What mattered was the disappearance itself.

He stood in the dark before the bathroom mirror. At his feet, a line of light illuminated his shoes and the cuffs of his trousers. Maiko must have been pacing the hallway, for every few minutes a shadow blotted out the light and rolled across the floor. He tried to convince himself that whatever he saw in the mirror, once he turned on the light, would be okay for him. Anything was better than what he was before. As his eyes adjusted to the dim room, his fingers pinching the light switch, he watched the light at the base of the door, and then his gaze wandered up: first to the doorknob that was not locked and did not move; then to the sink, with strands of Maiko's hair pasted to its curved walls, and the faucet that dripped steadily; then to the bar of soap glued to a saucer with a collection of chewed-off fingernails; and then to the metal frame surrounding the mirror.

He saw the outline of his jaw, his own picture frame around

his own face. His fingers flicked the switch, and the room exploded
into light (had she changed the light bulb?). There, looking back at
him in the mirror, was his new face.

The prominent feature was a chiseled jaw, as if he were an
ancient statue. His cheeks had become angular, and his nose a bit
smaller. The shape of his eyes was the same, but now he appeared
less like a toy and more like a person. His eyebrows arched down
from his smooth forehead, giving him an amused expression. He
tried to change his look and found he could make subtle movements around his symmetrical mouth. His hair was now close
cropped and not thick yarn. Instead it was slightly fine linen, again
looking more natural. The features he had before now seemed like
they had been made by a child. This new body was unlike anything
he had imagined.

All of this made him smile (and now he could smile). He
undressed and found his body sinewy and sturdy. His arms had
filled out, as if he had been infused with life. His waist was narrow,
his chest more full with slight tufts of hair and rings of short hairs
surrounding his nipples. And there, between his legs, the truest
sign he was no longer an adolescent.

"Are you all right?" It was Maiko, at the door.

"One moment," he said. He dressed again, examined his face
closer, noting there were no dents, no words of old newspaper
exposed. In the hallway, he found her waiting. She sighed and smiled.

"He really did a good job. Much better than I could have
ever done."

"Is it all mine?"

"Of course." She squeezed his arm and laughed.

"You have muscles. And a nice face. Look at that smile!"

"I can't believe it," he said.

"Come into the kitchen. Are you hungry?"

He thought for a moment.

"Yes, this new body is quite hungry."

24

HE SLEPT THAT NIGHT IN THE DRAWING ROOM, IMAGINING THE possibilities. There was no desire to see Mischa, but he did wonder if he went into the theater whether he would find Doppelmann. A letter composed itself in his mind to the artist, but soon after it was writing itself instead to his father.

Dear Father, he thought. *I may end up staying here after all...*

The next morning, before Maiko awoke, he left the apartment and headed for the fish market. A group of women looked at him, suspiciously at first, but from their expressions, they seemed pleased to have seen him on their morning walk, instead of repulsed. He found his stride to be more confident, and as he passed the bus stop, he noticed that he was a bit taller than before. Months ago when he stood next to the bus sign, his eyes had lined up right below it, and now he was above it.

Through the fish market, he passed the aquariums and buckets of ice with fish for sale and rushed past the trash bins of rotted shrimp heads, before entering the ship that acted as the office for Holloway & Holliday Cannery. Through the tunnels and down the staircases he went, no one stopping him. He walked with a purpose, swift and stable on even feet, and a few of the ship workers, seeing him approach, stepped aside. The interior maze was still engraved in his mind, so it was no problem finding the controller's office.

Only someone else was there. Behind the controller's desk was a young man with glasses and a tie.

"Who are you?" Michael asked.

"Adam," the young man said. "Can I help you?"

"Where's the controller?"

"I'm the assistant controller. Mitchell works down the hall now."

Michael turned to leave, but Adam ran after him and stopped him in the hallway.

"He's very busy now, and asked to not be disturbed."

"I'm here about the job."

"What job?"

"Let me through." Michael pushed past Adam, who recoiled when Michael's segmented fingers grazed his shoulders. What surprised Michael, though, was his new strength. He almost wanted to apologize to Adam, but growing embarrassed, he moved on. Several doors were open down the hall, and Michael peeked in each room until he saw one with a single bulb hanging from the ceiling, blocking the face of a man at a desk. He was punching away at an adding machine, and the tape was a stream of paper cascading onto the sooty floor.

"Who's there?" The controller grunted.

"I'm here about the job. For a bookkeeper," Michael said.

The controller's fingers paused above the machine's buttons. Did he recognize Michael's voice? Surely he did not recognize Michael's face. Then Michael recalled how months ago the heat each day had dried his throat and warped the mask's paint. Whatever Doppelmann had used to paint his new skin seemed heat resistant, and this helped keep Michael calm.

"The position's filled."

"I wondered if you needed any more help," Michael began. Adam barged into the room and apologized to the controller, who waved them both out.

"I recognize you," Michael said in the hallway to Adam. "You had flyers posted for your bookkeeping business."

"That's me," Adam said. "But after working here on a contract for a month, they hired me as assistant controller. Are you a bookkeeper? I could let you know if I hear of any other jobs. I know it's tough to find work these days."

Michael considered this: a normal life to go with his normal body.

"Are there any other job openings here? I'd be willing," he began, but paused as someone carried two buckets full of fish guts down the hall. "I'd be willing to help in other areas if needed."

"Not at the moment," Adam said. "And I would know because I process all the payroll."

On the ground, fallen from the bucket, was a spine attached to a fish head.

"I could do a better job than that," Michael said.

"Sorry," Adam said. "I don't do the hiring."

It was strange that Adam looked so similar to the old Michael, with his thin frame, blue shirt, and caramel tie. Adam was the perfect fit for the cannery.

He wandered the streets back to Maiko's apartment, glancing in the windows of the shops and restaurants, considering the places with the HELP WANTED signs. He could never work near steam or sinks, he thought. Or pudding. Even though his body looked better than before, he didn't want to risk being close to water.

As he climbed down the steps to the drawing room at Maiko's, he could hear her, behind the curtain that separated the rooms, on the phone. She spoke rapidly, in another language, her voice intense. He slowly sat on the horsehair sofa to avoid making any sounds. He misjudged the new weight of his body, and a spring in the sofa creaked.

"Michael?"

"I'm here," he said. She said a few more words into the phone and then hung up.

"Where have you been? We need to go."

"What for?"

"I think I found you a job."

He leaped up. They had talked about this the night before, while she cooked. Maiko had suddenly become very charming and catering to him, constantly touching his shoulders and ruffling his short hair when she walked by. She had laughed several times, telling him stories of her childhood and the trials of moving into the city. He smiled too, and from her eyes, the bitterness he had seen that evening had vanished and they were brimming with excitement. That night he had told her of his plans to get his old job back and start a normal life with no fear. She remembered the melted paint and had brought up his safety on the streets but said nothing more when he said, "Look at me! They won't even notice what I'm made of."

He parted the curtains that separated the drawing room from the kitchen. Maiko was seated at the table, the one on which he had lain to dry out that first night so long ago, and she was tying her shoes.

"Did you go to the cannery? Please tell me no. I found something better." She grabbed his hand, and they both leaped back: an electric shock, human skin touching paper fingers. He looked at her apologetically and shrugged. She reached again and they ascended the stairs together.

25

MAIKO LED THE WAY. THEY WALKED UNDER THE BRIDGE, WHERE they had first met months ago, and emerged into the bustle of the shoestring street. In Front of many businesses, cardboard fences had been set up along the street and already had plenty of posters glued to them. Many were simply advertisements for city nightclubs and cigarettes; some were for the neighborhood ("We Offer Breaks for Businesses" and "Help Us Build a City Above the Clouds!"); others were phone numbers and declarations of love (MC+ASG). Since she wouldn't discuss the job prospect, Michael read the signs aloud, "FM+AB," hoping she would say something, "JE+LT," wishing she would give a hint—"GGM+JB." He still doubted that she forgave him for being away, even though he had had no obligation to stay there. With his new body, though, she treated him differently. Less like a little brother.

"These walls, will they really keep the north out?"

"You tell me," she said. "You're made of the same material. Could you keep the north out?"

They arrived at a set of stairs that zigzagged along the side of a building. Up to the third floor they climbed; below, he watched, with a small delight, the heads of pedestrians oblivious to his eyes.

Inside the building, they used a dolphin-shaped doorknocker and then entered a lavender-scented office, where they were greeted by a woman, also dressed in lavender, who hugged Maiko. She gestured for them to sit in a pair of chairs across from her desk. Michael let Maiko choose her chair, and he took the other one, careful on the slippery leather that nearly caused him to slide off. He steadied himself by locking his arms against the arm rests.

"Now, tell me what you have here," the woman said to Maiko. She unsheathed a pen and turned over a sheet of paper.

"This is Michael, my," and here Maiko paused and darted her

eyes. He tightened his grip on the arm rests. She continued, "He's my friend who moved here a few months ago. And he lost his job because of an accident. He's fully recovered now and is ready for work again."

The woman, who had been writing, stopped to quickly glance at Michael then scribbled more notes onto another scrap of paper.

"Go on," the woman said, looking down and still writing. As the pen continued to scratch against the paper, Michael began to feel itchy.

"Without work, Michael will end up on the streets. We all know it's not safe out there right now, so that is why I called. You said you might be able to help us out?"

He watched Maiko's hands, stationed on top of her knees, flutter every time she spoke. He imagined clasping her hand like a bird in his, calming it.

"I heard about something like him. An artist made a splash the other day with a similar model at a gallery. These paper men are popular commodities right now."

Maiko swiveled her eyes at Michael. The woman stared at him too. She squinted and then made a declaration.

"He's perfect."

"Really?" Maiko said.

"Perfect for what?" Michael asked.

"This is why. The city is all about protection right now. And he's made of a kind of armor. The mannequins don't cut it. Sales have been slow since we switched to them. He's perfect except for his face. He needs to look tougher. It's too soft, too pretty. Can you put a new one on him?"

Michael leaped up and his chair toppled over. He still wasn't used to his new body size. Standing up, he was taller than he had remembered, his feet far below.

"Yes. I can make a mask for him." Maiko tugged on his sleeve.

"Excellent. And could we switch them out if needed?"

"I suppose," Maiko said.

"What's going on here?" Michael finally spoke.

"This is the window dresser for Willard's," Maiko explained. "She wants to help you."

"And he can move in most positions? He's not too tall for the display window? You would know, dear."

"You saw me walk in," Michael said. He balanced himself by placing his hands on his hips. "Maiko, are you selling me?"

"Of course not. He works a regular day, like any other job, right?"

"Yes. Bring him here by nine every morning. We will give him the clothes to wear and explain what he needs to do."

"I'm not a piece of junk you can sell," Michael said. He wanted to push the chairs and desks over and assert his presence in the room. He stepped closer, and Maiko leaned back, a wave of fear or astonishment spreading across her face.

"Please, Michael. You can come back to the apartment at the end of the day. Besides, it might be fun. Don't you think?" She grinned.

"I'm not a fur model. In fact, I'm the opposite. I want people to stop looking at me."

"Is he not interested?" the woman asked.

"He's very interested."

"He doesn't seem interested."

Why didn't she talk to him directly?

"I don't know what other work he could do right now. The display window is completely safe, there are no liquids, and we're turning what initially seems odd into a leader of a trend."

"Indeed," the woman said. She looked impressed with Maiko's statement.

"I don't suppose you'd take me back as a fur model. If the mannequins haven't worked out." Maiko brushed her hand along the edge of the desk.

"I'm sorry, dear. No one's shopping for furs right now. And we still can't pay you for what you're worth."

Maiko blushed.

"Have you thought any more about the perfume counter?

There's one spot left. They could really use someone with your personality. The other girl is a little too cold."

"I'll do what you ask if you work too," Michael said.

Maiko stood up, stiff. He put his hand on her shoulder and pulled her a little closer. He didn't care what the lavender woman thought. Maiko shook her head.

"This isn't fair."

"It's only temporary," he said. What a surprise to be the comforting one.

"We'll need him for three months," the woman said. "If it works out, we can extend. Will you sign this contract?" She pushed a pink sheet of legal paper to the edge of the desk. "He starts tomorrow."

Using a thick fountain pen with blue ink, Maiko scribbled her name at the bottom of the paper. At the top, Michael noticed the words CONTRACT OF SERVICES.

"This would give him a work permit for the city, correct?"

"Yes, I'll take care of that. This will be marvelous. He's our new citizen. Protected on the outside, constructed by a storm of words from newspapers, the voice of the city." The woman tucked the pink sheet inside a folder. "And now I have to go home. It's good working with you, Maiko. This could increase our sales, get the city going in a new direction. Maybe I could run for mayor. Do you know, no one has seen him in ages? They say he's sick. I personally think he's left the city."

She reassured Maiko. "In the winter, they'll ask for fur models. Now, tell your mother hello the next time you speak with her. It's been ages since I've seen her."

In front of Willard's, they stood before the empty display window. Across the glass, a banner said NEW LOOKS COMING SOON.

"Tomorrow will I be in there?" he asked.

Maiko nodded. In the glass, he saw his reflection, his eyes

pools of darkness. This was what he looked like when others really saw him.

"I need to make you a new mask tonight. If it means anything, I kept one of your old masks after you left."

"I need to hide myself again?"

"Think of it as a costume," she said. "You can take it off at the end of each day. Your face looks fine now. No dents."

Maiko motioned to their reflections, staring back at them in the night. Michael only saw dark puddles for his eyes and leaning closer to the glass made them spread across his face. He pressed his paper cheek against the window. He was an object now, sold and stationed like any other static commodity. This was why he had run from the art gallery. He wanted a job where he was hidden, not in front of others, not trying to lure others into a masked life.

The street that headed north was lined with magnolia trees and pasted along the side of the gutters were discarded leaves and scraps of ink-stained paper—shed skin of trees and newspapers. Cardboard walls on the sidewalks obscured many of the buildings.

"Let's take a taxi home. That's what I used to do when I worked here."

She waved as a taxi approached and then helped Michael climb in. He bowed his head into the pool of darkness that made up the back seat. It was as if he were stepping inside the shadows in his eyes.

———————————

He lay on the couch in the drawing room while she searched the apartment for materials to make the mask. It was very late now. The streets were silent and the apartment building didn't creak. The room smelled like fresh dirt. He lay in his shorts, dazed; his pant legs were like ribbons on the couch.

While he wanted to be happy to have a job and begin to live a normal life with Maiko, it seemed entirely hopeless. Working in the display window would make him a circus freak.

"Remember the drill?" she said, carrying her sewing box and a stack of newspapers.

"Please be careful," he said. "I don't want anything to happen to my new face."

"And neither do I," she said. "It's such a nice face."

"Will you tell me?" he asked. "What happened the night he painted your portrait?"

She looked into the kitchen, thinking for several minutes. He tore the newspaper into bits and mixed the bowl that was for glue. The room was silent otherwise.

"Never mind," he said.

"I knew he wanted to use me," she finally said. "All along. I hadn't seen him in years, and I thought I would be different this time. He tried to paint me after seeing me in the display window. There's just something about having someone look at you that way. At first, it feels like they're admiring you, but then you start to become nothing more than a bunch of pieces put together."

"Will I be that way?" he asked. "In the display window?"

"Of course not. You're a man now. They don't look at men the same way."

He reclined on the couch, and she rubbed the cold jelly that protected his face from the approaching bits of newspaper. As he lay there, he imagined himself like a statue, immobile and expressionless.

26

AT WILLARD'S THE NEXT DAY, THE DISPLAY DIRECTOR GAVE instructions to Maiko as Michael stood beside them. In between, she explained her theory on colors, complementary items required to make a display successful, and how to deal with the variety of lighting. Clouds, apparently, severely impacted her display.

"I'm right here, you know," Michael said, but the woman ignored him. She showed Maiko the small door that led to the inside of the display window, went over the breaks and daily shift schedule, and emphasized that he was not to acknowledge anyone staring at him.

"That is the most important thing. He cannot break the illusion for those looking in." She climbed into the display area. "Our window is like a three-dimensional painting. It is a means of attraction, but must retain a sense of mystery."

"Yes, I know this already." Maiko squirmed inside her tight-collared dress, similar to an aeronautic attendant's uniform, the required outfit at the perfume counter.

"Excuse me?" the woman asked. She emerged with the paper sign NEW LOOKS COMING SOON crumpled in her hand.

"I already told him everything last night. He knows what to do."

Why don't you talk to me directly? Michael asked the woman, again. She tightened her grip around the sign.

"Very well, then, let's put him inside." She waved for him to enter.

He was wearing a tuxedo and dress shoes with paper-thin soles. The bow tie, too big for his neck, had been pinned in the back. As he lowered himself through the doorway, the bow tie choked him. What if he suffocated in here? He took a deep breath. The new mask covered his face. It was strange to have this extra layer on him. Before, the masks he had worn had become comforting, but now this one was too tight on his cheeks. He turned around, and

Maiko's hands reached in to pet him.

"Good luck with the new job," he said.

"See you tonight." From her glance, he knew that she wanted to be the one in the window.

"And he knows what to do with the mannequins? The man will incline to the blond, then pause, then incline to the brunette. Pause, then repeat."

"I know this," Michael said.

At this point, the woman actually looked at him, but he had the sensation that Maiko had described before: she didn't look at him as a person but as an assemblage of pieces. It made no difference that he was a man.

"Just remember that the imitation of art is the perfection of nature," she said.

The door shut. There was the click of a lock. He brushed his segmented fingers over the edge of the door, now seamlessly flush with the wall. An arm's length away was the window, a large transparent canvas, begging to be painted. The room itself was decorated as a mock balcony, with dark walls and ceiling to represent a night sky. A few oversized stars were painted above. To his left, stood two female mannequins, one blonde, one brunette, both wearing cocktail dresses, next to a table set with martini glasses and fake food. Over their dresses were pink bulletproof vests fringed with lace.

"Hello there," he said to both of them. They stood, stiff and silent, their eyes vacant and minds absent. Because of his own condition, he half expected them to turn and speak. Outside the window, speakers crackled and began playing the radio's orchestral music. Did the north not have any other music to play? The same songs cycled through each day. Whoever was controlling the sound turned it up extremely loud. Michael leaped back. The martini glasses rattled.

He tapped on the wall. A moment later, the music lowered. The pair of mannequins watched him with their unblinking eyes.

Their frozen smiles chilled him. He tugged at the bow tie, clawed at the mask.

"So I'm to dance with you," he said to the blonde. She stared back, smiling.

For a while, he waited in the corner, not sure where to begin. People passed by the window, but none of them looked inside. It was as if he was an everyday object that had become part of their route. But then one of the people paused. He noticed she wore lavender and was banging on the window. Her mouth moved, but the music drowned out her voice. The shape of her lips, though, told him everything.

Get. To. Work.

He took the mannequin's icy hand and raised her off her stand. She was lighter than his paper body. With both hands, he held her in a waltz position, something he had seen a couple do in the city park. Her arms were resistant, and he found it difficult to hold her comfortably.

Slowly they began to dance to the music. The waltz was in a minor key with plaintive strings playing the melody. The mannequin's cocktail dress brushed the floor, his shoes scuffed the paint. The lace around her vest was like a cloud pressed between their chests. From the corner of his eye, he saw someone stop before the glass.

"They're watching," he said. "They're watching us." He swayed the mannequin in time with the music, and quickly a small crowd gathered. He tried not to think about them. "Don't worry, pretend you can't see them," he said to the mannequin, but he knew he was talking to himself. He realized his movements would be much more fluid if he was wearing better underwear.

As the waltz climaxed, he spun the mannequin. Her legs almost kicked the brunette. A small crowd had their eyes glued to the window, mouths open, teeth showing. They were like hungry animals. He bowed as the song finished, placed the mannequin back on her stand, and then he slowed his movement and stopped mid-stride. It was as if he had come to life to dance and now was returning to a normal catatonic state.

He also did this because he didn't know what to do next. Would they let him out now? Even though the window dresser had gone over the schedule, he couldn't remember when he would be given a break. Outside, the music continued to play, but the crowd was clapping.

They were clapping, but he could not hear them, as if their sound had been turned down. The look in their eyes reminded him of when he was in the art gallery after Doppelmann had unsewed his eyes, but having a piece of glass between him and the crowd made everything better. He felt safer in here and far enough removed from them. It gave him the distance he needed to observe what was happening, not just with them but within himself as well: the glass gave him the ability to see his own movements in its slight reflection, and this critical information helped him make adjustments to his body movements.

"And now this news flash," the radio barked. It was the voice of the one-eyed man. "Walls continue to build up around city streets in an attempt to deter visitors from the north. A small scuffle near the isthmus inspection point led to northern officers arresting three city dwellers. We will announce the names as soon as they are filed."

The music returned, and the man's voice faded from Michael's mind. He remembered the thing, the entity he had been, upon arriving in the city. How distant that day seemed, just as the sound outside the glass seemed distant.

He did several dances that day, alternating between the blond and the brunette. With the music outside, it was as if he was underwater in the display window. The crowds became larger as the day went on. At dusk, the little door snapped open, and a hand waved for him to come out. It was the window dresser who helped him undress from the tuxedo and gave him an envelope with cash.

"We're going to pay you this way."

"Don't tell your bookkeeper," he advised.

Maiko arrived as if in a trance. They walked home in silence. He wore the mask still, and by the end of the day, it had made him feel safe again. Wasn't this his situation months ago? He looked at the people they passed, their gaits and mannerisms for carrying groceries and backpacks, or even children. The way people's feet landed and jutted away or fell closer to their bodies. He walked as if he threw each foot like an anchor, his light body dragging behind.

In the apartment, Maiko set the table and served their dinner in bowls. They ate in silence. When they were done, she moved to the sink, her back to him as she washed the dishes.

"How did it go?" she asked later.

He didn't know what to say. Would she be jealous? Angry?

"There isn't much room in there," he said.

She made tea and returned to the table. He stared at her hands around the mug and remembered the pale arms of the mannequin and her silky blonde hair.

"How was it working at the perfume counter?"

She took a sip of her tea.

"Terrible. The other girl is incredibly mean. They expect us to harass every woman who walks by. By the end of the day, I was nauseous from all the smells."

"It's only temporary. Soon we can switch. You in the window and me at the counter."

"The window dresser said you were a hit. They already want you for next season's lineup."

"I'm sorry," he said.

She took her tea into the bedroom.

Later, in the drawing room he lay on the floor, listening to people arguing on the street above. Maiko never turned on the radio anymore. In his mind, he continued to replay the walk of Mischa, that day they had met at the diner. It was her movement, her confidence, and the right amount of wind through her hair that had nearly everyone staring at her. She seemed to expect it. He didn't understand how someone like her and someone like Maiko could want to same thing—to be the center of attention. He thought he could hear Maiko down the hall, sobbing over the argument outside. On the table sat his mask, staring up at the stained ceiling.

After his first week, the scene in the display window changed. He was dressed in a light trench coat and helmet for a desert expedition. From the ceiling dangled nylon strings holding paper cutouts of clouds. Early fall fashions were already on sale in the store. The wall behind him had been painted with a long airport runway. Only the blonde mannequin was with him, wearing a kind of knit sweater with a hood. Her feet sported a pair of camouflage boots.

As Michael and the mannequin reenacted a scene from an old radio play, the voices for their characters were played on the outside speakers.

"You must leave," his voice said to the mannequin.

He felt odd to have his voice outside of his body. He turned the mannequin to the right, as if she were walking away. Then he pulled her close to him, and she was supposed to squeeze his body, but since her limbs were very stiff, it looked more as though she were clamping onto him.

"I never want to let you go," her voice said.

They walked slowly in place. He explained that she must absolutely go on without him.

She resisted.

He turned to her and said through the speakers:

"You have to go before they get here. I will stay behind and stop them from finding out you've left, until it's too late."

He took her to the corner of the window and leaned her against a toy airplane.

"Stay with me," her voice pleaded outside the glass.

"I've got bigger fish to fry," his voice said. "Good bye."

The mannequin stared at him, smiling, never changing. Although it was crazy to think, he suspected she was mocking him, and his insides tightened. He empathized with the voice of the actor, suddenly remembering the day, ten years ago, when he had taken Mischa to the train station and how she had rushed away from him. She had never said anything, not even *good bye*, and he had watched the train disappear down the tracks. She had seemed so perfect then, and he remembered every part of her that made her whole: her uneven stockings on her legs, her tendency to favor her left hip when running, the short boyish hair that didn't move in the wind.

He walked away from the mannequin, his paper palms pressed to his eyes. He littered the ground with cut-out paper tears, large droplets of blue paper. He had cried that day when Mischa had left. The dialogue stopped, and orchestral music started up. He froze in place, dropping the last of the paper tears, inside fighting back the urge to cry real ones. *Not even a good bye.* Glancing between his fingers at the crowd, he saw an enormous number of people before him. One woman at the front of the glass caught his eye: she wore a black cat mask and was crying, the tears dropping from her exposed chin. She was not the only one.

The music swelled and then stopped. Someone approached with a camera and a bulb flashed. It blinded Michael, and he nearly lost his balance. Everyone clapped, and this time he could hear the skin of their hands pressing together to make the sound of gentle rain.

27

MICHAEL PERFORMED MORE RADIO PLAYS OR DANCES OR SOME-
times just improvised with no sound. The one-eyed man's voice
continued to interrupt often, sharing the latest news of the north
arresting people from the city. The crowds grew and the attention,
at first intimidating, became exciting. He was so popular that the
department store paid for a taxi to drop Maiko and him off at their
apartment and pick them up. Once, while leaving the store, he was
swarmed by a crowd of eager fans, demanding pictures with him
and autographs. They called him "The Paper Man," the epitome of
flaunting art in the face of adversity. Some of the women had begun
wearing velvet vizards—masks that covered the upper half of their
faces. They used fans to cover the lower part of their face, fluttering
them to reveal flashes of their red lips. He tried to run away, afraid
of any camera lens, but they caught up with him and overpowered
him. He even received fan mail.

"That's what I was like when I was a fur model," Maiko said.
She leaned toward him, but he had to hold her face back from his
paper neck because it was wet with tears.

Who was this guy in the display window, he asked himself.
Was it really him? It was unlike anything he had ever done. He
began to understand why Maiko missed working there. Beneath all
of this was a flooding feeling that frightened him: that he was an
object, without true character of his own, and everyone projected
themselves onto him. They defined him, they categorized him,
boxed him in.

During his time in the display window, he had begun to transform again. His new skin, new hair, new body—those were simply
superficial changes. What was most significant was that his relationship with his body had changed. It was no longer a source of
anxiety and no longer the source of his problems.

This became his life for many weeks. The money allowed them to buy new furniture not stained with rainwater, and Maiko was always there for him. She helped him with everything. Once or twice, her hand lingered on his shoulders, and he wondered if she would embrace him. It would be nice to be held again by a human, he thought, instead of the cold skin of a mannequin. His gaze lingered, he hoped she could understand his curiosity, but her eyes would close and she would walk away.

The streets, as they drove to and from Willard's in the taxi, were calm, and these were the only times he was outside. He missed the outside air. From the taxi window, he glanced at the tall buildings, just as he had done on his first day in the city. He never imagined himself hiding in a basement apartment, a kind of local celebrity.

A few days later, the *City Mirror* included a front-page picture of Michael in the display window. The article was not what fascinated him. It was the caption that cited the amateur photographer as a name he recognized: Adam. Michael tried to remember if he had seen Adam in one of the crowds, but there were too many people to single him out. The picture was what people began using to ask for his autograph.

One night, after he had finished dancing and the crowd had left, many wearing small eye masks, he saw a shadow split from the dark street. A figure walked up to the window, removed a red marker from its jacket, and proceeded to scribble something on the glass. When it was done, the figure smacked the glass and ran away. As soon as Michael's shift ended, he ran outside to see what it said. He hadn't been able to read it backwards inside the window because the writing was so messy.

Michael gasped and collapsed onto the stained sidewalk. The marker said, in a frantic scrawl: *PAPER MEN BY DOPPELMANN*

Then, across the street, he saw a crowd gathered before the cardboard wall covering the glass of a store that had gone out of business. He approached them. What could they be looking at? Lying on the ground was the figure of a man—a paper man—made of invoices. Upon closer inspection, Michael discovered they were Holloway & Holliday Cannery documents.

"What is this?" Michael asked.

"It's the paper man!" a mustached man shouted. Everyone turned to look at him.

"Two of them?"

"It's the truth," an older woman, in a bonnet that framed her vizard mask, said. She pointed to the invoices. "Paper proof that the tuna cannery has been smuggling weapons and gear to attack us here in the city. They're working for the north."

"What are you talking about? They were trying to hide this from the north."

"That's impossible. This right here says it all."

"Who did this?" Michael said.

"The same guy who made you, David," she said, and pointed to the back of the paper man's neck. Scribbled in red ink was the same name as on the glass. It unnerved Michael that there were two paper men in the city. He wanted to tear him to pieces.

"Why did you call me David?" Michael asked.

"He said that's your name. Do you mind if I have your autograph?" She presented a paper napkin and pen to him and sheepishly smiled before hiding her mouth with a paper fan.

28

HE WOKE UP STARING AT THE WATER STAINS ON THE CEILING. THEY were a constant, haunting reminder of the rainstorm, only months ago. He realized he had not heard a train in a long time. Had they become part of the sound of the city? Had he really adjusted to life here? And just as he was adjusting to yet another version of life in the city, Doppelmann had appeared at the display window and seemed to be reclaiming Michael or staking an ownership in him. Marking the glass with his name—Michael knew what now haunted him was the squeaking of the marker as Doppelmann had written his name on the glass.

He had tried to take the paper man, this Invoice Man, but Maiko and the taxi had appeared and shuttled him away. When she had asked what the matter was, he couldn't tell her. As soon as they were home, he had thrown the mask on the table and said he was tired of being someone else.

"People now think my name is David," he said. "They don't even know my real face."

"But you are someone else when you're in there. That's the job. Then you leave that behind when you come home."

"Why is it always between two things? Inside, outside. Why don't we ever go outside?"

"It's not a difference between here and there. Things are more complicated than that."

The next day in the display window, he couldn't concentrate. Even with the blonde mannequin clamped to his side, as they stood on a fake cliff overlooking a beach, his thoughts were all about Doppelmann. If he appeared again in the crowd, by the time Michael got outside, Doppelmann still would be gone. Michael's new life was in a waterless aquarium. What was next from Doppelmann? A signature on Michael's body? A price tag on his head? A wire hanger on his shoulders? A label of materials used to make him and the year he was created?

During the day, he noticed that across the street many people swarmed around the Invoice Man, but he couldn't hear them over the music. More people in public had begun wearing masks, some of them simple bandit style eye masks, while young women wore vizard masks. Someone was there and photographed them, then scurried off just as a kid torched the Invoice Man. The flames leaped up into the air and set the roof of the building on fire. Minutes later, a fire truck parked and doused it with a blast of water. Several people threw objects at the truck. They hid as the fire dissolved to smoke. Of the Invoice Man, only a pile of blackened pulp remained.

Toward the end of the next evening, Michael waltzed with the brunette mannequin. In his aquarium, he watched pedestrians stop cars that drove by and harass the drivers. In his aquarium, there seemed to be no passage of time, while outside the city was clearly on the verge of something new. Nearly half of the people on the streets now wore masks. He regretted ever giving the invoices to Doppelmann. Again he questioned himself: was that really me, back then, taking the papers, innocently believing they would buy repairs to a damaged body? He couldn't remember the feeling of that body any longer. The dents, the thin limbs, the hairless stretch of painted newspaper skin. All of that was gone.

The side door opened, and someone tossed in his fan mail, paper packets heavy with photographs of him and requests for his autograph. The one thing he wished for at that moment was a letter from his father. *Dearest Michael. We haven't heard from you in months and want reassurance that everything is all right.*

He and the mannequin danced around the envelopes. As the number of onlookers increased, now with cardboard signs professing their love for his shows, Michael tried to ignore them. Some headed into the street as the music ended and they joined the few people harassing the cars. His fans always seemed to beg for him to acknowledge their presence, but he stuck to the rule of not breaking the illusion.

Dialogue began playing on the speakers, and so Michael strolled with the mannequin down an imaginary street under an umbrella, paper snow falling from above. A mirror lit up behind them. He turned the mannequin to face the window, and they stared out into the small chunk of the city that lay before them.

"I remember when you could see the water from here," the actor's voice for Michael said. He was surprised by this dialogue—was it from a radio play?

"Now there are only walls. Everything is separating us from the sea."

The mannequin never stopped smiling. What was this script from?

"Attention listeners!" The background music stopped and the voice switched. A young man spoke quickly and urgently. "This radio station now belongs to us!"

Michael's hand slipped from the mannequin's waist.

The young man continued: "Support the south. The city is ours! Oppose the north!" And then he screeched and the speakers crackled.

A moment later, a woman stood outside in an aeronautics outfit—the same that Maiko wore. But it was not Maiko. It was Mischa.

She had three young masked men with her, circling her, smiling, asking questions. She had paused before the glass and was watching Michael. The man on the radio continued shouting, but the speaker was damaged, and now only low frequencies could be heard.

Mischa must have been the other perfume counter girl. He felt something boiling inside him, starting in his gut, radiating to his hands and feet. She stared at him, smiling like a mannequin. One of the men looped his arm around hers, trying to get her to join them in the street. She nodded at Michael. She seemed to be approving of his new look, his new life in this container.

Michael whispered to the mannequin, "Pardon me, I need to use your leg," and tipped her over. Yet he still wasn't used to his strength and misjudged the distance. Her head cracked on the floor, and her body snapped apart, arms and head and legs scattering as if she had been struck by an invisible bomb.

No time, he thought. He turned to the window and swung one of her legs at the glass.

There was a loud crack. The jolt nearly knocked him off his feet. The men with Mischa were frightened and stumbled back. They stood before her, as if they were protecting her from a monster. The other onlookers had gathered in the street, perhaps bewildered to see their hero becoming violent. Michael swung again, this time starting low, and he felt immensely powerful, that he could do anything now, and with another smack the glass shattered and exploded into icy chunks onto the sidewalk. Fresh air poured into the display window, and its stale air rose out.

Mischa was hypnotized, her eyes large and her smile tight.

"You made it," she said.

"I hoped I would never see you again."

"But look at you! Even with that mask you are beautiful. I've heard so much about you. I've been waiting to come over here and find you. And now, did you hear?"

He shook his head. He still held the leg of the mannequin. The onlookers had approached the broken window and were peering into the display case.

"There's a revolution happening. The city is really splitting apart. The city dwellers have taken over the radio station. And they overtook the inspection point in the north. And all I hear from people is talk of you. You've inspired them."

"How so?"

"They think your name is David and that you're a symbol for resisting the behemoth that is the north. We're all like you, taken over by paperwork and blind to the lies that are buried in paper. But look at that Invoice Man and what he told everyone. Parts of the city—the tuna cannery—were turning on the city itself. What you gave Doppelmann has woken everyone up."

"I didn't do this," he said. "The tuna cannery was trying to hide from the north. No one understands."

"Mischa, come on!" The young man glared at Michael then tugged on Mischa's elbow. She stared at Michael again, her eyes shining.

"I'm so proud of you. Come join us!"

Then she scurried off. The three men chased after her.

Michael climbed into the display window and looked at himself in the mirror. He saw his masked face, and behind him, in the reflection, someone had set a small sedan in the street on fire. He tore off the mask and stomped on it with his new boots. He tossed the mirror onto the floor and it made a terrific shattering.

The remaining onlookers ran off.

The sparkling jewels of the shattered mirror looked like the tips of waves, ready to push him outside. He braced himself, took a breath, then leaped over the toothy edges of the window. He was escaping the case that had framed him and dashed through the palpable air faster than a paper bag in the wind, weaving in surprising patterns past the burning car, after the pack of men and Mischa, a blot of darkness the same liquid shape as Michael's shadow.

29

Distant voices led the way. The shadow he followed soon melted into other shadows, and the trees waving in the night wind confused his eyes. He relied on the singing that was carried by the wind to find his destination. As he got closer, he recognized the singing was the choir from the trees that lined a familiar street. Michael hurried and the singing increased. From the leaves and branches emanated the voices. At the end of the road stood the abandoned theater. The two statues on each side, NIGHT and DAY, glowed from the warm incandescent light pouring out of the marquee. The initial shock of seeing it—the place where he had been destroyed—passed and he hurried in.

Within the theater, the choir trees could not be heard. He passed the door to the projection room and continued on his way. He wouldn't let it bother him. He was someone else then, and now he was someone new.

The long hallway curved from left to right like a horseshoe. The familiar red carpet glowed along its edges from the shallow lights in the wall seams. Eventually he arrived at the string of doors, and this time he noticed they were all installed with peepholes and mail slots. But rather than looking out, the peepholes looked in.

At the first door, he observed someone painting a canvas by beating it with a broom. The painter, a woman, was muttering words with each strike. Inside the next room, a man was dancing on the walls. He wore red tights and a hat with a red feather. At one point, the light revealed that he was suspended by clear wires. The following room had a pianist, who may have been the controller from Holloway & Holliday Tuna Cannery, wearing only a tiger-print bikini obscured by rolls of skin around his thick stomach. Perhaps he had been fired because of the stolen documents. A lamp of whale oil burned beside him.

Michael continued looking through the rooms. One of them was dark, and he discovered it was a coat room. He found a black pea coat and tried it on. It fit perfectly. He left some pieces of the mirror he still had with him on the floor, and their sparkles faded as he closed the door.

Other rooms had other artists, musicians, writers, and they were all working. It disgusted him. Here the city was falling apart outside and they were absorbed by their work. They were in aquariums just as he was. There was no difference, he decided, between art and artists. Neither had control, and both lived in the same kind of environment.

He found a door with the name MISCHA carved above the mail slot. Michael peeked through, but it was covered by cloth. He tried the doorknob, and it opened. Inside it was very quiet. He swallowed hard to clear his throat and to hear his body operate.

The room had a small kitchen, including a sink and hot plate and mini refrigerator. Two doors on the right seemed to be a bathroom and closet. The room was littered with paintbrushes and soiled towels with different colors. Several blank canvases leaned again the long wall. There were two twin beds, a nightstand between both of them. This was not the room she had taken him to months ago.

On one of the beds was a shirtless man. His skin was tan, his hair was long, and he had a slight beard. Dark hairs spread across his chest like an eagle in flight and trailed down his stomach. His face was covered with a black mask with a long nose that was a black paintbrush. This was likely another man for Mischa. How typical of her to leave him waiting. She was probably in another room down the hall with one of the other men and would be here next.

The man sipped a glass of whiskey and casually looked over at Michael.

"I'm looking for Mischa," Michael said.

"She's not here right now," the man said.

"I'll wait," Michael said, and sat down on the other bed. He didn't want to go back outside.

"You'll be waiting awhile," the man said. "Might as well take off your coat. Do you want a drink?"

"Yes," Michael said. He slid the pea coat off and set it beside him as if it were his pet dog. Did the man come from the crowd that had surrounded Mischa?

The man leaned over to the nightstand to pour from the whiskey bottle into another glass. As he moved, Michael saw the ink of a tattoo on his bicep, and on his back were deep red lines, creases from the wrinkled blankets beneath him.

"Is this Mischa's room?"

The man laughed as he handed Michael the glass. On the rim, it had an imprint of lipstick. Did the man notice that Michael was different? Did he know him from the display window?

"Did she say this is her room?" The man sat on the edge of the bed and looked directly at Michael through the eyeholes, glancing at his stitched clothes.

"Her name is on the door."

"She's staying here with me," the man said.

It made sense to him now: she wanted to be the object of affection for everyone. She didn't want to be a person. She wanted to be their object of desire. And look how many of them fell for that, including Michael.

"How do you know Mischa?" he asked the man.

"Probably the same way every guy knows her. Probably the same way you know her too."

Michael took a sip. The smoky liquid made him cough. He spit it out on the concrete floor.

"Take it easy," the man said, and tossed over a sock. "Use this to wipe it up."

Michael wiped the spot with the sock, hard as a dried sponge. He threw it aside.

"Are you an artist?" Michael asked, motioning to the blank canvases. He didn't want to point out the man's paintbrush nose.

"Yep. I've been here for a few days now, waiting for inspiration to strike. I like this room. It's perfect for incubating ideas. It's quiet, warm, no distractions. You're my first guest."

"Sorry to bother you. I just need to see Mischa."

"I haven't seen her for a few days. She might not come back."

"But the door says...."

"She's always marking things then moves on. I bet that door feels special, but it doesn't know yet that she'll never touch its knob again."

Michael laughed. It felt very strange to do so. He touched the corner of his lips. His new mouth... he wasn't used to it just yet.

The man studied Michael a bit then put down his drink.

"I like nothing better than a blank stare. You know why? Because then I can write all over it." The man continued to study Michael, staring at him from behind his mask. He announced: "I'd like to paint your nose."

"What for? You mean put a red dot or something on it?"

"No," the man said, "I mean, paint your nose on a canvas."

"Just my nose?"

"The rest of your face is nice, but I want to focus on your nose."

"The city is falling apart outside. Shouldn't we do something?"

"What can you do at this point? I've put my art out there. Creativity is nothing more than transferring emotions, mostly anxiety and fear, to the outside world. Let them make sense of it."

The man grinned and gathered up a thin paintbrush, palette, some cans of paint, and a small canvas. He put them on his bed. He leaned forward with the brush and held it out. In the air, he gestured the strokes that would make up Michael's nose. He then swished the brush across Michael's face.

"That tickles," Michael said. The man continued to brush in quick, light strokes. Michael closed his eyes, and the brush explored his face like a dry tongue. The bristles slid over his closed eyelids. Suddenly the brush was gone, and he felt the warmth from the man's body very close.

He opened his eyes to find the man's eyes aligned with his, his long nose pointing over Michael's ear. Their faces were so close it took a moment for Michael to realize they were about to kiss. He leaned forward, and their lips touched. If he wasn't careful, he would give the man a paper cut.

"I thought," Michael said, "you were here with Mischa."

"We don't need her anymore. What has she done for you or me lately?"

Only tear my body to pieces, he thought. He was over that. He had survived it, been remade; perhaps he would thank her one day. Would he be here, doing this right now, if she hadn't done that? He didn't know. They kissed again, and then the man's arms were around Michael. They fell back on the bed, which squeaked like a shocked animal.

The man playfully pinned down Michael, not the way Mischa had, his long hair hanging over his face so that he appeared like a dark smudge above Michael. For a moment, Michael thought his vision was blurring. But no, it was just dim in here. Dim and dream-like. The man removed Michael's shirt and stroked his new skin.

"Those fingers," Michael thought. The finger pads felt like corduroy, and they stroked him with firm waves of gentleness.

Michael sat up.

"I know who you are," he said.

The man smiled.

"When did you know?"

"These hands," Michael said, and caught both of them in his. He held them up between both of them. "You were the one who repaired me."

"Yes," the man said, and peeled his mask off and tossed it on the floor. He felt the contours of Michael's body. Soon their clothes were off, and they were under the covers, and it was unlike anything Michael had done before.

Later, they lay there, Doppelmann sipping more whiskey. He was sketching Michael's nose on a canvas.

"What if Mischa comes back?" Michael asked.

"Let her come back. Nothing surprises her."

Michael glanced around the room.

"Now what?"

"You can stay here if you like." Doppelmann put the canvas aside and pulled himself closer to Michael.

"I can't."

"You can do whatever you want. You left that display window on your own, right?"

Michael thought for a moment.

"I did. But what will they say?"

"I think," Doppelmann said, whispering now, "you should fake your own death. Leave some scraps of newspapers, some old clothes. Put them in the display window, and let everyone think it was them who did this to you. They were the ones who destroyed you."

"Yes," Michael said. "And then?"

"Then you can find who you really are."

30

A FAINT MEMORY OF LIFE IN THE DISPLAY WINDOW ROSE INSIDE him, as though it had sunk deep within his mind and was now breaking free from its anchor, floating out of him with his breath. And it had only been a few hours earlier. Outside the room, he could hear the hum of electricity; inside himself, he felt the same level of energy, a charge of potential he had not felt before. But what would Maiko think? That he had abandoned her again? She would always be stuck, he thought. She was so afraid of change. She would be trapped forever.

He rose from the bed, shocking his feet on the coldness of the room's cement floor, dressed, and stepped out into the carpeted hallway, a passage that seemed to go on forever, lined with its hundreds of doors and hundreds of recessed lights. Along the way, he found the carpet littered with random bits of garbage, including rolls of yellowing newspaper, torn cardboard boxes, and old clothing. He took off his own clothes and put on the found ones: a striped shirt, a pair of jeans, a wool sweater full of holes. It was like shedding a layer of skin. Then he stuffed his discarded clothes with the scraps of cardboard and newspaper until he had made a headless version of himself.

Outside the theater it was dawn. He dragged his effigy back to the display window. Michael managed to swipe an extra copy of the *City Mirror* that a newsboy was delivering along his route—and with it, he now had enough paper to make a fake head. He crumpled several sections of the newspaper together into a large mass, as if his head had bloomed open. This he stuffed into the neck hole of the effigy's shirt. Gently, he laid the body on the display window floor, next to the pieces of mannequin, and stroked its split head. He thought about what Maiko had said to him about how people view women and men. And here were the plastic women, broken on the floor, and he was still whole. He poured a handful of broken mirror over the body and watched, fascinated, while the passing trucks' headlights flashed and illuminated the bits of glass.

Someone was approaching. Michael ran across the street, past the charred car, his shoes crunching on the spray of glass crusting the sidewalk and, with the old clothes he now wore, managed to blend in with his surroundings. A few trash collectors were in the street and slowly passed by. Soon after, a group appeared before the broken window. The people were visibly upset, as though their hopes and dreams had been destroyed. A man blew his nose on white tissue paper and a woman cried into a handkerchief. Michael recognized the navy handkerchief. It belonged to Maiko. So she was here too. He held his breath and stood very still. She climbed inside the display window to hold his effigy, believing it was his dead body. Could she not see that there was nothing of him in that shell? Yet she clung to it, and she kissed its roll of paper that was its neck. The others tried to comfort her. When she gathered up a stack of envelopes from the floor, he realized he had left his fan mail behind. A part of him wanted the letters, to remember his days working there, but another part of him was ready to leave all of those memories behind.

Eventually, as the morning progressed and more cars appeared and the city came to life, the others helped Maiko out of the window. Her nose was red and swollen. Above her, the radio speakers dangled, lifeless of sound. As she climbed out, she cut her hand; walking away, she smeared the blood on the marble wall. The shattered display window was like a broken eye.

The truth, he realized, was that he no longer needed her. The theater seemed more like a natural home for a paper man. He had learned enough from her on how to survive but was stifled from learning any more about the city, about life. She was better off without him.

Just then, a truck stopped in front of the window. Michael had to stand beside the charred car to see what was happening.

"Everyone show us your identification papers," an officer said. Three other officers jumped from the back of the truck and began reviewing the documents. From their uniforms, it was clear they were a new presence in the city.

"Who are you?" someone shouted.

"We're from the north. This city is now an annexed territory."

"Get out of here!"

"We're here to help. No more antics like this. No more vandalism."

Someone tossed several chards of glass at them. The officers turned their faces but ignored the gesture.

"A new rule is in effect. Those from the city's southern district are not permitted in the city's center any longer."

"But I'm not an immigrant!" Maiko shouted. They seized her papers, striped red from her bleeding hand.

"Doesn't matter."

"I belong here in the city too."

"Get in," they said, and forced her inside the back of the truck.

"Wait!" Michael said and people's head's jerked around. He immediately realized his error and ducked. He imagined the officers looking for the source of his voice. He listened to shuffling of everyone's feet, but no one came searching for him.

From the side of the car, he watched the truck turn around and head south, Maiko sitting with a few others, her head bowed and her hair draped over her face. It was the same face forever captured in Doppelmann's portrait.

Part Four:

ADAM

31

IT WAS AN UNSPOKEN DEAL: MICHAEL BECAME DOPPELMANN'S assistant. He now officially lived in the theater, claiming one of the empty rooms in the curved hallway. As assistant, he often stood or sat for long periods of time, watching Doppelmann paint a canvas or sketch a new idea on sheets of blank newsprint. Michael's job was to move these art objects out of the way from Doppelmann before he tried to destroy them, or he was tasked with simple things, such as cleaning Doppelmann's brushes, or making frames for new canvases.

Once, while waiting for Doppelmann to sign a new painting—
D. Dpplmnn—Michael asked, "Why did you tell people my name is David?"

"Because I modeled your body on the body I wished I had."

"But your body is fine." He had been watching Doppelmann, shirtless, painting for hours, watching the muscles in his back flex and fatigue over repeated positions and the long veins that rose to the surface of his skin in his arms and hands.

"Don't we always want what we can't have?"

Even though Michael had his own room, there were some nights he stayed with Doppelmann. There were days Doppelmann only worked on his paintings and sketches, but then he would turn to Michael, who became his only focus. The sheets rustled like newspaper, and Michael's skin felt he was a part of everything in the room.

And then there were times when Doppelmann got very moody and asked Michael to leave.

"Did I do something wrong?"

"It's not always about you," Doppelmann snapped.

Much further down the hall, Michael discovered that Mischa was still living in the theater. She never returned to the room with her name carved into the door. She had unofficially given that to Doppelmann. One of her boys from the night Michael escaped the display window was still with her, whom she fed as if he were a pet. He never said a word, but some time later when Michael went to visit her, he learned the boy had run away, saying he needed to leave and fight the cause.

"What cause?" Michael had asked.

"Those invoices and Invoice Man really riled people up."

"Why don't you talk to Doppelmann?"

"He's all about you now," she said. "He doesn't want to see me. He only talks about you." Then she laughed. "What am I saying? It's me. I don't want to compete for the attention."

Michael went out one night and discovered more cardboard walls had been put up. Already there were plenty of secret doors cut into the cardboard. They were painted like fake doors or window frames. People could be seen entering and exiting different parts of the city. The new police force from the north patrolled the streets but seemed to not care about the walls. From the theater, he could hear occasional explosions and shouts, brief fights that ended in silence.

And the southern district? Michael wondered about Maiko. He discovered from the copies of the *City Mirror* usually discarded in the alley behind the theater that there were now three zones in the area: the southern district, the rest of the city, and then the north. The southern district had most of the city's poorer immigrants, and they were easy to manage by the north because that area had a natural divide: the bridge. Michael remembered the pigeons and rats under that bridge, the giant puddle that had nearly drowned him. The remainder of the city continued to debate their borders, and several iterations of cardboard walls were built and razed by northern officers.

Then one day in the newspaper, he saw a photograph that shocked him. It was of citizens wearing crude paper masks. The fabric ones he had seen worn by onlookers at the display window had been replaced with paper. These masks had uneven eyeholes and large mouth openings, so the maskers could stick out their tongues. In the article, it cited the Paper Man, David, as inspiration for people to become anonymous in the city, as a solution to fighting back against the north. It was a way to show solidarity in anonymity.

The article went on—that at first masks had been a source of humiliation and shame in public. The people of the city had been able to single the Paper Man out and identify him as the one outsider who was pretending to belong. Through his work in the display window, masks suddenly became a fashion statement. Masks were now truly multipurpose. They could protect a woman's complexion from the ocean-side breezes to be a kind of armor, as the Paper Man had used one, or to conceal and disguise; to correct the misshapen face he once had and to give alternatives to identity or celebrate the multiplicity of identity; to show nothing is fixed unless made permanent, like art.

And in the front of the theater, the postal service still left deliveries every day, mostly for Doppelmann. Michael was vigilant in retrieving them. He was afraid that if people discovered they lived inside, they would be attacked. He learned that Doppelmann was not well liked in the papers. Holloway & Holliday Tuna Cannery had been kicked out of their ship by the Northern Shipping Authorities. In the *City Mirror*, a photograph of the Invoice Man had spread the news to the city that a business of the city was working for the north. But in another edition of the paper, Holloway & Holliday said they had been double-crossed. They hadn't realized that the contact paying them for smuggling the arms was actually from the north and that all of this was a ploy for them to take over the ship and the jurisdiction of the city's harbor. That article included a photograph of one of Michael's notebooks found on the ship and his attempts at sketching Mischa.

"That's how you picture me?" Mischa had asked, reading it over his shoulder. "Stick to your day job."

In the mail, Michael found a letter from the man in the deckle-edged suit demanding that Doppelmann pay for the storage of his art.

Dear David Doppelmann,

This is my first and final notice for you to pick up your artwork and pay the storage fees for the last two months. This gallery has limited space, and it is time we move on to new art. Your reputation in the city has ruined any chance for us to sell your artwork. Strangely, the missing piece of the Paper Man is what people have asked to buy. You should know that we commissioned you to make that new piece, therefore all proceeds should be directed to us. We believe you have stolen him for yourself and used him in the display window at Willard's. They claim to know nothing of how he got into their window. We know they are protecting you, and thus, we will proceed with legal action if you do not cooperate.

Sincerely,

Filip Fowles

The Gallery by the Sea

Sometimes, Michael heard children rattling the chains that locked the theater. When he peeked through the ticket booth, he saw that even children wore masks: theirs were made to look like elephants or more likely gas masks. They played a strange game, taking turns capturing each other, then demasking the caught child and painting streaks across his or her face. They stripped the leaves off the choir trees that led the way up to the forest and glued them to their bodies like armor. In the sky, seagulls seemed to be fleeing.

All this time, for once, Michael felt safe and in a bubble. The theater was large and had plenty to explore. He had the body he wanted, he was free of having to work, and he was admired by the city now instead of repulsed. But what next? He was too recognizable. Once, while outside, he found himself walking through an alley that led to a view of the north and its iconic radio tower. Before he was at the end, a masked man turned the corner and started running toward him. Michael stepped out of the man's way, and a moment later, a crowd of unmasked officers chased after him. One of them held a rolled-up newspaper that was lit like a torch.

"Burn him!" someone shouted.

The man stepped in a pothole and fell to the ground. Michael pressed himself against the dumpster and watched, afraid to move. The man who fell had torn his pants at the knees, which were bright with blood. The crowd threw the torch at the man. He screamed. Michael held his hand against his own mouth to stifle the voice of his own fear. He couldn't believe the smell of burning hair.

"Wait, it's not him," one of the officers said.

"He's not made of paper," another said.

They dashed off as the man, his whole body on fire, ran back to the main street. The crowd was gone; a moment later, the man was immediately hit by an oncoming bus.

Michael had been holding his breath all this time. Now the stench of burnt flesh clouded the alleyway. Michael slinked back to the theater carefully, staying close to the walls.

He often thought of his brief life in the display window. That life was not for him, but he was surprised how quickly he had fallen into it. Now he was free, as Doppelmann said, to be whoever he wanted to be. How could that happen, though, while he incubated inside the theater?

"You're not forced to stay here," Mischa had said. She seemed interested in his new body, often stroking her varnished nails along his arms. "You can go outside whenever you want. You can come to my room whenever you want."

"Is your pet boy back?"

"He brought me breakfast. But that shouldn't stop you."

She was studying him, but from the shifting of her eyes, he could tell she saw him only as a surface, an object.

And while he watched Doppelmann paint canvases, shirtless, exposing his speckled tan skin—despite the fact he never went outside—Michael composed more letters to his father on scraps of paper. *Dear Father, I believe I'm seeing things like I've never seen before. I thought I knew the path I wanted to take, but now that has changed.*

Doppelmann turned, grinned, pleased with the progress of his painting, and walked over to kiss Michael.

I've learned so much more about the world and myself and options I did not know are now there for me to take.

Without saying anything, Michael moved away the latest painting and set it in the hallway to dry. He hoped this meant that Doppelmann was done working and they could climb into bed. He had the energy of an adolescent again. Often, all he wanted was to be with Doppelmann, alone, naked, one dim light on.

When he returned and tried the doorknob, though, he found it locked.

He started drawing again. The ledger of city life was out of balance. Michael craved the days he was in the cannery ship drawing in the ledger notebooks or even the days at home when he drew in his first notebooks. In his free time he made more sketches on discarded pages he found in the empty rooms, of the people he saw outside, especially the children in the paper masks. He tried making paper doll versions of them. Using scissors was still a bit difficult with his segmented fingers.

At night, when he lay in his room alone, staring at the ceiling, he was haunted by an image of a dark, dry background, almost like a dried stain of night. It was streaked by red. He tried to draw this a few times, but it didn't look right, more like a traffic sign. Once he attempted painting this image on the wall, but he couldn't get the background color right. It wasn't solid; it had some sense of hovering depth, like the night sky, which was nearly impossible to see now. Outside spotlights and the sweeping beam of the lighthouse cut through a dense fog that nevertheless blocked any view of stars or clear sky.

One night, Doppelmann joined him outside the theater, but at any sound or appearance of people walking by at the end of the street, Doppelmann would rush inside.

"Why are you in hiding?" Michael asked. He made sure the chains were in place to keep the theater doors locked.

"It's not safe for me."

"Now you're concerned about safety?" Michael laughed. He tried to touch Doppelmann's shoulder but was afraid he might shrug his hand off.

"You should be, too."

"Not when we're here in the theater. I thought you said I was free here."

Now Doppelmann laughed.

"You're so gullible."

"You have to continue with your paper art. You're really making a difference in this city. They respect your work now."

"My work is more respected than me. My work is more famous than me."

———————

One day, Michael gathered the mail just as he saw a crowd of masked children rushing down the street toward the theater. They had now removed the cracked concrete to expose the choir trees' roots. They banged on the theater door and tried to break in. They were shouting in a language that Michael didn't understand but was nevertheless familiar. Their mouths covered by their masks, it was the new, muffled language of anonymity.

He began reviewing the correspondence. There were several

requests for interviews and a few invitations to lesser-known artists and their upcoming shows. Life still went on despite the presence of the north in the city. Another letter from the gallery, another threat from Holloway & Holliday Tuna Cannery. And then there was a letter, and as Michael read it, his entire body trembled and vibrated, and he felt sick but knew there was nothing inside him to throw up.

The letter, written on a typewriter, praised Doppelmann's work and requested a chance to meet with the artist. The writer identified himself as an amateur photographer whose pictures of the Invoice Man had recently appeared in the *City Mirror*. He wanted to interview Doppelmann for a longer story he planned to write. The letter was signed *Adam*.

32

MICHAEL WENT TO THE CITY COLLECTORATE TO MEET ADAM. HE
wore an open-collared shirt with an extra button undone at the top
to reveal a puff of his new chest hair, made of fine linen threads.
Then he took a fountain pen and tattooed on each finger of a pair
of gloves (why didn't he think to wear these before?) a letter, and
spelled out on all ten fingers:

D O P P E L M A N N

He even drew the serifs on the letters to make them appear
typed. He thought of the time when it had been easy to remove his
body parts. Doppelmann had given him the perfect body and now
Doppelmann was the inspiration Michael needed to find himself.
He would be the inverse of Doppelmann. He had the body Doppelmann wanted, and Doppelmann had the self that Michael craved.

Lastly, he needed a mask. He had to blend in so no one would
recognize him as the Paper Man in the display window, and for a
moment, briefly, he missed Maiko. He would have had his pick if
he still lived in the damp basement with her. Instead, he made a
generic mask based on one of the photos he had seen in the paper,
struggling with even the simplest design.

He bought a pack of cigarettes. As he walked, he slouched, a coolness and carelessness sliding off him. He lit a cigarette and held it
carefully in his gloved hand, bringing it to his mask's lips but not
inhaling. The cigarette butt didn't fit—a mistake he now realized in
his design of the mask.

He stood on the steps and stared at the diamond-shaped building. People were now working there again. Nearby, at the other end of the grass square, construction workers were busy with a crane placing a large bronze statue on a marble stand. Below, on the streets, other workers poured concrete, using jackhammers to break apart old sidewalks. All of them wore navy uniforms to signal that they came from the north.

In the grass, there were still scattered sheets of paper stuck and dried like desiccated carcasses. Adam approached—or at least who he assumed was Adam—a man wearing a narrow slate-gray mask, narrow enough to allow him to still wear glasses over it, and a plain charcoal suit—and looked hard across the street. To see all the construction was exciting and heartbreaking. The news on the radio had announced the night before an immediate pledge of aid from the north to help rebuild the outdated infrastructure of the city. However, as he overheard from pedestrians on his way here, everyone in the city suspected this as just another ploy for the north to further infiltrate the city's administration and architecture. They would make the city now more like the north. The city, Michael realized, was changing along with him.

"Dddlmnn?" Adam asked in the muffled language of the masks.

"Hello there!" His own voice sounded clear within and he wondered how people tuned their ears to this new language. Michael exchanged his cigarette to his other hand and shook hands with Adam, who gushed

"It's such an honor. I didn't expect you would actually meet me."

Michael acknowledged the compliment with a slight shrug and even slighter bow, as he had seen Doppelmanndo a hundred times.

"Shall we walk?"

"Certainly," Adam said.

It was exactly like the display window, Michael thought. His voice was removed from his body. Filtered through something, and the words not part of him. He was also surprised how easy it was to talk like Doppelmann. With the mask, it made it easier for him to change his voice. He realized with a little practice, he would have it down. Trying to emulate someone who was real and successful was more admirable than making a new identity that failed.

———————————

They walked along a rolling line of street, which had a gradual curve and never seemed to arrive at a horizon. Surrounding buildings appeared far off, looming on a sharply curved sphere. It was as if the world was aquatic, a little ball that they strolled on, or the city was the center of its own planet, and its southern point would be overlapping with its northern edges. The curve was so steep any sharks in the bay would likely fall out.

Michael said these observations to Adam, who nodded and approved, and tried to contribute by stating his own analogies. The city was not on a curved ball. It was on a sail tight with wind. Soon it would deflate and everything would be normal, and the shadows of seagulls would soar in a straight line across the city's surface. Michael attempted to outdo this by suggesting that the curve of their eyeballs had changed due to some invisible pressure, and they were seeing a perfectly straight city, with perpendicular buildings and streets, as a convex landscape.

"Did it recently change like this? I don't remember this happening yesterday," Adam said.

"It's because of the time of day," Michael said. "In the afternoon, this will all settle itself. Now I have to ask something important of you. Please do not let anyone know where and how we met. I'm of particular interest to many people right now, and need some anonymity to move about in the city."

Adam scratched behind his ear.

"I hear you. You know, the photograph I took of the Invoice Man got on the *City Mirror's* front page. It's what broke the story to the city! I can't believe what it's done."

"At least the story came to life," Michael said.

"You mean, you were trying to..."

"It doesn't always work. Not even for me."

Power surged through him as the amateur photographer tagged along. He wanted to keep moving and stride in the style of Doppelmann, yet something peculiar was inside him, a strange feeling that was unlike anything he had experienced before. It was difficult for him to identify because he was so used to pain on the outside of his body, the blurry visions of colors, but now it was inside. He didn't recognize it as pain, though, only as a force originating in his joints and radiating down into his digits. He continued moving to try and shake the sensation out of his limbs.

"Do you know anything about that statue at the other end of the square?" Michael asked.

Adam's mask muffled his laughter. "It's a northern poet. Can you believe it? He's never even been to the city. But the north adores him, and seems to think the poet deserves commemoration as art here. I heard it's not even made of metal. It's only painted the color of bronze. Underneath it's all plaster."

"Is that so? Now the north is making art?" Michael asked.

"By the way," Adam said. "What do you think of my mask?"

"Did you make it yourself?"

After a pause, Adam said: "I bought it."

They walked a set of steps, and Michael laughed as Adam's tie flipped up into his face with a gust of wind.

"I'm on my lunch break," Adam said. "You must have a nice flexible schedule. Take breaks when you want, work when you want."

"Yes, but it's deceptive. You are constantly looking for the focus and ability to get things done right. Sometimes you spend a lot of time on something, only to throw it out and start over. But the greatest feeling is when things fall into place and you see everything balanced."

"I know exactly what you mean." Adam laughed and then just as quickly quieted down. After a while, he spoke again. "Do you mind, if I ask a personal question, about a certain painting?"

"Yes," Michael said. "What about it?"

"There is a portrait hanging in the Gallery by the Sea. Something about the expression of the woman's face. It broke my heart."

"Oh, well, it was meant to show the look of defeat in a woman who has tried to love too much of the wrong thing."

"What do you mean?"

"She was trying to love someone and make him into one person, but then she discovered he was really someone else, and all her efforts had failed. There was nothing else she could do. That moment, that expression of emotions on the face of a human being, that is what the Maiko painting captures."

"Was it based on a real person? Is her name Maiko?"

Michael trembled and stubbed out his cigarette. They stood at a street corner and a jackhammer started up. He waited until they crossed the street and passed another construction site before speaking.

"Yes, there was a model this was based on."

"And where is she now? Does she still look like this? Is she still defeated? Who broke her heart?"

"Why all these questions? Where is this going? I do not see why you are so interested in the source of this painting—the original art piece, if I could call her that."

Michael waited. It was uncanny how this was playing out. He was on the other side. This was what it felt like to be Doppelmann. Adam had fully replaced the old Michael in this city, and now Michael was the substitute for Doppelmann. But could there be two Doppelmanns?

"I recognized her," Adam said. "One of the fur models at Willard's. She was always my favorite. Out of all of them, she was the most beautiful. And then one day, she was gone. I wished I had talked to her. To see her now, with that look in your painting—it just pains me to think she's so unhappy. You said her name is Maiko?"

Michael paused at the steps. They had returned to the City Collectorate building. He squeezed Adam's shoulder. It seemed so long ago when Michael had torn Adam's flyers from the streets.

Then they had met in the cannery ship—and who was Michael then? Not the person he was now, standing here, not the one Adam photographed in the display window.

"Thank you for telling me this, it's very honest. You're much different than how I was, when I first came to the city. I do know Maiko, and yes, she lives here. She's happier now. We should all get together for lunch. Perhaps next week. I could see if she is available. She is just as lovely in person."

"That would be wonderful!" Adam said.

"Excellent. Well, I suppose you don't want to hear any more about my art."

Adam hesitated. "I'd love to, but I have to get back to work."

"I understand completely. Let's meet in a week. I know a diner we can go to next to an outdoor sculpture garden."

They made the arrangements, and then Michael watched Adam walk off. There was a change in him. The subtle change was fascinating, a little spring in his step. Michael had created that within Adam. It was an amazing, intoxicating feeling to think of how he could manipulate not just materials but emotions to get the new gestures that Adam now exhibited.

Michael sat on the steps of a building and considered things, but the thoughts weren't coherent in his head. They smeared and dried too fast, like some watercolor painting, and soon it felt like it wasn't words in his brain but splotches of color and texture, something he could not translate into any language. Inside him still was the strange feeling he could not figure out. This was the first time he isolated the feeling as actual discomfort and continued to watch the construction work around him. The city was shaping up. In a few months, it would be as if nothing had happened, and the new buildings would be a part of regular life. Just like a sickness or illness a human went through, they recovered and were more revitalized because of it. Perhaps he was ill and that was why he felt this sensation. But forget the pain. Look at all the new jobs he had created! In the sidewalk below him, he saw several handprints and initials carved into it. Everyone wanted to mark things that didn't belong to them as their own.

He walked back to the theater slowly, eventually approaching a woman moving slower than him. From behind, he thought she might be Maiko, the way she leaned into each step with her left leg, but it turned out to be someone much older. This was found out by asking the woman to remove her mask, which seemed like an offensive request, but he found a way to charm her and suggest he found the rest of her beautiful and only wanted to see her beautiful face to inspire his next painting. The woman obliged, and he was saddened to see it was not Maiko. She seemed disappointed as well that she was not what he had hoped for underneath her mask. He continued onward, passing the department store and seeing banners displayed in the window, with only the words: BIG SALE and CLEARANCE. The city indeed was looking better and better. The buildings looked so vibrant and alive. It was almost as if they were covered in a membrane that pulsed with life. This was a great place to live, he decided. He would capitalize on his life here as much as possible. As Doppelmann, he was so comfortable. This was the skin he had always wanted. This was the attitude and stance he had been searching for. It was so natural; he wanted to be this way forever.

33

HE CRUMPLED ANOTHER SHEET OF PAPER. HE HAD BEEN TRYING to draw Adam, with his strange, flat expression frozen on his mask, but it was not coming out correctly. His own mask was on the nightstand in his room, staring up at the dark ceiling. The image of the dark night with the streak of color was still in his mind. He tried to sketch a new scene, but he felt constricted by the boundaries of a page. He tossed this on the floor, now covered with balls of paper.

Without much thinking, he started something new. First he poured some glue into a can and added water until he had a soupy mix. Then he unrolled some wire mesh, found a pair of scissors, and cut the thin metal until he had a piece the size of a living room rug. What could he do with this? He stared at this rectangle a long time, walking around it from all angles, projecting mental images on it, until he saw a shape. In his own paper body were the memories of being built, the first time ten years ago, then recently by Doppelmann. Yes, he thought, staring at the wire mesh, inside that square was a human figure with an extra arm. He cut down the wire further, rolled sections to make the limbs, and soon had the armature standing beside him.

It would be taller than him once he added a head. For now, though, he pulled down a stack of newspaper from the closet shelf and soaked it in the bucket of glue. He tore strips and, starting from the feet, covered the wire mesh with a layer of paper.

It took all day. He didn't stop. It was easy to lose himself in the process and for once something felt natural. With no windows, it didn't occur to him that another night was over and the sun was rising. When he finally did pause for a break, he walked down the long hallway and returned to the front atrium of the theater. The pain in his joints throbbed distantly. When he passed Doppelmann's room, he realized that, for once, he did not want to see him.

Outside he found Mischa, smoking. She nodded to acknowledge him.

"I need your help," he said. It felt good to talk without wearing a mask.

"I've done enough for you." She stubbed out the cigarette and turned to head back inside.

He grasped her arm, again surprised by the strength inside him. She froze, and he felt in her muscles she was startled, even though her face looked amused, waiting to see what he would do next.

"Something has happened, and I need you to pose as Maiko."

"What? Your girlfriend from the perfume counter? What's happened?"

"This guy, Adam, contacted Doppelmann. I met with him instead."

"No!"

"He recognized Maiko from the portrait."

"This sounds familiar."

"Will you do it?"

Mischa looked at her varnished nails. She shook her head.

"Will you do it?" Michael repeated. He yanked her hands into his. She glared back at him.

"What happened to Michelangelo?"

"What?" He withdrew his hand from hers.

"Did you not learn anything from being torn apart? That was your chance to start over and find yourself. Are you so lost that you need to impersonate an artist to become one yourself?"

He closed his eyes. He tried not to remember the sensation of being torn apart.

"That's what you're doing, right? Don't be so modest. But where is Michael? After all that's happened, is he even here?"

"I'm right here," he said. He clamped onto her shoulder, pressing harder until he felt bone. "Listen. In two days, we'll meet him for lunch. You must do exactly what you did with me. Write a note and tell him to meet you in the bathroom. This is the first test."

———————————

That night, Michael went to Doppelmann's room. He found Doppelmann asleep, a light still on, beaming on a new painting. For a long moment, he observed Doppelmann, his naked torso, the blanket twisted around his legs, his lips pinched as if he had tasted something sour.

What did their relationship mean? What kind of loyalty did Doppelmannhave toward his creation?

"Doppelmann," Michael whispered, "are you awake?"

"What now?"

"I haven't seen you for a few days." He wanted to tell him about the paper figure he had started building, but from Doppelmann's expression, he could tell he was annoying him. Michael headed for the door.

"Well, what is it?"

"Nothing," Michael said, and stared at the painting. It was familiar. Then he realized that the painting on the canvas was the exact swirl of colors in his brain.

"These colors," he began, and pointed at the stroke that started in the lower left, a deep blue, and rose to the top to become almost white. "These colors you have here. I see them in my head."

"Really?" Doppelmann was alert, and putting on a shirt. He stood next to the canvas. "What should the next stroke be? I've been stuck on this all day."

Perversely, Michael hoped that his imitation might be sucking away Doppelmann's creativity. Did the artist sense any of this? Michael took the brush from Doppelmann, who stepped back and smiled. Michael focused on the canvas, comparing it to the image he had seen. They were nearly the same, but yes, the one in his mind had a splash, a drop of red, that trickled down. He dropped the brush and dipped his finger in some red paint, got a thick swab of it, and held his hand above the canvas.

"Yes," Doppelmann whispered and clenched Michael's hips,

where the pain inside had returned but dissipated from Doppel-mann's touch. His mouth was now next to Michael's ear, the heat from his breath on Michael's neck. He let himself go and leaned back, pressed himself against Doppelmann.

Yes, he repeated. Or was that in Michael's head?

Michael waited, and Doppelmann continued to breathe heav-ily into his ear. And then—the paint dripped and skidded down the canvas, a long red trail thick and invasive over the dark, dry background.

34

ON THE APPOINTED DAY, MISCHA WORE A WHITE FELT MASK, BLACK silk dress, and red high heels, and Michael wore clothes he had secretly taken from Doppelmann: black slacks, brown shoes, and tortoiseshell glasses over his flesh-colored mask. Several times, Mischa stumbled down the sidewalk, and when she grabbed Michael's elbow for balance, he noticed she was soft and light like paper.

"Maiko didn't walk that way," he said to her. "You need to be a little more confident. Walk as if you are on display. As if you're draped in expensive furs."

She glared at him. Mischa was not one to take directions. She lit a cigarette that smelled of apples. As they made their way to the diner, in between corrections to her performance as Maiko, Michael gathered several fallen flowers and the seed cones, like little red pineapples, from the magnolia trees.

"Doppelmann would find a way to make something out of these," he said.

"You think he's the smartest artist."

"No, but smarter than most."

"Is that why you're pretending to be him?"

He ignored her, but for days, he had been thinking about this. Why not imitate one of the best artists in the city?

As they walked, the pain he'd been feeling returned and stayed. It occurred to him that something deeper was wrong. Perhaps something was faulty when Doppelmann had reconstructed him. Perhaps only his father could build truly functioning paper men. *Dearest Father, How long do paper men live?* There were enough distractions, though, for him to not dwell on this.

They found Adam already seated inside the diner.

"Adam!" Michael shouted across the room. Several people at a large table turned in unison; they were all wearing paper bird-face masks, with small sparrow beaks, their lips exposed beneath. Here was a new trend, manifesting in animal spirit masks that seemed to express people's attitudes toward food and the rituals of eating.

"Look what you've done, Doppelmann," Mischa whispered.

Adam stood up and met them in the middle of the diner. He moved cautiously and held his hands close to his gut, as if he might vomit. Over his face was a slate-gray mask with simple cutouts for eyes, nose, and moveable mouthpiece.

"I made this mask," Adam said.

"Hmm. Needs work. Now for you," Michael said, and handed over the magnolia flowers and pineapples. "I made this. Found art."

"I see. Thank you, then?" Adam reluctantly accepted his gift, quickly put it on the table, and turned to Mischa.

"And here is your old fur model, Maiko." Michael placed his hands on her shoulders. Mischa dipped forward, her mask moving slightly from her face. Swiftly, Michael tightened the knot behind her head.

"Hey, Adam," she said, her mouthpiece opening wide to expose her teeth. She seemed unfamiliar with talking through a mask as well. "Nice to meet you."

Michael cringed. She sounded vulgar, but in the language of the masks, it didn't matter. She was whoever Adam wanted her to be.

"I," Adam stammered. "I'm so happy to see you. I've been a fan of yours from the first time I saw you."

"And when can I see you? I bet you're a handsome man, Adam."

"It's so hard to with these masks." They both turned to Michael. He added: "I mean that in a good way. I know, Mr. Doppelmann, that you started this."

"He's the smartest artist," Mischa said.

Adam burst into laughter. "Is that really you?" One of his hands shot out and tried to touch her mask. Mischa politely patted his hand away.

"Not here. Shall we eat?"

They ordered food, but no one was hungry when it arrived.

"It's so different now than when I first moved here," Adam said.

"This place is awful," Mischa said. "Something has to give."

Adam listened, nodding carefully. Michael wanted to impart an important message and searched his mind for something that was fitting of Doppelmann to say. Help society start afresh with a new attitude? "It should be unity, not individualism that is the priority."

Masks were becoming the unifying force in the city. As the *City Mirror* had said, gone were the days when people in town wore masks to hide birth defects or deformities. Now it was an oddity to not wear one. The mask had lost its sinister suggestions. It was sometimes a cosmetic accessory, sometimes a disguise, sometimes a form of protest. The waitress, wearing a mask herself, came over and removed their untouched plates.

"Express what we all have in common instead of what sets us apart," Mischa added.

"Very good, dear. But enough of this coffee house talk. Shall we go see some real art?"

"That's not art?" Mischa said, motioning to the people outside.

"I'll get the chit," Adam said. Michael and Adam's hands crashed as they reached for the paper bill left behind by the waitress. It sent a jolt through Michael.

"Of course not," Michael said, holding the bill up in triumph. "I'll be right back."

At the cashier, he remembered how he had seen Doppelmann remove something from his nose and wipe it on the counter. Michael's paper nostrils, however, had no debris inside, no mucus, nothing. Doppelmann had told him always leave a piece of yourself wherever you go. And what would Doppelmann do if he had a paper nose?

Michael plucked a piece of his linen hair and rolled it between his fingers until it frayed. Then he tossed it onto a plate of sugar figurines that the waitress was carrying to a table.

He glanced at the others in the diner. All of them were masked.

At that moment, he wondered: with all these masks, what did everyone look like naked? He was thinking about sex again, wondering how all of these people appeared in private. Did they take their masks off then? Did they ever expose themselves anymore?

He returned to the table to find Mischa writing on a napkin. His heart nearly stopped.

"What are you doing?"

It was perfect. It was the same thing she had done for him when he was in Adam's place.

"Writing a haiku," she said. She folded the napkin and stuck it in the eye slit of Adam's mask. She giggled. To Michael's surprise, it sounded just like Maiko: a peal of bells. He was impressed.

Adam plucked the napkin from his mask and gently cradled the triangle of paper in the palm of his hand. Michael found Adam's handling of it tender and sweet. He immediately wished the paper had been the part of his body he had left behind instead.

They walked inside the museum, and Michael paid for their tickets then led them to the outdoor pavilion. The sun was so warm it felt as if everything would melt. Adam dabbed at his mask to check if his paint was softening. Around them, the trees and bushes were amorphous, like plushy piles of green, and the branches drooped close to the ground.

They made their way to a shady spot where the sculptures stood.

"It's not good for art to be out in this weather," Michael said.

"It's much better for it to be locked up, right?" Mischa said, glancing at him.

They approached a blob of a sculpture that barely rose from the ground. It stretched across a block of concrete, and it was a bright yellow slab that either looked like a melted stick of butter or a pool of urine. The piece was named *Untitled*.

"Tell us everything about this, Doppelmann," Mischa said.

Michael thought for a moment before opening his mouth.

"It's very interesting. It appears to be a pure surface."

"But underneath?" Mischa asked.

"All the expelled vitamin shells. All the leftovers. Crystals, skins, carcasses."

"Wow," Adam said under his breath. Michael turned and patted Adam on the back.

"You'll see art differently soon enough. Don't you worry. Now, tell me. Do you like this piece?"

"I do now," Adam said. "I've always wondered, though, for those older paintings from thousands of years ago—do they have them here? I've never understood why they paint so many people with the same face. Don't they all look alike? Did the painter only have one model?"

"That is correct," Michael said. "He only had himself."

Adam nodded then seemed to do a kind of agitated jig.

"I'm sorry, but I will be right back. This heat is too much."

"We'll be here," Michael said. But when he turned, Mischa was gone also. Soon enough, he spotted her heading for a squat building that was wrapped in the arms of an ivy bush. And heading that way, he saw, was Adam.

Around him were others in their masks. He noticed that people were becoming more expressive with their eyes. They looked at things intensely, and without a mouth or eyebrows exposed, people had begun to channel emotions into their eyes. The masked people here had eyes with large pupils, and he realized they were projecting the same emotion: desire. Everybody wanting something, art, attention, affections. He wanted to run his hands along their masks, feel their different contours, and feel where they were the same. For a second time, he saw a woman he thought could have been the real Maiko and discovered that she was beginning to haunt him wherever he was in the city. Her presence was felt, but she was nowhere here—still banished south of the bridge.

He was hot with his own mask on and wished he could throw it off.

After staring at the yellow sculpture a few minutes, not seeing any empty shells or carcasses in the sculpture, but only dried bubbles, Michael quietly turned and found himself heading for the building as well. He opened the door to the men's room softly; inside, he avoided his reflection in the metal doors that made up the stalls. He immediately recognized their voices. He slipped into the last stall then squatted down to watch their feet.

"Take off your mask," Adam's voice said.

They were kissing.

"You're more beautiful than I remember," he said.

They continued kissing. It went on for a long time until Michael saw their feet step away from each other.

"Is he your boyfriend?"

"I'm his muse," she said.

Michael rubbed at his jaw.

"Will he wonder what's taking us so long?"

"There are no strings. I can do whatever I want."

"I want to see you again."

"Of course. I already had that in mind. Meet me tomorrow outside the hotel one block before the lighthouse. I'll be there at 7 P.M."

Someone else entered the restroom and took the stall between theirs and Michael's. He saw their pairs of legs rush out. He waited out the pain that was throbbing deep in his joints. He almost fell to the floor and had to brace himself between the stalls. It wasn't what he had overheard that hurt him. Something was terribly wrong with his body. The wave of pain passed, and he followed them out, leaving the dim restroom and finding himself sucked into the bright, blinding sunlight.

35

MICHAEL STOOD IN THE LONG HALLWAY OF THE THEATER, STUDY-
ing the highway of ants that were climbing the wall and disappearing into the ceiling. But never mind the ants, he was still thinking of
Adam. So it was set. Adam was planning to meet Mischa as Maiko
the next day, and he wouldn't know that Michael was showing up
first. If it went according to plan, Adam would follow them into the
forest, just as Michael had done to Doppelmann and Mischa.

"Where have you been?"

It was Doppelmann. The sight of him, scraggly beard, stringy
hair, shirtless and covered in spots of paint, thrilled Michael. His
paper joints tensed up.

"I've been out," Michael said.

"And work? Have you started any of it?"

"In fact I have," Michael said. Doppelmann stepped closer, and
Michael found himself recording the movements for his later use.
He realized then, as he stared at Doppelmann, unsure if he was
going to hit him or hug him, that it was easier to be someone else
than create a new version of himself. What was known was easier.
It was a path already defined so that he'd eventually find a trail that
would lead to his real self. This way he didn't have to spend time
wandering, wasting time to locate the trail head.

"What did you work on?"

"Your correspondence and your invoices."

"What about the frames?"

"I will get to those tomorrow."

"Are you keeping something from me?" Doppelmann cocked
his head to one side. "You're acting very strange."

"Not at all," Michael said. It was difficult to restrain himself.
He only wanted to feel Doppelmann's body. The artist didn't seem
to believe Michael and stepped closer until Michael found himself

cornered against the wall.

"Is something going on?"

Michael wanted to pour it all out of him. He would rather have Doppelmann be excited for this next phase in his life. But he wasn't ready just yet. He knew the story wouldn't make sense.

"Well," Michael said. He was slipping.

Doppelmann presented his ear to Michael's mouth.

"I'm listening."

"I've actually," Michael began. Doppelmann was exuding body heat. Michael leaned closer.

"Tell me."

"I've started making my own art."

Doppelmann stepped back.

"Why haven't you shown me?"

"It's not ready yet. But after that, I want you to see it."

"That's great. I look forward to that. I once made the decision to destroy all my old work, and that was when things really changed for me as an artist. You might be on that same path." He was smiling for a moment, then his face became solemn. "But don't let it take up all of your time. I still need your help."

In his room, Michael continued working on his sculpture. By working, he avoided the pain, which faded in and out. He added more layers to the figure, and while he waited for them to dry, he started another one. They couldn't have been more different. The second one was much shorter and thicker, with one arm and three legs. Side by side, they looked like opposites. Day and night. He gave one a spear and the other a cardboard shield. After they were covered in several layers of paper as a base, he began giving a more defined shape to the fourth layer. This included noses, ears, eye pits, and thicker biceps and thighs. He gave the tall one male genitals and the short one female genitals. He added a final layer on top to strengthen all of it. It was important, he thought, to keep all of these strong so that nothing could make them easily break. The first construction of him, while good, was not enough, and that was why Mischa had been able to tear him apart.

When their paper layers had dried, Michael painted the figures. He cracked open the containers of used paint and made do with what he had. One of the figures started out blue, but because he ran out, he switched to brown and then yellow. The short figure he painted all green. While he waited for them to dry, he wandered the curved hall, picking up debris discarded on the sides. He found several sticks, pizza boxes, and broken closet poles, and brought them back to his room. He couldn't fit everything inside, so he left it outside his door as a stockpile of materials.

What exactly had his father done to keep him alive in his body? His father had refused to talk about it. Certainly, Michael concluded, you couldn't animate something that had never lived. But once his father had encapsulated him, did he think Michael would live that way forever? Did he not think that life would catch up in the form of physical pain, finally attacking his body and leading to death? By this time, he was exhausted, and so after kicking away the loose material scattered on the bed, he covered himself with the sheet and went to sleep. At one point, though, he woke up, immobile, the pain surging through his body, and he was terrified to see he was just as still and lifeless as the figures surrounding his bed.

Later, he took the figures out into the hall and stood them as guards to his door, similar to the statues above the marquee. Then he set to work on another two figures.

For each pair, he made them complementary. One would have an elongated mouth, while the other had no mouth. One would have three eyes; the other would be a single eye. Tall and short, thin and fat, male and female, angry and calm, they all came out in pairs. It took a few days to make each pair. Soon, though, he had them crowding outside his door in the hallway, blocking several doors past his room.

While watching the cars drive by, he was struck with an idea. He would place the figures throughout the city at night. It would be his present, his contribution. Yes, he realized, he could be a useful member of the city and give it more citizens. The city had latched onto him when he was in the display window. Why couldn't there be paper figures everywhere? He went back inside and finished painting the last pair. While they dried, he went in the hallway and lined the pairs on opposite walls, so the tall one was on the left wall and the short one was on the right; the faceless one was on the left and the double-faced one was on the right. They looked like an army. He had twenty of them. He brought out the last pair and put them in the back. Then he went inside to sleep.

36

THEY MET AT THE CORNER OF THE HOTEL. MICHAEL WORE HIS DOP-pelmann clothes. Mischa, dressed as Maiko, had been waiting, smoking an apple-flavored cigarette. They pretended to chat until she spotted Adam, at which point Michael leaned in and kissed her—so odd! Her softness against his paper lips. Doppelmann's lips were a better match.

"Here we go," he said and took her hand. It was also odd to know that someone was watching them and that he wasn't allowed to look back. Like his work in the display window, when people pressed their faces to the glass to get a look at him, but he wasn't allowed to look either. At least Adam would keep a distance, and the whole city was their display window.

They sat in a restaurant, Michael's back to the window. The room was filled with the scent of cloves. Mischa stared out the window, her necklace pendant of a mermaid flashing whenever it picked up the glint of the candlelight. Around them, the other customers all wore paper masks, some with single eye slits and simple nose holes. Others had two eye slits and large grins cut into them, like carved pumpkins.

"He's watching us," Mischa said. She was in her element, Michael knew: she was the exclusive thing of someone's attention, even if it was for just this moment.

They ate slowly. Mischa rubbed her foot between his legs, holding his hand and staring at him. But he knew she wasn't really looking at him. She was searching for Adam, and Michael was too because then he would know how he himself had looked when this had happened to him. How many opportunities in life do you get like this, he wondered, to turn the mirror on your own past and replay it?

"Let's get out of here," he said.

"But I'm not done."

He paid the chit anyway and they left. They took the shoe-string street to the lighthouse park. Michael couldn't help it at this point and glanced back.

"Don't do that," Mischa hissed. "You'll break the illusion and turn into something worse than paper. You'll turn into salty sea foam."

He pulled her closer to him then bent and removed her shoes. He looked up, and, because of the way she smiled at him, he had to remind himself that none of this was real.

They ran up a dirt path that led into the eucalyptus forest and disappeared between the trees. Eventually Adam showed up, and Michael briefly hid behind a tree, as Adam quietly brushed aside branches and crouched low whenever he walked through an open space. He looked so confused. Was his Maiko from the past playing games with him? Why, he must have thought, was she not alone as they had agreed? Michael had a lot of advice for Adam, but not today.

Further in, Michael caught up with Mischa, who had stopped under the apple trees. He pulled down an apple and sniffed its bottom. It was so ripe, his first apple in a long time, that he pulled it off the branch and took a bite. The apple cracked, and the sound echoed throughout the forest. Nearby, they could hear the barking cliff dogs.

"Get down," Michael said when they arrived at the same spot where he had seen Mischa and Doppelmann months ago. He pulled off his sweater and lay it on the ground.

"Wow," Mischa said. "New paper muscles! Doppelmann really went all out with you, didn't he?" She touched his arms. "Stop shaking."

Indeed he was—he had wanted this moment so long ago—but now, as Doppelmann he had to fake his confidence. He pushed Mischa onto her knees and lifted her dress.

"He's over there," she said. "Ready? Do it. Now. Fuck me."

He put his hands in his pants and tried to arouse himself. It did nothing. The birds in the branches, the crunching of the waves on the rocks below, dogs barking, it was all too distracting. Most of all, though, was the awareness that Adam was watching them.

"What's the matter? Can't you get it up?" Mischa asked. "Isn't this what you wanted?"

"I'm trying," he whispered back. It still did nothing. Somehow he knew it was not going to happen. Here he was, with the girl of his dreams from high school, squatting before him on her knees, and he was useless.

He tried to take in more of her. He unzipped the top of her dress, and it spilled open her soft skin. He touched the ridges of bumps from the slight chill in the air and from her anticipation. Then he pressed his hips against her, and still nothing happened.

"Just pretend, then," she said.

He made the motions, yet the whole time it seemed ridiculous. His impressions of how this should have occurred were much different than hers. Then he felt a tug and then realized her hand was searching in his unzipped pants, pulling him closer, stimulating him.

"You're hurting me," he said. It wasn't only her movements that hurt him; the joint pain had returned. His shoulders seemed swollen and his elbows were ready to break off from the fiery pain pulsating inside them. He wanted to scratch at all the spots where this pain came from, but he'd have to dig into his skin.

"I don't care." She pulled harder.

"Please stop."

"You're pathetic." She thrust herself back against him and made sounds that caused the barking dogs to be silent. He tried to match her rhythm, but it was awkward and they had no coordination.

"Yes," she said a few minutes later. "He's masturbating. He's really doing it. Call him over here."

That would have only made things worse, he thought. As Doppelmann, he forced himself on her, faking it the whole time, imagining he was punishing her for everything she had done to humiliate him, but she cried out as if she was enjoying all of it. He realized she probably was.

He ran his fingertips along the coating of her skin and tasted it. She was flavored like apple juice. He leaned forward and licked more off her back. The taste was so surprising and incredible, he wanted more and more. There were so many sensations he had yet to experience, he told himself, and this was only the first.

But she was slowing to a stop. She turned over and lay on the sweater, looking up at him. What was he supposed to do? As he crouched there, tempted to seek out Adam, she grabbed his head and crushed his masked face into her chest. They couldn't even do this with their masks off. Adam might see that Maiko's face was someone else's. She tugged at him in spots where his paper joints creaked, and the pain was shocking. He tried to leap up, but she held him down. He thought he was losing consciousness, it was all so much. And then the joint pain, the neck and spine now part of it as well. His fingers were locked because moving them caused his wrists to feel inflamed.

"He's coming," she said.

Michael looked up and was hypnotized by the wave of the branches, the swinging apples...

His vision was a mass of colors that brightened, brightened, lightened. He closed his eyes.

He found Mischa standing before him, dressed. His pants were still around his ankles. He yanked them on and shook out the leaves and dirt clinging to his sweater. He felt like a shell, a carcass. The pain inside had drained him of any additional energy.

"How long have I been out?"

She rolled her eyes.

"Where is he?"

She said nothing. Instead, she led the way through the trees back to the dirt path. She swayed her hips in a new way, as if he had put something inside her that had changed her walk. But he knew he had failed at that, too, so all of this was her performance.

"This didn't work," he said when they arrived back on the street.

"Relax. Everything went as planned. I'm all ready for Adam now."

"I thought you weren't going to do that part."

"Of course. I have to. That's what happened with you."

"It doesn't have to be exactly the same."

"Yes it does. In the name of art. In the name of finding out who you really are. You can't do some things and not the others. You'll ruin it."

"It's so easy for you," Michael said. "But do you have to sleep with him?"

"Do you want to instead?"

She linked their arms together. They walked the rest of the way in silence, his feet numb from the dirt path now turning to concrete. His joints still hurt, and there was a hot pain throbbing in his crotch, but he set aside the rising panic—that he was ill, that he was dying—to watch the city. It was still light out when they returned to the streets, and everything pulsed with life. People walked by in their masks, cars drove with masked drivers, and from the nameless, covered façades of dozens of restaurants, grills sizzled and the scents of cooking meat and boiling broths wafted out to meet them. Somewhere too, he smelled mushrooms. Clouds of flies swarmed at the garbage bins. In the distance, he heard shouting, but he couldn't tell whether it was in celebration or distress.

He stopped to peer between the boards of a fence and witnessed a confusing scene: restaurant workers rushing to a naked woman, coated in sweat and not even wearing a mask, bent over a cutting board on the counter. They were crowded into a back alley, the restaurant's kitchen door throwing light onto the scene. The staff shouted at her to hurry, and Michael saw that she was giving birth to fish—yes, there were fish emerging from her body—which were immediately put on plates and rushed into the kitchen. The woman's face was pale, and her hair was pulled back like a wet rag. The workers yelled at her again, and she made the effort to birth another.

Mischa saw none of this as she dragged him from the fence. The illness he was feeling washed over him, and he doubted what he had just seen. Was it possible for a paper man to be feverish? What disgusted him the most was distinct sound of people, eating. He kept spotting them through holes and windows in the cardboard walls. Most of their masks had been altered so they could remove the lower mouthpiece. Their fleshy chins quivered as they ate from white plates or sat in cafes picking crumbs from muffin wrappers. He imagined the food on their plates, normally as passive art on a wall, suddenly coming to life and biting their eaters back. It would be a much different world to try to survive in if that could happen.

37

HE KEPT GOING TO THE THEATER ALONE, WHILE MISCHA STAYED behind to find Adam. The plan was for her to seduce him and take him to the hotel on the corner where they had met. He realized that had he been able to perform, she might not have gone with Adam. On his way back, he caught a vague whiff of mushrooms and resisted the urge to follow a woman who looked like Maiko. His old friend seemed to be everywhere now, and every time he recognized a similar appearance, he felt magnetized, drawn to confront the woman. Small details, from too much hair on the arms, to thicker waists, to narrow shoulders, all let him know that he was wrong again.

He dragged the first pair of his figures to the front of the theater. This took a long time. He eventually found a shopping cart that he used to transport the next pair. It was too difficult to move them together, so he switched to moving them one at a time. It took several hours just to get them down the long, curved hallway to the lobby. When he opened the front doors, he saw it was evening and the balance of light was shifting to darkness. He was pleased that this no longer bothered him. In the larger scheme of day and night, there were equal amounts in the world, even if he couldn't see it.

Joints aching, his head cloudy, Michael dragged the figures outside. He put one on the cart and ran out into the city. He placed it next to a stoplight on the main street. He ran back and retrieved its partner and placed it across the street beside a short building.

The next pair he decided to cut off their legs and attach them to building walls. Another pair hid behind bushes that lined the library. Two pairs were placed on the square outside of the City Collectorate building. Another pair went outside the ship of the Holloway & Holliday Cannery. The gallery was the farthest and most difficult to get to. A long cardboard wall covered several intersections and bus stops, but eventually he climbed through and boarded a cross-town bus. Inside, he took the pair with no face and a double face and brought them onto the bus with him. The bus driver demanded that Michael pay for three passengers, which he did. There were two others on board, including a woman with frizzy hair, who cooed and petted the figures. Her face was disguised by a white mask with large, red spots to designate apple cheeks.

"They are so lovely," she said. He couldn't tell if she recognized him as a paper man. "You're building an army of them. Things are going to get better here. The city will expel the north, and we'll start over."

By now, the gallery had been repaired. The plastic tarp was gone, and a new window and door were there and red paper lanterns hung from the roof. It looked as if there had never been an accident. Construction in the city was an easy way to erase its history. He heard Doppelmann's voice: "Nothing is more beautiful than the scaffolding surrounding a building under construction." Michael attached one figure to the gallery's new window. Then he decided to break it and put the other figure inside so that it was halfway inside and halfway out. The breaking glass made a terrific, loud sound. This was the sound the one-eyed man had found so liberating, long ago when he smashed the funeral home's window. Nothing stirred except for the outline of a stray dog, picking its way down the foggy road blocked by orange traffic cones.

When he was done, Michael trudged back to the theater on foot, taking short cuts through cardboard walls. Everywhere he looked, masked people seemed to be meeting, conferring, assessing. At the theater, he hurried to Doppelmann's room and, without knocking, entered. The painting he was working on floated in the room like a ghost, covered by a white sheet upon its easel. Doppelmann was in bed, twisted in the covers. Michael lay beside him. Doppelmann, eyes still shut, snatched Michael with his painter hands and pulled him closer.

"I have a surprise," Michael said. "I want to show you something."

"Let's wait until later," Doppelmann said. "Time to sleep and incubate more ideas."

Michael lay awake, letting the pain in his body subside. He watched Doppelmann sleep, tried to hold this image in his mind—if he was to die, this would be the one place he would want to hold onto forever.

———————————

The next afternoon, down the theater hall, he saw Mischa sauntering toward him. She was so relaxed it was as if she were floating down the carpet, her mask off and her skin glowing.

"Michael!" She shouted and waved. He paused, too late to turn back, and waited. "Oh, Michael, you won't believe it! I had the best night ever."

"I'm busy," he said. They began walking the way he had come. He noticed her hair was undone from its crab clip and spilled across her exposed shoulders, which had small red scratch marks.

"You don't want to know how thrilling it was? To hear him whispering my name into my ear? He kept saying *Oh Maiko, Maiko, Maiko!*" She laughed. "It almost sounds like your name. And then—"

"I don't want to hear this." He stopped before one of the open rooms. Some of the doors to the rooms in the hallway had been ripped off, used by Doppelmann as new canvases. Inside Michael grabbed a stack of yellowing newspapers. Mischa ignored him and continued.

"He also said he's a playwright. He's written a play and he wants me to play the lead in it. He carries the script with him. Look..."

She opened her bag and presented a stack of crisp pages. Without thinking, Michael dropped his stack of newspapers and latched onto the script.

"I'll take this."

"Don't bother. He's in the main space of the theater."

"Adam is here?"

She nodded.

"Get your mask." He rushed back to his room and found himself moving down the hallway like Doppelmann. No more imitation. It was becoming his own walk.

38

ADAM WAS FRESHLY SHAVED, HIS HAIR STILL MOIST, HIS GLASSES foggy over his slate-gray mask. He stood near the first row of seats, looking at the stage. When Michael arrived, they shook hands, tapped their own masks. Michael opened a folded seat in the front row, and it screeched, echoing throughout the room. Mischa appeared, her mask slightly crooked, and she sat in one of the side seats.

"This play," Michael began, "it's very interesting to me."

"I've been so afraid to have someone read it."

"And yet you gave it to Maiko."

"I trust her," Adam said. "And you."

"When did you write it?"

"I finished it last week. I've been writing it at my job in between tasks. They don't know."

"At the tuna cannery?"

"How did you know?" Adam asked.

Michael drew an invisible grin across his mask and tapped his head.

"Don't you remember when I went by there one day?"

Adam shook his head. "I was probably too busy thinking about the play."

"So are you looking to have this performed?"

"Some day. It seems impossible, though. Especially now with the way the city is."

"You could use this theater," Mischa said.

Adam staggered out of his seat. His hand reached out for Michael's.

"I am so honored," he gasped. "And glad. This really validates my work. It validates me. It makes my existence," he paused, glancing at the stage, "it makes it all worthwhile."

Michael pulled away his hand.

"Let's not get carried away."

Adam sat back and shrugged. But Michael was thinking otherwise. He was certain the constant pain that followed him was a message from his body that he was dying. He no longer felt he was imitating Doppelmann. The mannerisms he had studied and practiced were his own now. They were all Michael, and he was desperate to use them, to make Adam his greatest project before it was too late.

"Long ago," Michael said, "I had your uncertainty. And I looked to others to validate myself. What you really need to do is take a long look at yourself in the mirror. I don't mean a quick minute. I mean a very long time, especially in a space where the sunlight changes so you can see the different shadows on your face. Soon they will become shapes instead of spots on your face. Then you will see yourself. Don't use others for mirrors. Use your own reflection."

"Simple enough. I feel I should write this down, though."

"Stop that. I'm not dictating a code of living to you. Only things to think about. Let's get started."

The large room held heavy, stale air, and the sounds of rats squeaking in the rafters. He told Adam to climb onto the stage, where scraps of small papers were scattered like dead moths. He handed the first few pages of the play to Adam, who now stood above him, towering as a near shadow, masked. Adam cupped the pages of the play in his hands. Michael settled into his seat, a small pocket that quickly sucked in his body heat and pressed it back against him, making him drowsy.

"Take off your mask," Michael said.

Adam hesitated—his hands were occupied with the pages. It took him a moment to decide to lay the pages on the stage floor and then use both hands to untie the mask from behind. When he pulled it away, he revealed his glistening face, young and pale, frightened and naïve, imprinted with sweat and an outline of grease and grime. With his forearm, he wiped himself, using the corner of his t-shirt as the final polish. The mask was dropped to the floor, as if it was a huge weight that had become unbuckled from his body. This new lightness made him stand taller. He scooped up the pages of the play.

"Tell me the basic story," Michael said.

It was about a mermaid who envied humans walking on the beach. One day the mermaid climbed a rocky cliff and flopped through the streets to the city's fish market. There she envied the legs of all the people running away from her. She returned to the water but soon made regular trips to the fish market. And then one morning, as she always went in the early morning to the fish market, a doctor appeared, and luring her with a pair of high heels, caught her in a net.

He took her to his studio and kept her in a large aquarium. He took samples of her blood and shavings of her skin, and with a special collar, he placed around her neck, he was able to operate on her. He gave her pig's lungs to breathe air forever, and the bones from an ostrich for legs. Her skin grew over the bones, and she had her own pair of legs. She was soon walking into the city on her own two feet and doing what she had always wanted: to walk along the coastline.

But then the mermaid became famous, and everyone in the city was following her. The attention became so unbearable that she stayed all day in the doctor's studio. She wanted to return to the water, to become a mermaid again, but he wouldn't let her. And though he was sorry to imprison her, she was simply too valuable a creation; she meant too much for his career.

One day she managed to escape. But she was followed by someone who was lighter and faster than any of the humans in the city. He was faster and lighter because he was made of paper.

Michael interrupted. "Have you met her? Who told you this story?"

"What do you mean? I based it on what I read, in the newspaper," Adam said.

"Read the first page to me," Michael said.

Adam squinted as he shuffled the pages.

"I've never done this before. I'm not an actor."

"If the author himself can't read it out loud, it's not worth hearing."

Mischa's chair creaked. Adam's brow creased, his hands wiped at his temples, where hair stuck to his skin, and he walked in place. His hands continued to touch his face, and soon enough, the corner of a page jabbed him in the eye. He stumbled as Michael watched, fascinated. For a moment, Michael wondered if this was part of the performance, but then he knew that this young man was just like him, just like the nervous, naïve version of himself when he had arrived in the city, and was not used to being under everyone and everything's scrutiny. Michael said nothing, only watched as the struggle spread from Adam's hands to his face, down his arms and trunk, down to his finger tips and twitching feet. And then, with one eye open, one eye watery, Adam started speaking, stuttering and stumbling, unable to get beyond the first word.

"M-m-m-m-m," Adam said. "M-m-m-m-my..."

The sound of M echoed in the theater, against the open seat boxes on the side walls, mumbling through the balcony and murmuring in the front row. Michael rocked in time to the sound then swung his head side to side, like a metronome, trying to guide the M sound out of Adam's throat. He gestured with his hands like a conductor. Adam, wide-eyed but cyclopean, stared at the single seat occupied by Michael. His terror brimmed in all his appendages.

"M-m-m-m-my," he tried again.

He paused. He closed his open eye, squinted with his watery eye, and within a few seconds, the stage was silent. All the rattling from his clothing, all the creaking of the stage floorboards had stopped. Then, the entire theater became quiet. Outside, the sounds of vehicles, chirping birds, and a barking dog seeped in. With both his eyes closed, his lips puckered, the line finally discharged from him:

"Might kill my gills up there."

Michael stood and his seat snapped shut. He cleared his throat.

"That line is nonsense. It's a piece of shit."

"Wh-what?"

"And what's with the stuttering?"

Adam looked small and defeated on the stage.

"I don't like to hear my own work. And it's intimidating up here."

"This play needs a lot of work," Michael said, and collapsed back into his chair. He sighed, not because he felt it was something Doppelmann would do in this situation but because he felt something in himself changing. There was no longer much difference, he concluded. He watched Adam scurry down the side of the stage and stumble down the aisle, landing in the seat next to him. He smelled of salt and citrus.

"Is it really bad? I thought you liked it."

"The concept is there, but I have to say that the execution is terrible. I wanted you to hear it out loud, outside of yourself, but that's obviously not going to work."

"Please, I'll do whatever I can to learn from you."

Michael ruffled the hair on Adam's bowed head. He stroked his shoulders in long, concentric shapes, felt the knobs of his spine embedded in his flesh. The paper tips of his fingers paused over a knot near his shoulder. He pressed a little harder to work it out. He looked over at Mischa, whose blank mask watched all of this. She was digging her nails into the arm rest of her chair.

"Don't look so upset," Michael said to Adam. "You need tougher skin. I can't help you with everything, but I'll give you some guidance. You need to experience more, go to darker, deeper places. Your characters live underwater, yes?"

"Some of them."

Adam clung to the moist pages of the script. The paper was like putty in his hands, pressed against his chest. Michael placed his own paper hand between them and could feel Adam's rapidly beating heart.

"You should come with me. Now."

39

MICHAEL LED THEM OUT OF THE MAIN THEATER SPACE TO THE curved hallway. Adam walked hesitantly, anxiously glancing at each door they passed as if a monster would jump out and scare them. Michael wouldn't have been surprised if a monster had.

"Where are we going?"

"Here."

The broken projection room, with its missing wall. Michael had avoided the place since Mischa had torn him to pieces, but somehow it felt good to be back. The room had racks on opposite walls, brimming with all kinds of supplies: buckets of paint, rolls of fabric, bags of stuffing, and stacks and stacks of newspaper. Adam's eyes narrowed as he took in his surroundings. Mischa moved closer to the edge and looked out over the missing wall, a panorama view of the stage and the rows of empty seats far below.

"Maiko? What is going on here?" Adam asked.

"What are you doing to him?" she asked Michael. He ignored her. Standing behind Adam, he threw a blindfold over his eyes.

"Adam," he said. "We're going to help your art. You need to be broken in a bit. Then your play will be ready for your new eyes."

"Maiko?" the blindfolded Adam asked, pinching the air with his hands. Mischa clasped his wandering fingers into hers. She glared at Michael.

"We can't do this."

"But we can," Michael said. "It's too late to break patterns."

Adam tried to walk, but he blindly headed straight for the ledge. Mischa grabbed his shoulders and forced him in another direction, only to lead him into a coiled rope on the floor. His feet became tangled, and he collapsed into a heap.

Michael rushed to tie Adam's hands behind his back, and

Adam, who didn't resist, sighed gently. When he was done, Michael handed a pair of scissors to Mischa.

"Do your thing," Michael said.

The door opened, and Doppelmann entered. He had a big grin and held a camera with a small lens.

"I thought I heard people in here. Michael? Is that you?" he asked, tilting his head. He came up closer to Michael's masked face.

"I can't do this," Mischa said. The scissors she held plunked to the floor.

Michael laughed, a chuckle he recognized as his own, and nobody else's. "I was just curious if you would do it to real flesh."

"Maiko, please help me," Adam said. "What is he doing to me?"

"May I ask what game you all are playing?" Doppelmann went up to Adam, kneeling in the middle of the room and stroking Adam's hair.

"This is my work," Michael said. "I was trying to tell you about this."

"He's your art?" With a gentle nudge, Doppelmann pushed Adam over.

"Let him go," Mischa said.

"We're not done here," Michael said. Until he was in the room he hadn't known what he would do. Now he did. He began opening cans of paint.

"Quit this, Michael, before I use the scissors again," Mischa threatened.

Michael saw that Mischa was going to be a problem—but so too, potentially, was Doppelmann. What was it like to tear something down to its barest self, unpeel it like a banana, and see how it would recover? Michael felt this curiosity, pure and authentic. Doppelmann, suddenly, felt like the imitation. A wave of sickness washed over him, and he didn't fight it. Somehow, it was giving him strength too.

"He's coming with me," Mischa said, setting Adam back on his knees, resting her hands on his shoulders. Michael pulled her toward the door. Mischa yelled out.

"What is all of this?" Doppelmann asked. "Who is that behind the mask?"

Adam screamed out: "Maiko, I love you!"

His words echoed in the open theater space before them. Mischa shook her head and held her hand over the mouth of her mask.

There was only one thing to do. Michael grabbed her wrists and pushed her out the door and locked it. Again, he was surprised he had such strength, even with his paper arms, and the pain inside his joints and gut.

"Don't go, I'll do whatever he says," Adam yelled, turning toward them.

Banging came from behind the door, demanding to be let in.

"Very good," Doppelmann said, who now stood in the middle of the room. He continued stroking Adam's hair.

"What are you doing to me?" Adam asked the room.

"We're here to help you," Michael said. "This will make your play much better."

Doppelmann pinched Adam's arm, and Michael swatted at his hand.

"He's not very permeable."

"This is my project."

Doppelmann rose up and faced Michael. "Take off your mask."

Michael was used to moving things for this man, and he didn't think twice. Doppelmann lunged at his mouth and kissed him so hard he thought his paper lips might tear. They fell to the ground beside Adam. Michael was dazed and surprised by Doppelmann's weight as he climbed on top of him. He felt heavy, as if he were made of stone. The door rattled and shook. Mischa demanded to be let back in. Doppelmann tore Michael's shirt apart at the buttons.

"You need to work in your own skin," Doppelmann said. He pulled off his boots, then socks, then tore free his own shirt. He grinned. "Then you'll really feel alive."

"You're suffocating me." Michael placed his hands very carefully on Doppelmann's chest and then shoved with all the force he had left.

Doppelmann stumbled. "You're coming alive, Michael. Don't let anything hold you back."

Michael removed his pants, and Doppelmann copied him. Michael removed his underwear, and Doppelmann did too. Michael grabbed a paintbrush, and Doppelmann brought over an open can of paint and handed it to Michael. Doppelmann kissed Michael's neck as Michael stood there, regarding Adam, both his subject and object.

"Please," Adam said. "What's happening?"

Doppelmann prodded Michael to move him closer to Adam. Adam's head turned blindly at this exchange. Michael held the can above Adam's shifting head. The weight of the can brought on the pain in his joints again. He spread his toes to stabilize and disperse the pain throughout his body.

Despite the open wall, the air was thin and constricted inside the room. It smelled like dog's breath. The can of paint was full and heavy, and Michael saw that his hands were shaking and the can would slip any moment. Doppelmann flashed a single eye at him, his other obscured by an instamatic camera. He clicked it several times, and Michael let the paint go, which coated Adam's neck and shoulders.

Adam screamed.

"We must reproduce the effects of nature on the object. At least, that's what the masters say."

The splash echoed in the theater space.

"Where did you get that camera?" Michael demanded.

"Don't hate me," Doppelmann said. "The Northern Authority gave it to me, commissioned me in fact, to do a documentary project."

Anger welled up in Michael, and from the rack of paint cans, he grabbed another and poured it over Adam. Then he striped entire buckets across Adam's body. The paint splattered on the walls, got in Doppelmann's hair, covered the fine linen hairs sewn into Michael's arms. Doppelmann rubbed some of the loose paint on his own body. He walked over and rubbed more into Michael's chest, digging into Michael, permanently staining his paper tissue. He was becoming a kaleidoscope, an echo of a rainbow. The pressure activated the pain inside. To avoid focusing on it, he studied the colors that swirled together and pooled around Adam's knees and feet. For once, the colors were real, outside of him.

"That's it! You finally look happy to be doing this," Doppelmann said. He pointed at Michael's groin. The sight of his own erection would have startled him before but it no longer did. Doppelmann laughed and threw more paint at him.

The paint formed a shallow puddle that reached for the open ledge, then rolled off like a waterfall. Michael opened up stacks of newspaper resting on the shelves and wrapped sheets around Adam's arms. This is really happening, he thought. *Dearest Father, I can see it all through your eyes now. When things made of flesh and bone turn to you for help to change, life is never the same again.*

He felt something transferring out of his own body into Adam's, and once it was all gone, he would be so light he could float off the ledge and out of the theater, past the cliff dogs and the apple trees, past the lighthouse, and out of the city. Yes, perhaps he was seeing now that he did not belong anywhere in the city. Dying, he decided, might be the best thing that happened to him.

Doppelmann turned to Michael, and their bodies stuck together from the paint. We're equals, Michael thought.

They slid in the pool below them and crashed against Adam, who cried out, the three becoming a tangle of limbs and materials, all joining and separating, with Michael unable to tell if paint or glue or saliva was entering his mouth or leaving his ears or filling his eyes. He and Doppelmann grappled. All the gentleness gone. Michael felt his face was being pushed into the paint. He couldn't breathe. Drowning.

"Stop!" Michael commanded, but the words only appeared as

bubbles in the rainbow of paint. He thrashed his arms around and struck Adam in the groin. Then he saw Doppelmann's face. With red and white streaks around his lips, he looked like a terrible clown. His eyes were bloodshot, and he had solid pupils. Michael found the paint-splattered instamatic and raised it to his face, framing a shot on Doppelmann, and snapped a photo.

"Don't do that!" Doppelmann screamed, slipping again.

"You forget whose project this is," Michael said. With all his strength, he swung the camera into the ground and smashed it. Doppelmann scrambled to retrieve the scattered pieces of metal and plastic and the long roll of film, like a long, diseased intestine, exposed and swallowed by the creeping paint. The paint was everywhere now, a lake. Just like the flooded drawing room in Maiko's apartment, Michael thought. So much had changed. He grabbed at his chest, trying to push back the pain.

Adam lay unconscious, his face covered with striped layers of drying paint, his nostrils blocked, his mouth opened, his teeth different colors. A large blue bubble formed around his lips, expanded with one large exhale, then burst, and ringed his mouth.

40

"I SEE YOU'RE DOUBTING YOURSELF NOW," DOPPELMANN SAID. "Don't listen to that voice inside you. Listen to me. When painting on a canvas, we leave in too much. But when painting on a body, we need to eliminate. Take out anything that's not essential, not totally relevant."

Michael pressed his palm to his forehead then remembered his hands were coated with paint. The paint fumes were dizzying.

"I wasn't trying to make something," he said. "I was trying to save it. That was my project."

"What's the difference?"

He remembered what Mischa had asked him. After she had torn him apart, where had Michael gone? Where is he now?

"Stop thinking and feeling so much and just do your art. You'll learn by doing, not by thinking about it."

"The city's falling apart thanks to your art."

"You don't think it would have happened otherwise? The city knows how to heal itself. It's a mix of so many things anyway. One thing can't bring it down."

Michael thought of the mermaid, stopping traffic on the highway. It was so easy to impose yourself on others and make yourself their problem. It was easy to push someone to the limits of their self, interrogate them until they were beyond themselves.

Adam suddenly spoke.

"Doppelmann?" he said, his voice hoarse and slow. "Please? I can't see."

"You're going to be fine," Michael said.

Doppelmann, who had another can of open paint in his hands, stood up. He rose and appeared taller than ever before, bristling, his chin pulled in.

"He called you Doppelmann."

It was difficult to read the artist's face, smeared with paint. Around Michael's feet, the paint was collecting so thickly it could easily begin climbing up the threaded hairs on his legs. He shook his head, hoping to let the interior pain out.

"Are you pretending to be me?" Doppelmann asked. He jabbed the painting knife at Michael.

"I was using you," he said honestly. "The idea of you. Trust me. You'd approve."

The painting knife jabbed again, and the jolt knocked Michael back. Doppelmann's nose flared with each deep breath. Then Michael shoved back. How strong was his new body after all?

Doppelmann slammed him against the wall. Punched him in the gut two times. Threw him into the paint. They glared at each other, and Michael wondered:

What would he say, the real Michael? What would he say about all of this? For a moment, he was dazzled, lost. And that was when he knew. There was nothing left of what was once called Michael.

Doppelmann charged again, but this time, his foot sank into the thick paint pooling on the floor and he slipped. Most vivid in that moment was how Doppelmann's eyes widened and how Michael saw something he had never seen before in Doppelmann's face: fear. The fear contorted into pain, as Doppelmann winced and his naked body fell into the paint.

From the force of falling, he simply slipped. And slid off the ledge.

He was there, then he was not.

Michael heard it before he saw it. Doppelmann's body crashing into the seats, a loud *bang*.

The pain in Michael's joints pounded and his chest pulsed. Behind him, Adam twitched in the pool of paint. Michael rushed for the camera, only to remember he had shattered it. When he looked over the ledge, it took a moment to make sense of what he saw. There, below him, draped on the seats, was his true creation. Nothing less than a tragic accident could create this. And no one but a paper man could have transformed Doppelmann into what he was now.

For plastered to the seats below was Doppelmann—his body pressed flat, thin as paper, like tissue placed upon a seat, or worse, a thin skin upholstered directly to the chairs. Michael had to look away, and the only thing he could focus on was Adam. More than the physical pain was the stickiness of guilt accumulating inside him, and then the dry dizziness of hopelessness.

———————————

At this time, the projector room door, which had been shaking on its hinges, burst open like a sluice gate. Mischa flooded in, seething, her eyes shining.

Adam groaned and coughed up painted phlegm.

"It's too late," Michael said. He sank into the pool of paint, staining his paper skin. He held out his numb arms and studied the streaks of colors across him. They had mixed so much that his body was now stained the color of sea sludge.

"Where's Doppelmann, Michael?"

He pressed his hands to the floor and hoisted himself out of the pool of paint. Then he pointed out, past the open ledge, to the sea of chairs below.

Part Five:

MICHAEL

41

To each other, they said no words. Mischa gave one glance to Michael—a glance that held so many things: disgust, horror, perhaps even a glint of admiration. She hovered over Adam's unconscious body for just a moment and then dropped down into the paint. When she looked again at Michael, he knew what to do. He dressed quickly, the fabric sticking to his painted body, and helped Mischa lift Adam up. Between them, they carried him out of the room.

Dear Father, This distance between us has allowed me to make something of my own. It isn't perfect by any means, but what accident is?

In the hallway, they stopped several times. Adam's body was heavy. The weight of the paint seemed to increase as it dried and hardened, making Adam himself increasingly difficult to move. Yet he was still alive. They could tell by the occasional blue bubbles that formed around his mouth and bulged from his nostrils and which Mischa unclogged with her pinkie.

The dim lights in the hallway suddenly went out.

"What happened?" Mischa's voice in the darkness said.

"Power must be out on our block," Michael said. "Or the city."

"Hurry, then."

They crashed into the debris on the carpet: all the pizza boxes, empty paper cups, and food wrappers. Following the hallway's continual curve, each new section they entered felt like the section they had left behind.

"It never ends," Mischa cried. She was out of breath.

Michael nodded. It seemed like they were being surrounded. There was a muzzled shuffling and buzzing, as if out of the darkness insect creatures were coming, their antennae sweeping before them.

Father, I always wondered why you did what you did. By the time of the accident, you had given up painting long ago. But photography and my accident wouldn't work together would they? So you went back to paper, and painting, back to an art form you had abandoned. All because of me.

They paused once more to catch their breath. Mischa searched in the dark for Adam's mouth and checked his breath. She placed her hand on his painted chest.

"He's still alive," she said.

"We have to get him some water," Michael said. "We might be able to get this coat off of him. He hasn't entirely dried."

They kept on until they reached the staircase that led down to the front doors. Mischa kicked them open, and Michael lifted Adam's body in his own arms. Outside the air felt sluggish, colder than the womblike warmth of the theater. Even though the sky was overcast, it had been too long since he'd been outdoors, and he had to squint and guess his footing along the street. They stood outside the theater and listened to the near silence of the city. In the distance, the faint call of a train rang out.

For years, the sound of a train always frightened me. And now, it does nothing. Now it can even make me smile.

He was carrying Adam's heavy body, and the struggle of holding on to that much weight was enough to buckle his paper arms. Where had all the pain gone? He wasn't ready to say it had left him for good, but his joints were suddenly free of what had become a persistent, nagging discomfort. Somewhere within his pulpy insides, his body told him perhaps this meant something, that perhaps he had finally reached the end. When he lived inland, old herding dogs had a sudden resurgence of energy and spirit just before dying.

The body of Adam stuck to him, and with each step, the sticky adhesive sound of the paint against Michael's paper body became a kind of rhythm. Could it wake Adam up? What would happen if he was responsible for Adam not surviving? He nearly felt crushed, not from the weight of Adam's body but from the guilt stacking on his weakened shoulders. But covered in paint as he was, he was still acutely aware that they were exposed now and might be caught by some patrolling group from the north. However, the city had become eerily quiet. Their own movements were amplified. Only one streetlight flickered, animating shadows of immobile cars. There were no leaves left on the trees to tumble in the slight breeze, which instead carried the hiss of a radio voice: Remain indoors. The city has been occupied. Wear your masks...

I sometimes wonder if that old me, the one who is afraid of train whistles, is still there, in your house, clothed and safe and dry. If he is, please don't let him out.

Mischa's voice interrupted: "Let's get him to the sea. We'll wash him in the water."

"What if someone sees us?" If the city had been occupied it wasn't safe, especially not for them.

"There," she said, and pointed at an abandoned shopping cart further down the street. She brought it back. With her help, Michael lifted Adam into the cart. Adam's lips puckered and pulsed like a fish out of water, leaking paint.

"Can we make it?"

She didn't say anything. Instead she pushed the cart as fast as she could, breaking out into a full trot. Without Adam's body in his arms, Michael was lighter and flew alongside her, feeling entirely empty. He was no longer Doppelmann; no longer Michael. No longer.

In fact, if that paper boy is still there, make sure you take his photograph. Because he could change before you know it.

They skirted the cardboard walls that obscured and in some cases now barricaded most of the eastern part of the city. The cutout doors were soft and lined with black mold. Above, vines of morning glories had overtaken the top ledge and hung like a massive flowering octopus. Mischa peeked through the door and, seeing no one on the other side, tried to lift Adam's body through it. Michael helped push him through a flap that covered Adam like a fish mouth. They heard him crash onto the dirt on the other side.

He grabbed her arm before she could climb after him. "Why does it matter to you?"

"What?"

"Him? Saving him?"

"You really don't get it?"

"When you did this to me," he said, "you tore me up and then left me there to die." He said this, at least partially, to dispel some of the fear he had that Adam could die too.

She narrowed her eyes.

"You tried to preserve him like a relic, like a piece of art. But he's human. And you know what?"

"I was human, once—"

"But you've never been real. You're just a sculpture. Doesn't matter what kind of body you're in, flesh or paper! You're stuck in it and always have been. You had everyone going that a paper man could be a creator. But I never fell for it. It was just you on display all along."

He wanted to tell her about Doppelmann—his one true creation, folded over the theater seats, but why bother? He realized that Mischa had not wanted to look, had not looked on purpose, and even if she had looked she wouldn't have acknowledged what Michael had caused to happen. He almost laughed then, and as he grew more hopeless, he also noticed he was growing stronger. No pain, and almost a lightness, began to fill him.

Mischa leapt up and disappeared though the flap. Michael heard the soft thud of her body on the other side. He used the shopping cart to help raise himself and climb in after them. The inside edges of the cutout door were soggy cardboard, so limber that the weight of his body seemed ready to split it. With a kind of rolling motion, he forced himself over the ledge and fell through, the cardboard flap sealing shut behind him.

Cloaked in sudden darkness he blinked, trying to adjust his eyes. He found Mischa looking down the road, toward the bay. The water was visible despite the dense fog in the sky, a vague shimmer on the horizon. She wasn't looking at the water, though. She was watching a stream of figures approaching.

42

THEY WERE SURROUNDED BEFORE THEY KNEW IT. ONE OF THE masked members held a boat anchor with a knitted rope. The others held fishing poles and spears that clicked together as they made a tight circle around them away from the stream of passing people, a massive crowd marching along the shoestring street and headed south. Many wore elaborate gowns and suits: lace-fringed sleeves, top hats, hoop dresses, hats with ostrich feathers, sewn-on jewels. All of them, needless to say, hid their real faces behind masks. Everything from plain paper jobs to elaborate animal faces.

"Where are your masks?" The tallest man in the group stepped forward and lit a match by striking the cheek of his mask.

"What brings you to the south?" another man said.

"We're from here," Michael protested. His mind searched for a hint—a sign predicting the moment when they would be attacked. But he inhaled to steady his breathing, stood taller, and said the first thought that came to him: "We were attacked and need to get to water." He motioned to Adam's stiff body pressed against Mischa. "He's been drenched in paint."

"Our masks were lost," Mischa added.

The group conferred, mumbles emanating from their moveable mouthpieces. Michael never thought a day like this would come, a day in the city where *not* wearing a mask was more dangerous than wearing one. Even more surprising, though, was that no one recognized him as the famous paper man. Did they not know who he was?

Mischa pulled Michael's ear and hissed: "We need to get out of here." Her breath smelled of dirt. They dragged Adam forward, past the small group, onto the pavement, where they were enveloped by the larger, flowing crowd. Two men from the group with identical dolphin masks picked up Adam without saying anything.

Michael gratefully accepted the help, but Mischa tried to pull Adam back down. The small commotion quickly attracted the attention of a car driving by in the opposite direction. The driver slowed the car to a stop and rolled down his window. His face, with no mask, shined with sweat, and he stared at them as if they were part of a pleasant landscape or still-life.

"Can I touch you?" a woman in a brown leather mask asked Michael. "Why are you so many colors?"

"Like a peacock!" the driver of the car said and everyone laughed. He grabbed a mask made of newspaper from his car and placed it over his face. Hands began reaching for Michael, curiously touching his body and discussing his wonderful disguise. Mischa reeled back from the hands.

"Amazing costume," they said. "Brilliant!"

"We need to go. Please put him down," Michael said. So it was settled, then. No one remembered who he was.

"You're not going to the masquerade?"

"What are you talking about?" Mischa asked. She placed her hand on Adam's chest. Because her legs were shorter than the men carrying Adam, she had to practically run to keep up. "His heart's beating faster! You're scaring him. We need to free him from this paint."

"There's a masquerade at the City Collectorate building," a girl in the crowd yelled. She wore a black vizard mask—covering her face from her forehead to her nose and revealing the skin of her sharp jawline and full lips. She grinned and exposed her teeth. Someone closer leaned into to Michael and Mischa and whispered, "It's a takeover. We're taking it over."

The girl in the vizard mask placed her index finger to her lips.

"What's that thing?" her companion, wearing a spangled caul, asked. "Did you make it?" She pointed to Adam. The men carrying him raised the body of Adam higher onto their shoulders. Balanced on the tips of their fingers, he seemed to narrow into a multicolored flag in the shape of a man. People reached for him. "Offer him to the

Collectorate," someone shouted.

"Stop that," Mischa said. "We need to get him to the sea. Put him down."

"You should really be wearing a mask," the girl scolded them both.

Trapped in the current of the crowd, they were carried along the street. To the east was the languid bay water, a few ships parked along the docks. To the south, the street was a clear line extending to the bridge that divided the city. A few blocks before the bridge was the City Collectorate building, still illuminated from its interior office lights. The front of the crowd was not too far ahead of them. If they could get ahead of everyone, perhaps they could take Adam and break away from the crowd and make for the water. But what would happen there? He was beginning to realize that accidents seemed to be the only solution in his life, thus far. Must he force another, final accident?

Directly above them, in the apartments that lined the streets, the latches of windows opened—*click click click*—and people leaned out, cheering when they saw the crowd. Those in the windows wore masks, which meant that people were hiding their faces even in private. Was it a show of solidarity, or something else? From the doorways, people emerged waving and carrying candles, torches, gas lamps—anything to brighten the foggy evening that was quickly transforming into night. None of the streetlights were illuminated.

"The masquerade!" children cried from behind pastel-painted masks, peeking over the edges of balconies. Everyone pointed at the painted offering, now being passed further along, hand over hand, as Mischa and Michael struggled to keep up. The children especially shrieked in delight.

Michael saw that with no light, the roaches began to scurry into the street. They were like a brown ribbon, their wings flashing small diamonds of light, reflecting the candles from above. Mischa groaned in disgust. The woman in a vizard mask laughed, reached down for a handful, and tossed one into her mouth.

"If the north thinks we're vermin, then vermin we are!"

"You have no idea," Mischa growled back.

Then, from the apartment windows, paper began falling. Napkins and paper doilies floating down like snowflakes. The children tore construction paper and burst their confetti into the air. As the pieces dropped, Michael realized he was not the only one making a last stand. Here, too, was the south, making its final bow before the inevitable takeover of the north.

Solidarity for the citizens of the city came, not in anonymity, but in transformation. The human face was a canvas, or infrastructure, on which these modes of various identities were mounted. Their bodies, draped in adornments that made them amorphous figures in a contrived landscape, were now objects on the public stage: the shoestring street. The city had changed and so had the people. They were all like Michael: all were strangers. But what of their real faces? Under their masks, he could sense it—the fear, anxiety. Or was it something else, something worse?

What a sight it would have been for all those masks to come off at once. Beautiful or terrifying, he could only have found the idea of it overwhelming and distracting. With so much noise, he couldn't hear himself think. Men in roan leather masks used rolled-up newspapers to beat the hoods of parked cars like drums and the ground shook from thousands of foot falls.

"Adam!" Mischa cried, but he was getting carried off, an object of the crowd.

Mischa and Michael ran alongside the millipede crowd, passing one of the paper giants he had planted next to a building. *I tried to give the city something beautiful,* he reminded himself. Now his figures were ignored, as uninteresting and ordinary as lampposts. It was Adam's turn, on the shoulders of men who probably had once attacked Michael when he had first arrived, to be the totem. He heard voices muttering that the northern authorities were about to intervene. "From where?" people asked. "And how many?"

Above them, streams of paper from adding machines were

coiling in the lazy coastal wind, and then rolls of toilet paper were undone from the highest floors, slithering to the ground like interminable white snakes. People around him danced. Everyone accepted each other in the crowd. People put their arms over the shoulders of strangers, some held hands, and some paused beside the thin streetlights to press their masked foreheads together. In the midst of the celebration was Mischa, screaming anxiously after Adam. Michael watched for a moment before his guilt returned, and he rushed beside the dolphin-masked twins and reached for the stiff painted arm of Adam. He stretched his arms but felt the stabbing pain that resided in his joints returning. It was back. More powerful than ever before. A flash that reminded him of steel meeting steel, and his own precious but foreign self trapped in between. He crashed on the pavement. Pain throbbed in his shoulders and elbows, spread to his wrists and knuckles. So it happens here, he thought. No more accidents.

"Get up," Mischa yelled, stopping momentarily to glare.

Michael took deep breaths to push the pain to his edges, and it was as if the whole crowd was pressing his lungs. Buses, halted for the night for the curfew, were covered in the paper falling from the sky. Between the legs of the citizens, he noticed nearby another set of the figures he had created, emerging from a bank building. People in the crowd hoisted them too, cheering to have their new citizens be a part of their protest. The scene warmed him. His own creations were accepted after all, and they belonged, just as he belonged, in the city. He felt an overwhelming sense that he was part of an unorganized power that had tipped too far in one direction. The city was out of balance, and the people were taking it as far as they could. The ledger had to be unbalanced with this much demand for change. And he was a part of all of it. He smiled without moving. "Get up!" He heard Mischa's voice distantly, breaking apart his satisfaction.

The sharp briny smell of kelp wafted through the legs of the crowd. Fellow marchers picked some of the confetti from Michael's head. Michael wiped off a napkin that had stuck to his brow. His joints were growing extremely tight, and again he thought his hands might burst. Around his knees built a tension that made it nearly impossible to stand. He immediately thought about the time that Mischa had torn him to pieces. If Doppelmann had not given him a new body, would he be here in this moment? He could hear Mischa's voice. *Do you see why I had to tear you apart?*

Mischa propped him up on his feet, yelling something at him that he couldn't understand, and that was when something broke inside his sleeve. Michael suddenly felt extremely hot. He tore off his jacket, which was swallowed by the crowd behind them, smelling it and searching its pockets. A desire, deeper than the pain within, or perhaps a part of it, came to him: for water or rain to pour on him, just like the day he had arrived in the city.

"We're losing sight of Adam," Mischa said. She tore the buttons off Michael's shirt. The people around them pulled at Michael's shirt too, and the fabric tore apart at the seams. They were undoing him; in a moment, he would internally combust.

"So warm," Michael claimed happily. It was as if he were disintegrating, becoming part of all the paper falling around them. Adam's shape bobbed further ahead—he was only a speck of color now. When his shirt was removed, also disappearing in the crowd, Michael saw that his elbow had cracked open. A dark wound in his paper skin, oozing a sap like oxidized glue. A series of small hands, from masked children who had joined the crowd, reached for his arm, and with their grasping nails, they peeled away another part of his arm's skin.

"Bring him back," Michael moaned but it was no use. His temperature continued to rise. Somehow people had lifted him off the street and made him part of the current again, like a leaf on the surface of water. For a moment, he was overwhelmed with a feeling that he couldn't identify or explain. Not much longer, he thought. And it was almost blissful—the chance of dying. More fingers were on him, pressing his back to move him forward, make him a part of them, but he only felt heavier and heavier.

"We've lost Adam," Mischa said. "You need to move faster." Mischa tugged on his other arm.

"I can't," Michael said. Nausea peaked in his stomach, and he keeled over.

"Adam is going to die," she cried. "We need to get him out of here." She motioned to the bay, the darkness to their left. Adam, though, was already too far away, and this made Michael's stomach feel worse.

"But I'm dying," he managed to laugh. "Don't you see it?"

Mischa ran her fingers through her knotted hair, as if she were ready to tear it off her head. She was about to open her mouth, and he anticipated the harshest judgment yet from her. But instead, she simply turned and left him, racing after the bobbing offering that was Adam, disappearing among the hats and swept-up hair.

I'll never see her again, he thought. No one caught him as he fell, and his head smacked the papered pavement. Legs stepped around him. His gut felt heavy, as if it were one sack full of inky poison. He imagined his insides bursting and pouring toxic paint throughout his body. His throat clenched. He laughed at the macabre truth of it. Here was a real performance, not like the ones in the display window. This time, he really was suffering the pain of his character. No musical soundtrack played. Only the sounds of the city and the trail of revolutionaries taking over the street.

It was too late for Adam. He knew this. He would become an object. Just as Michael had been an object, Adam would be the new one of the city. And Michael would die as an object too, trampled on the street and mashed into pulp. *We are all the products of terrible accidents,* he thought.

On the ground, he watched the passing feet. He felt the vibrations in his ear and cracked elbow. A memory returned—his first day in the city. The rainstorm, his collapse under the bridge. And now the people passed him, the people laughing, masked, ignoring him, not even aware there was a body in the way. No one looked down, and that, he decided, was for the best. After several minutes, the paper snowing from above began to collect around him. It wouldn't be long before he was buried. Rejoining paper, he prayed for a storm—for rain to disintegrate him.

Then, as he was allowing himself to drift off, an image caught his attention—so strange that it stood out even in this masked crowd. A mushroom cap, bobbing, and attached to it were two cardboard antlers. From its eyeholes glittered wide animal pupils, black as night, before dropping out of sight again. Then it was there, staring into his face.

Before she spoke, he recognized the scent of mushrooms.

"Need a hand?"

43

SHE PRESSED HER HAND TO HIS UNMASKED FACE THEN FELT ALONG his neck and arms. "What's wrong with you?"

"Please, take off your mask," he said. "I want to see your real face."

"I can't. It would be bad for business."

"What do you mean?" He studied her mask closely and noted the exceptional detail: the antlers, the precise cuts that made the eye slits, the delicate curve of the nostrils. "Maiko."

"The one and only."

The crowd parted around them roughly, knees and shins knocking against them.

He moved to touch her, perhaps hug her, but the pain had a hold on his body, and he could only flinch. She observed him with her mute mask.

"Where does it hurt?" she said.

"Everywhere." He wanted to distract himself from the pain by asking her more questions. "Where have you been? They had put you in a truck headed for the south. How did you get back here?"

She snorted, or laughed.

"I really wanted to help," he added. "But there were too many of them."

He put his hand on her shoulder. If only he had followed her to the south. Things would have turned out much differently for him if he had been patient.

"Maiko," Michael said. He took another breath and his lungs locked, not letting him exhale.

"What has happened to you? And where are your clothes?"

"I am dying," he said.

"How can you be dying?"

"It's inside me. It's spreading." He knew he didn't have enough time to explain all of this. She raised him and placed his arm over

259

her shoulder. One of her antlers sliced at his scalp. When he leaned back to avoid it, she seemed to understand and unstrapped the leather thong holding her mask in place under her chin. Her face was reluctantly revealed. She was so close, just as the night they had sat in her bed and she placed her first mask ever made on him. He could see her freckles, the mole shaped like a mushroom, and her eyes that were moist.

She tried to break them from the crowd, but it had swelled so much that the entire street was full of people. They took a few slow steps out of the crowd, closer to the bay, when he felt his arm cracking more.

"It's too late," He crumpled to the ground. She tried to catch him but he fell anyway. When he looked above him, he noticed that she had his arm still in her hand. It was falling to pieces. No rain had done this. No outside force. This time it was from the inside. The pain was all his own doing, he told himself. No accidents. He wondered if in a strange way his death would coincide with Adam's last breath, which, he was certain, was coming. He closed his eyes.

"Look," Maiko commanded. She tossed aside his paper arm, and he screamed as it fell to the ground. Even if he were dying, even if he could not feel it, he still preferred to stay in one piece. *Throw my paper body into the bay*, he thought, *and I'll sink to the bottom as one being.*

"Not at that," Maiko was giggling, reaching for his chin and shifting it back down so he was gazing at the rest of his body. "You're not dying Michael," she whispered in his ear.

In place of his paper arm was something else, held there by Maiko: a pale appendage that was connected seamlessly at his shoulder. It took him a moment to understand what she was showing him.

"Your arm," she said, "underneath it's real skin. Feel it."

She took his other hand, his paper hand, and placed it on the five digits that were attached to the pale, fleshy limb. His paper hand climbed from there to his shoulder to find everything intact and connected to the rest of him.

It was true, then, as she said. Underneath he was something completely different than paper and pulp.

44

MAIKO STEPPED AWAY AS MICHAEL RAISED HIS NEW ARM AND GENtly moved it in circles. He became aware of the blood inside pulsing, flowing as fast as the crowd. He retracted his fingers and pressed his palm out, framed it against the dark water of the bay. He put it in his mouth, and tasted. Salt.

What had Doppelmann done to his body when he had recreated it months ago? He must have added something, some life-generating, cell-creating material. The pain that Michael had felt in his body wasn't the pain of dying but the opposite—he had been growing inside, a larva filling his paper shape and eventually outgrowing it. No longer would he have to be stuck in a paper body. This body had become what he had always wanted. He noticed his exposed hand had no finger nails. Even newborns have fingernails, he thought. A small detail, nonetheless.

"I've been inside this for so long." A dizzying mix of fear and elation nearly overwhelmed him. His life had become a series of exchanges impossible to keep straight. Who was ultimately responsible for this new body? Was it those outside of him or something original from his core—an original mutation, with its own set of intentions?

"I need to see Adam."

"Who is that?"

"I'll explain later." He grabbed her hand and dragged her back into the crowd.

"This is me," Michael said. He tore off the other paper arm, the one that had fallen off in the bus on his first day in the city. Then he remembered the dead mermaid and how the sight of her had been a kind of bad omen, that to try to change oneself would cost your life. However, here he was, not only alive but with an actual human body. He already knew what Doppelmann's fate was, but now he needed to see what would become of his other counterpart. *I have to see*, he kept telling himself.

Michael grabbed Maiko's hand and started running through the crowd. They pushed people out of their way, cutting their own path through the organs of the crowd creature filling the street.

He didn't immediately recognize the intersection they were at, but based on the amount of people climbing the cement stairs that led to the garden square, he was able to make out that the looming building before them, now bare with no glass and no recognizable architectural skin, was the City Collectorate building.

The building was nothing but a skeleton, its exterior torn to pieces and peeled off like an orange. All of the windows had been shattered and the inside cubicles knocked over. Papers flew out from the exposed windows: pages of documents streamed like miniature magic carpets. Chairs and desks were being flung from the highest floors, and smashing onto the street. On the sidewalk, someone was trapped under a fallen filing cabinet and, inside their mask, mutely struggled to free himself. Nearby, trees were stripped of their leaves, bent and twisted together. The glass glittered on the ground like stars reflecting in the streetlight. The evening sky was now dark. In the building, gaping holes reminded Michael of his escape from the display window. No one was here, though, to mourn the loss of the City Collectorate. They were here to destroy it. This, Michael realized, was the masquerade.

Across the grass square, the beheaded body of the bronze statue—the northern poet—was being dismantled. The sliced neck revealed a white moon of plaster that lay underneath its painted exterior. Michael felt a pang of sympathy. What looked impenetrable from the outside was actually soft as bread on the inside.

And above them, at the top of the stripped building, was the unmistakable shape of another sculpture—bright, striped with many colors, and hovering at the ledge. Stretched from head to toe, the sculpture already known to the revelers of the masquerade as "Adam" was perched at the ledge of the Collectorate building. How he had been taken up the many floors so quickly, Michael could not guess, but he was now the crowning monument of this desiccated headquarters, his back arched like a giant salmon or rainbow trout. Floodlights had been placed under the sculpture of Adam, illuminating him against the night sky, larger than life.

Michael stood frozen, transfixed by the scene.

"What are you looking for?" Maiko pressed closer to him. "I can feel your body heat," she said. "You're so warm."

She stepped back to get a better look at him, and that was when she was knocked over. A fight had broken out over the broken arms of the northern poet, and this group crashed into them. When Michael lifted Maiko, he saw her face washed in blood. A large, red gash stretched across her eyebrow. He used his paper hand to apply pressure to her wound, and it was immediately saturated in blood. Stunned, Maiko blinked rapidly at him in confusion.

"I need you to walk. Now," he ordered. "We're almost there."

He used his other arm, the exposed human arm, to drag her away from the boxes. The crowd swelled like a clogged gutter and pooled around the building. They stumbled toward the bay.

"Are you okay?" Michael asked. He held his hand over Maiko's forehead. She pushed it away and inspected his palm.

"Is it bad? Will it scar?"

"I don't know," he said, using his new fingers, which felt strong as steel, to tear part of her fur cape and wrap it as a bandage over her head.

"The bridges are still closed," she said. "But let's leave anyway. Can we? By tomorrow morning, the north will have shuttered the city and all of this will be over. I saw their police forming."

Michael laughed, feeling light even as he became increasingly away of his new mass, his powerful density. "What does it matter? Look at me! We'll do what we want."

Maiko did not respond for a moment. The hand pressed against her bandage grew tense.

"Michael," she finally said, "if they find me, this time I'll really be taken away."

"Why?"

"I made all these masks."

He took in all the faces around them, from domino masks to riding masks to netted maskers and scarlet veils. Leather, canvas, plaster bandages; animal heads, theater faces, long noses, helmets with single eye slits.

"All of them?" he asked dully.

She nodded her head. "Many. Only the high level organizers know its name: M&M Masking. City Security. It's run out of our old apartment. Of course I have a lot of people to help now. So many orders. Michael, I'm notorious!"

"How did this happen?"

"The night you left the display window changed everything. Anyone from the south had to stay in the south. I knew then that my life as a fur model was over, or had been over and I was only realizing it then. My only other skill was making masks for you, so I decided why not make them for others? They were inspired by you in the display window. I had created that. With the masks, I found a way to protect more people. Everyone looked the same, and no one could be in danger for being different."

"But look at them now. Look at what they're doing."

"That wasn't my intent at all. I wanted to protect everyone. They've taken it from me and made it into something else. It's not safe if I stay here anymore. The north will be going after the organizers, and my name will be given up. They already know who I am. I was followed into the masquerade and lost them, luckily. We need to get out of here. Now."

"How. If the bridge is blocked?"

"I know another way."

They headed away from the crowd, away from the buildings, and for the docks that lined the bay. The chanting from the crowd didn't fade, and when there was a loud explosion, Michael was tempted to turn back. Adam! he thought. And Mischa. And Doppel-mann. How could he just leave? Below the City Collectorate build-ing, on the street, masked faces flashed and looked like a pack of raccoons, something he had seen several times when living inland. They worked as one body, tearing the exteriors of buildings, expos-ing the inner workings of the city, and then papering them with their own marks. But Maiko pushed them forward. On the water, they found a small fishing boat with two sets of oars. Michael climbed in and noticed the shift in weight from his own body.

"So, it's quite simple. We head across the bay, and we'll be on land in less than two hours."

"You've done this before?"

"As a child. My father used to canoe for recreation. And we would come here and visit the fish market then be home by dark. Do you know how to paddle?"

Michael took a set of oars and tried them out. His muscles felt the resistance of the water and were filled with a burst of energy. He had real muscles. And he was using them to propel them away from the city. He couldn't believe he was with Maiko again. He watched her settle into the boat and listened to the sound of the oars hitting the water.

"I'm so tired," Maiko said after a while. "I might have to take a little nap."

"You have to stay awake," he said. "I don't know where I'm going."

She delicately touched her wrapped head. The blood had caked on her skin.

"You can't miss it," she said sleepily. "There's only land across the way. Don't worry. You can't go in any wrong direction."

She leaned back and closed her eyes. If Michael had known more about human health, he might have urged her to stay awake. But he didn't. So he allowed her to make herself comfortable, and he focused on the task at hand. Behind them was the surface of the water and fog billowing above it. He wondered if they would cross over the bay of bones, where the city buried those who died. All the citizens of the past lay under them as they skirted across the still surface of the water.

Despite the shouting from the coast, Maiko was already in a deep slumber. Instantly, she took on the appearance of an inanimate object, a sculpture, a statue. Everything he looked at from now on would always look like art, even if only for a moment. He couldn't believe the woman across from him, the woman who had helped him, was the notorious maker of the masks and a helper to the people now tearing the city to pieces. In the distance, he studied the city as if it were a diorama. The city would always be a mess—a struggle of multiple neighborhoods and groups. Had he really lived there and survived? Within a few hours, once the north had silenced the unrest, he could imagine the city looking like something completely different.

I myself am completely different.

With this realization, he tore at his face.

He ripped the layers of paper from his cheeks and ears and exposed his skin to the elements. The coolness of the marine air settled on his cheek, stinging the new skin. He dug into his scalp with his nail-less fingers, pulling away the paper shell surrounding his brain.

The paper he tossed into the water.

The diffused moonlight seeped into the fog and illuminated their boat and the still, glassy surface of the water. Michael pulled in the oars and looked over the side. He waited a moment for the ripples to calm. Leaning close, he saw in the reflection of the water a shape that looked familiar. The outline of his face was the same, but the exact features were new. He leaned in more. He turned left then right, taking in the shape of his eye sockets, the shape of his nose. He ran his fingers over his face, his fingers made of soft skin and hard bones that took in the shape of his lips, his cheeks, his eyebrows. He moved in closer to the water, and for the first time in over ten years, dipped his face into the cold liquid.

He opened his eyes.

ACKNOWLEDGEMENTS

Thank you to all of my family, especially my parents Mick and Joan Lawson and my sister Melanie Wuensch, for their neverending support.

I would have never made it to the finish line for this book without the tremendous amount of encouragement from all of my friends, especially from Mickey Birnbaum, Becky Chuen, Jess Feldman, Ross Helford, Julie Kelly, Michelle Ladd, Holly Rose McGee, Jen McGee, Amelia McGinley, Kasey McMahon, Judy Mei, Ron Reyes, and Steven Toner. Thank you for listening to all of my adventures in writing the book and kindly reminding me to keep working. Also, thank you to my piano colleagues in Pasadena, especially my teacher and fellow writer Christopher Brennan, and thanks to all the athletes in SMRC for your inspiration to keep on keeping on.

This book has been largely influenced by all the teaching and training from so many peers, faculty, and more. I'd like to especially thank from the University of Nevada, Reno the early encouragement of Gailmarie Pahmeier, Chris Robertson, Scott Slovic, and Bill Stobb. From the UCLA Extension Writer's Program, special thanks to Noel Alumit and the members of AAWG! Thanks to the Colgate Writers' Conference, especially John Robert Lennon. And to everyone at UC Riverside's Palm Desert MFA program, thank you for your support and guidance, especially Tod Goldberg, Mary Yukari Waters, John Schimmel, and Agam Patel. A very, very, very special thanks to Mark Haskell Smith, who really helped shape this book into something more than words on paper.

For the team that brought this book through its final metamorphosis, that had innumerable creative suggestions and tireless edits to make this book be the best that it can be, many thanks to the unstoppable and unparalleled Unnamed Press team that is Chris Heiser and Olivia Taylor Smith. And for the immense amount of help, support, expertise, and guidance, thank you Dara Hyde and the Hill Nadell Literary Agency.

And finally, for everything and so much more, thank you, Mr. Tim Walker.

GL

ABOUT THE AUTHOR

GALLAGHER LAWSON is a graduate of UC Riverside's Palm Desert MFA program. He has worked as a travel writer and technical writer, and plays classical piano. He lives in Los Angeles.